The Garden

The Garden

Elsie V. Aidinoff

HarperTempest
An Imprint of HarperCollins*Publishers*

Library of Congress Cataloging-in-Publication Data

Aidinoff, Elsie V.
  The garden / Elsie V. Aidinoff.— 1st ed.
    p. cm.
Summary: Retells the tale of the Garden of Eden from Eve's point of
view, as Serpent teaches her everything from her own name to why she
should eat the forbidden fruit, and then leaves her with Adam and the
knowledge that her choice has made mankind free.
  ISBN 0-06-055605-6 — ISBN 0-06-055606-4 (lib. bdg.)
  1. Eve (Biblical figure)—Juvenile fiction. 2. Adam (Biblical figure)—
Juvenile fiction. [1. Eve (Biblical figure)—Fiction. 2. Snakes—Fiction.
3. Adam (Biblical figure)—Fiction. 4. Free will and determinism—
Fiction.] I. Title.
  PZ7.A26922Gar 2004   2003015841
  [Fic]—dc22

Typography by Larissa Lawrynenko
1 2 3 4 5 6 7 8 9 10
❖
First Edition

To my husband

ACKNOWLEDGMENTS

As this is my first book, I would like to acknowledge not only the many people who have had a part in bringing *The Garden* to life, but also those who have helped turn me into a writer. I wish Miss Couser, my English teacher at secondary school, were still around; I would like to thank her, fifty-five years later, for making me memorize reams of Shakespeare and Milton, for introducing me to Lamb's "Dissertation upon Roast Pig," and for teaching me the importance, in both reading and writing, of every word.

Next Anne Greene, from whom I took a creative writing course at Wesleyan in the summer of 1990. At my first conference with her, Anne exclaimed, tapping my paper, "Well, you're a writer! What are you going to do about it?" It's taken a while, but *The Garden* grew out of that course.

I wish to thank the people who took me seriously, read my work, and gave me their comments on my first efforts, among them Roger and Cecil Jospe, David Black, and Toni Levy. June Roth and others in our writers' group patiently read snippets of stories (all I seemed able to produce at that time) and made helpful, tactful suggestions. I am especially grateful to Mike and

Cornelia Bessie, wonderful friends who have encouraged me in writing and in life for many years.

Thanks go to Ned O'Gorman, who criticized some of my early efforts as if they were the work of Henry James. To Stanley Crawford, with whom I took a writers' seminar in Santa Fe; Stan and his wife, Rose Mary, have become great friends and helpful, attentive critics. Their view of the world has enriched and broadened mine. To Virginia Davies for her thoughtful comments about religious questions, and to Jack Rosenthal, whose take on *The Garden* was marvelously invigorating. And especially to Jane Kramer, who urged me to write long before Adam and Eve entered my life, loved the idea of *The Garden* from the start, and still loves it eight years on. It is quite possible that, without her enthusiasm, this book would never have been completed.

Molly Peacock rescued me from discouragement— not writer's *block* but writer's despair: the sense that there was no way I could pull this odd piece of work together. I appreciate her careful readings, her suggestions and input, and her confidence in me. Thanks to my agent, Kathleen Anderson, who had the temerity to take me on—what a miracle!—a seventy-year-old new writer. Kathy edited mercilessly and educated me enormously, for which I am extremely grateful. And finally my wonderful editor at HarperCollins, Ruth Katcher, who has asked the sort of questions that have led me to rewrite sections, develop characters more fully, and delve into the book more deeply than I had before. Ruth shares with Miss Couser both a passion for literature and a focus on each word. It is a delight to work with her.

My warmest thanks go to my family, who have listened to me talk about *The Garden* for far too long, and must often have wondered whether anything would come of it. Several of them have read the manuscript at various stages; I hope they will have the fortitude to read it once again now that it is finished and, I trust, improved. I am especially grateful to my youngest son, Tom, for giving it a very close reading at a point where I could no longer see either the mountain or the molehill, and making a number of suggestions that got me underway again. And above all I thank my husband, Bernie Aidinoff, who has read, criticized, and commented on the manuscript—without ever treating it as a legal document—and encouraged me every inch of the way.

CONTENTS

CONTENTS

The Beginning

SOMETHING HEAVY ON my center, smooth against my skin, shifting very slightly within itself, stretched and retracted. Occasionally a tap to the side, always in the same spot. I breathed. Instantly the thing was still. I let out the air. Again I inhaled, deeply, and pushed against the heaviness as I filled my chest. The thing began to move. Slowly, stopping and starting, it wound back and forth across my thigh, around my knee, down my leg. It slid over my ankle, passed gently by my heel, with a little touch to my instep along the way. There was a swish. Again, silence and dark. I felt light, unburdened, empty, as if I might float away. Soft things swept my face, my cheek, my ear, wafted across my nose. My hands rose from my sides and brushed them off. There was a

1

tickle in my nose; I gasped, gasped again. A great noise burst from my mouth. My eyelids jerked open. And I saw.

At first there was only blue, limpid and luminous, stretching wide above me. A white, fluffy mass appeared, scudded across the expanse, tumbled into pieces, and melted into the blue. I lifted my arms, spread my fingers. Light came through them; the ends glowed pink. I curled a finger into my palm and felt it scratch the skin. On my arms fine hairs glimmered in the sunlight. Still lying flat, I turned my head to one side. Not far away several forms, tall and dark and topped with green fluff, stretched toward the sky. Scattered around me and floating through the air were weightless bits of pink, turned up around the edges: blossoms falling from trees; it was one of them that had tickled my nose. I caught a petal as it fell and rubbed it against my cheek. It was soft and smelled sweet. I raised my head and looked down. More new sights: two small, white cushions topped with pink, each with a tip that stuck out. A smooth, soft expanse where the weight had been. Below, something fuzzy and gold. Sitting up, I discovered legs, ankles, feet, toes with shiny ends just like the ones on my fingers. A petal rested on my foot; it slid away when I wiggled my toe.

That first day, of course, I did not know it was the sky

I saw, the wind that moved my hair, an apple tree that shed pink petals on my toe. Cloud, face, blossom: all were unknown. I had no knowledge, no words. Each time I turned my head and found, before my eyes, something I had not seen, the world expanded.

Bending my knees, I took my feet in my hands. The soles were tender and a little wrinkled. I lifted my hands and found my mouth, nose, eyes, and above, a tremendous load of stuff, soft and very long. I pulled my fingers through it and stretched my arms as far as I could reach, drew the stream over my face, and saw the world through a fall of gold. When I blew, my breath sent it ballooning in front of me. The sight, the feel of it, astonished me, and I laughed.

There was a rustle in the leaves, and I heard a sound like the one I had made when my hair billowed on my breath. I stood and saw, in the shade of the tree, a mound of coils sheathed in brilliant colors, moving and shifting constantly, topped with a feathered head. Two emerald eyes looked out at me from a brown face. The creature's mouth was open and its head shook. When it realized I had seen it, it stopped and flicked a green tongue over its lips.

"Well, little one," it said. "I don't mean to laugh at you—but it's amusing to see you wake from the silence and start to explore the world." It set its head to the

3

ground and moved toward me, straightening its body one coil at a time. In the sun it wound itself again into a circle and raised itself high, bringing its head level with mine. I reached out my hand and ran my fingers down its back, overwhelmed by its beauty. The creature stretched under my caress. Then it shook its head. "And you know how to laugh. And sneeze. That is a gift not given to gods."

"Gods," I said. "What are gods?"

"Never mind. It's not important now. Much more important to know yourself." It inclined its head to the left and smiled. "You," it said softly, "are Eve." It drew out the *e*: *Eeeeve*, with a little puff at the end. The name sounded beautiful and worthy.

"*Eeeeve*," I said.

"Yes," it replied. "I've been watching over you. I'm glad you're awake."

"Oh, it was you that was sitting on my . . . " I put my hand on the place where I had felt its weight.

"Stomach."

"My stomach."

"Yes. I hope you don't mind. I was listening for your heart to begin its beat. You were so soft and comfortable in the sun, I grew quite sleepy."

"But you're too . . ." I spread my arms wide.

"Big."

"Big to fit on my stomach."

The creature smiled. "Oh, I made myself smaller," it said. "I wouldn't want to squash you—especially not when you've just come to life."

"And who," I asked, "are you?"

The creature uncoiled itself and drew its body toward the sky so that it was nearly standing on its tail. "I," it said, "am the Serpent. God has given you to me to raise. He has placed you in my care. I am your mentor, guide, and teacher. For you are new to the world. You know nothing." The Serpent smiled as if it were paying me a compliment. "You are mine to form and to teach. That, for instance, is your foot." It slid over gracefully and licked the end of my foot. I looked at my feet, and then at my body, and cupped my hands under the cushions with pink tips. "Those are your breasts," the Serpent said.

"Breasts," I repeated.

"Below is your stomach."

"Stomach," I said.

"Legs. And these," it said, "are your toes. And toenails. Repeat after me. Feet."

"Feet."

"Toes."

"Toes, toenails, legs, stomach, breasts."

"Ah," said the Serpent. "A quick learner. Good. But

5

we won't rush. We have lots of time. You must be hungry."

"Hungry?" I asked.

"Yes. A funny feeling in your stomach. It means you need to eat."

"Eat?" I asked.

The Serpent sighed. "Come, I'll show you."

The Serpent's Lessons

○

THAT DAY WE ATE BY a lake, a lunch of dandelion greens and peanuts and bananas, and I watched the lily pads and their white and pink flowers opening in the sun. When we had finished, the Serpent showed me how to wash my hands and face in the water and dry them on the warm grass. Then we leaned against a tree and looked at the world around us, and the Serpent gave me names.

"This is a tree," it said. "A leaf, grass, water, sky. A cloud. Earth." It pulled up a dandelion and shook it. "Roots. They're underground. Trees have roots too." The words came flying into my head as if they had always been there. "Good, good," said the Serpent, and tapped the end of its tail on the ground. A small black creature climbed out of the sand and waved its legs in the air. "An ant," said the Serpent. "I've disturbed her nest—I *am* sorry, Ant—let's go a little farther on."

And so my life in the Garden began.

We lived on the bank of a stream in an open glade that looked out over a valley. The Serpent had piled leaves and straw under a tree for a bed. It was pleasant, but we had no protection from the weather, and it was often too hot or windy or wet. After a while the Serpent helped me make a covering of vines and eucalyptus leaves to shield us from the sun in the middle of the day, when the pools steamed with heat and we could not walk on the sand, and from the showers that sometimes came in the night. Little by little we improved the structure; we built a lean-to, and then a rough shed of branches, which I plastered with mud. Before long we were living in a hut, open on one side and thatched with straw. I cleared away the shrubs and grass in front and packed the earth hard with my feet to make a terrace. Here we ate and slept and talked, sheltering under the roof of the hut only during the rare periods of rain.

Our food was simple, fresh fruit—apples, bananas, pears, grapes—all nearby, dangling from trees and vines. Avocados and arugula, and tomatoes and all the herbs, and olives, and every kind of nut, and clear, cold water from the stream. Sometimes I made a sweet drink by squeezing the juice from a lemon, and adding water to it, and honey. The Serpent lapped water with its tongue, but that did not work well for me; I had to cup my hands and slurp the liquid into my mouth. *If only I could make something the same shape as my hands but solid*, I thought, poking my fingers into the red mud at the river's edge. The mud clung to my fingers; I plunged my hands in and drew out a great glob of it. I rolled the mud into a ball, pressed the ball flat, and finally managed to shape it into a wobbly bowl. This I set out to dry in the sun.

"What a good idea, Eve," exclaimed the Serpent, and I went on to make larger and better bowls and cups with handles.

One day we passed a herd of goats, and I spotted a baby ("A kid," said the Serpent). I had seen very few baby animals. "God doesn't want many; the Garden would get crowded if every creature had young," the Serpent explained. The kid was on its knees, nuzzling and butting its head against a pink bag hanging under its mother's stomach.

"What *is* it doing?" I asked.

"It's feeding. That bag is the udder; the mother's milk collects there, and the baby drinks through the teats."

I wrinkled my nose. "What does milk taste like?"

"It's good," the Serpent replied. "When the kid has had its fill, I'll teach you how to milk the goat. Run back and get one of your bowls."

When I returned with the bowl, the kid was sleeping

on the ground while the goat grazed alongside. "Go pet the goat," instructed the Serpent. I walked slowly over and began to rub the goat's back. The animal looked pleased; animals always like to be caressed.

"Good," said the Serpent. "I can't *show* you, but put your hand around the teat and squeeze gently from the top down." At first nothing happened; then suddenly milk squirted warm onto my legs. The Serpent laughed. "That's fine." It pushed the bowl toward me. "Now see how good your aim is." After a few tries, I was able to send a stream of milk into the bowl. Once I had gotten the hang of it, I set the bowl between my knees and used both hands. "Excellent," said the Serpent. "Don't take more than you need; be sure to leave plenty for the kid."

"Would you like some?" I asked, offering the bowl to the Serpent. I was not sure I wanted to drink white liquid from a bag hanging on the underside of a goat.

"Try it, Eve. It's good; you'll see." So I drank and liked it so much I finished it and had to go back to the goat for more. From then on we had milk for breakfast every morning.

We rose when light began to dull the stars, and washed, and stretched hugely, both of us reaching toward the sky. Then we ran—I ran with the Serpent moving beside me in its effortless, endless spiral (how I envied the movement, the ease!), savoring each ray of light. Shadows ran with us, reshaping themselves on rocks and trees. Flowers opened slowly; deer grazed. We picked an apple for breakfast and ate by a lake or brook. Afterward we strolled along the shore, and I gathered all the things that interested me: blue-and-white spotted eggs fallen from a tree, a brown stone striped in gray, a tiny purple orchid with a ball of earth clutched in its roots. I always returned with hands overflowing and often had to go back to pick up objects I had dropped along the way. Finally, exasperated, I managed to weave some supple grasses into a pouch, which I hung around my neck to hold the small treasures I found.

When we got home, I went for a swim while the Serpent sunned itself on the terrace. The stream in front of our hut flowed from the forest to the west and emptied into a pond just below the terrace. To me the stream was a pathway into the woods, like the trails made by the animals all through the Garden. Along the banks were open glades bright with daisies or tiny beaches curving yellow in the sun. Farther along massive trees crowded together, their giant roots clutched into the mud. The water was quite deep, and the current strong. Each day I swam upriver as fast as I could until I was exhausted, then gave myself to the stream and let it carry me down to the pond. Here, before climbing out, I lay on my back and found all sorts of creatures in the clouds.

After swimming we had lessons. The Serpent told me stories: how the world began, what stars are made of, why leaves are green and crickets chirp. It would not allow me to ask many questions. "Later," it said, "when you have learned the basic facts, you can ask all the questions you like. For now, listen." So I listened, to the words and to the rhythm of the words, to what they said and to the music they made; and as the Serpent spoke, I learned the tales by heart.

"In the beginning," said the Serpent, "God created the heavens and the earth and said, 'Let there be light'; and there was light.

"And God saw the light, that it was good; and God divided the light from the darkness, and called the light Day, and the darkness Night.

"And God called the dry land Earth; and the gathering together of the waters the Seas; and God saw that it was good.

"And God said, 'Let the earth bring forth grass, and the fruit tree yielding fruit.'

"And the earth brought forth grass, and trees of many kinds.

"And God said, 'Let there be lights in the firmament of heaven,' and God made two great lights, the greater to rule the day, and the lesser to rule the night; he made the stars also. And God saw that it was good.

"And God created great whales, which the waters brought forth abundantly, and every winged fowl. And God made the beasts of the earth, and cattle, and every thing that creepeth upon the earth; and God saw that it was good.

"And God created man in his own image, in the image of God created he him; male and female created he them.

"And God blessed them, and God said unto them, 'Be fruitful, and multiply, and replenish the earth, and subdue it; and have dominion over the fish of the sea, and over the fowl of the air, and over every living thing that moveth upon the earth.'

"And God saw everything that he had made, and behold, it was very good." The Serpent stretched itself and looked at me. "Any questions, Eve?"

"What is man?" I asked. "You said God created man in his image."

"Man is a human being, like you."

"Where *is* man? What's his name?"

"His name is Adam, and he lives with God. He's not really a man yet; he's very young—a boy—"

"The way a young goat is a kid," I interrupted.

"Exactly, and you are a girl. God is raising Adam, just as I'm raising you."

"Will I see Adam—and God?"

"Yes, of course, when you have lived a little longer."

In my mind I ran over everything the Serpent had told me about God creating the world. "Is all that true?" I asked.

"That is the story of the Creation," the Serpent replied. "Tomorrow I will start teaching you science." And the following day it began again: "The sun is a ball of flaming gases in a galaxy of other suns. Aeons ago parts of that ball broke away and formed planets. There are nine of them, and they revolve around the sun in great circles. Our world is the third planet, Earth."

"Earth," I muttered. "But earth is also this." I crumbled some soil between my fingers.

"Yes," said the Serpent. "That soil is a part of the Earth, and so we often call soil 'earth.' Long ago a piece of the Earth broke away and became the moon we see at night. As we revolve around the sun, so the moon revolves around us. The stars we see are other suns spread out across the sky, far, far away."

I traced a circle in the sand of the terrace and drew a line through it. "So which is true?" I asked. "What you told me yesterday or what you've told me today?"

"One is myth; one is science. Each has its truths and its realities."

"Isn't it hard sometimes to know what's real and what's make-believe?"

"It is," said the Serpent. "But we can try." And the Serpent explained light and darkness, day and night, rain, clouds, lightning, wind, dry land, and oceans. Grass and trees and seeds, and how they grow. The orbit of the sun, the moon, the stars. Then living creatures: fish, birds, animals. Some I knew well: the dogs that occasionally played with me, the squirrels that scampered in the trees around us, the goats we milked. Others I had seen from a distance, grazing on the plain; some, like the great fish of the sea, I did not know at all.

Often we walked in the fields and forests, searching for the animals we had discussed in the morning. The Garden was crisscrossed with trails, large and small— alleys tramped out by elephants, paths shaped by the webbed feet of geese, tiny roadways formed by ants trundling seeds to their nests—and we followed those we could wherever they led. When we came upon animals, we walked among them quietly while the Serpent commented. "See, Eve, as I told you, the deer and cows have strong, square teeth that enable them to chomp clover and grass. The cats prefer the shrubs in the hills; they have long tongues to lick shoots from the branches, while the bears live in ravines and woodlands and have sharp, pointed claws to scrape berries from the vines or bark from the trees."

At dawn and at dusk most animals came to drink in

the river or roll in the mud and play together. The gazelle with their curved and pointed horns raced after swift, spotted cheetah, sending clouds of dust in the air. Baby deer and lion cubs rolled together on the ground, paws and hooves waving in the air. "Serpent, won't they hurt one another?" I asked, for I sometimes stubbed my toe or hit my elbow on a rock, and I knew it could hurt.

"Maybe a little bump or bruise, but they won't do any real damage."

"But they're biting each other!"

"Only in play. Don't worry, Eve; they're just having fun."

The Serpent taught me to keep myself clean, wash my hands before preparing food, scrub my fingernails in moss to remove the dust and grit that collected there in the course of my day. But on one matter the Serpent was unable to give advice: my hair, which tumbled well below my waist in a tangled, curly mass. The Serpent watched bemused as strands whipped into my face or got caught in low branches. "You'll have to figure that out yourself, Eve," it said, shaking its head. "I have no experience of hair."

I tried calming the mop with my fingers, but it did little good. Finally I found a shrub with short, stubby branches, which I managed to whittle (with a sharp piece of flint) into a rough comb. Every day from then on, after working the tangles out with the comb, I played with my hair, experimented with plaiting it, or wound it around my head and fastened it with vines. If the Serpent was there, it often watched. "Miraculous!" it said, waggling its ears. "Leave it that way today; it looks nice."

In the afternoons I gathered reeds and long leaves and grasses both green and dry, and plaited them to make bracelets for myself, or necklaces that I slipped over the Serpent's head. "Instead of hair," I said.

"How foolish you are, Eve!" It laughed, but I noticed that it went to the pond to look at itself, twisting its neck one way and the other to get a full view.

I experimented with mud of all sorts and colors. At first I made useful things: cups and jugs and plates. When I had enough of them, I began to amuse myself, molding figures or making designs in the damp clay. I drew pictures of birds and shaped clumsy forms of animals. One day I found that rolling clay between my palms resulted in a long, thin cylinder I could coil or stretch out in undulant spirals. Add a head, ears, feathers, a mouth slightly open, tiny agate eyes, and there before me was a miniature Serpent. Enchanted, I made a series of them in various poses and lined them up before the hut. When the Serpent saw them, it shook and shouted with laughter while tears ran down its cheeks. "Eve, Eve! The things you do! You're an artist!"

"An artist?"

"Never mind," said the Serpent, wiping its face on the grass. "Artist or not, you have a wonderful way of looking at the universe. I believe," it added, tilting its head to one side and looking at me with tender, teasing eyes, "you have brought humor into the world—an attribute God overlooked in his Creation."

In the evening, as the birds stilled their chatter and the fish sank to the bottom of the stream, the Serpent asked me, "What did you see today that you'd never noticed before?"

"I saw the morning glory open when the sun rose and close in the heat of the day. I saw a shooting star mark its trail in the sky. I saw salmon leaping in the waterfall."

"And what did you learn today that you had not known before?"

"I learned that ants carry their food into their nests, walking all in a row, and that bees stick their noses—"

"Proboscises," said the Serpent.

"Proboscises into the flowers to drink, the way I drink sometimes through a straw. And Serpent, I learned that something stirs here"—I pressed my hands beneath my breasts—"sometimes, when I see an eagle or an elm, or clouds moving across the sky, or hold a lamb in my arms—"

"A mixture of elation and joy and love—"

"And sometimes when I'm watching you, or you tease me and laugh."

The Serpent smiled. "That's nice," it declared, and we lay on our backs and listened to the frogs sing as the stars made patterns in the sky.

Solitude

ONE AFTERNOON the Serpent told me it was going off by itself and would be back for supper.

"Where are you going? Can I come with you?" I asked.

"No," said the Serpent. "I have things to do, things to reflect upon."

"What sort of things?"

"Occupations. Ideas."

"And what am I to do?"

"Eve," said the Serpent. "You've been with me for three full moons: ninety days and ninety nights. Now I give you a gift, two gifts: solitude and silence. Look around you: you have a world to explore. Go out into it. Use your eyes: observe all things as they are. Don't place a twig in the path of an ant or whistle with the bird. Instead hear the voice of that bird, watch the walk of that ant. If you do, you'll truly know its nature."

The Serpent was quiet, and I thought it had finished. But it went on: "And then, when you're exhausted from so much looking, lie down and close your eyes and listen. Hear everything. Not only the doe in the thicket, the chestnut falling, the moth as it bursts forth from its chrysalis, but the mole underground, the fish at the bottom of the stream. The chaff and the grain in a blade of wheat. Apple blossoms as they open to the sun. If you listen long enough and are very lucky, you will hear . . . nothing."

"Nothing?"

"Silence. That is best and rarest of all."

So that day and whenever I was alone, I watched and listened. And it was just as the Serpent had said. I came to know the mossy feel of a bee on my finger; the tickle of dandelions; the movement of wind and water in my hair; the smell of lemons and strawberries, cedar bark, clover, and garlic; the taste of pear, peanut, pomegranate; the crunch of corn between my teeth and gravel between my toes. I perceived the slightest quiver of a butterfly's wings, the twitch of a dragonfly's tail, the pointed tips of the tiger's ears in the tall grass. I heard a trout flick its fins in the lake, a black bear yawn, a petal lost in the wind.

What is it like, I wondered, to *be* a butterfly? An otter? I lay on the ground and thought: I am a snake slithering through the grass. On my belly with my hands against my sides, I swayed my shoulders and legs back and forth and gazed into the tops of the grasses as if they were trees and, at eye level, watched the ants scurry by, waving their feelers in the air.

I thought: I am a hippopotamus. My four flat feet are buried deep in the mud; when I walk I go *shlurp shlurp*. I lay immersed in the brown river with only my eyes and my nose sticking out.

I thought: I am a big white bird with thin legs. I have a long, curved bill instead of a nose, and I pluck the green plants from the bottom of the pond and eat them. I tiptoed around the edges of the pond, raising my head and lowering it. Pushing a reluctant heron from its nest, I perched cautiously on the eggs, legs folded, elbows squeezed against my ribs.

I thought: I am a giraffe. I galloped, moving my neck forward and back as giraffe do, and spread my legs stiff and wide while I bent to catch grass in my teeth or stretched my neck to the treetops. I thought: I am a gorilla. I moved sideways across the ground, using my knuckles for support, and cradled a bundle of straw in my arms (the mother gorillas would not let me take one of their babies), and pounded my chest with both hands and roared.

I thought: I am a monkey. I chattered and climbed into a tree and hung from one leg, because I did not have a tail.

I thought: I am a trout. I lie in the shadow at the bottom of the stream and open and shut my mouth and flick my tail to swim. But I could not stay beneath the water long enough to be a fish.

Then I thought: if I climb onto the animals and ride, I'll move as they do, become part of their bodies. I dropped from a rock onto the gray back of an elephant and lay flat, clinging to its ears as the great beast lumbered through the Garden. I am enormous, I thought. With my trunk I can pluck bananas from the top of a tree and spray myself with water.

I clambered onto a pony: I am small and limber, with a long mane. I swish my tail to chase away the flies that tickle my flanks. I prance and lift my hooves high and arch my neck.

I plunked myself onto a billy goat, but it bucked me off into a fresh cow patty, and when I arrived home, limping, the Serpent refused to let me near the hut until I had swum and washed my hair.

In all these adventures I had no sense that the

Serpent was watching me, but one evening when I was staring into the upper branches of a pine tree, where a falcon was spreading its wings, I found it at my side, head tipped, ears raised. "Eve. No matter how much you want to, or how hard you try, you'll never be a bird. Don't even think of taking off from the top of that tree!"

"I don't know what you're talking about!" I said indignantly.

"Of course you do," replied the Serpent, and it slithered into the brush, making an odd noise in its throat. Before disappearing, it turned its head. "That's a chortle, in case you're wondering."

So I gave up my idea of trying to fly. Instead I began shadowing birds: I watched them eat, imitated their walk, made awkward attempts to peck at seeds with my mouth. I followed them to their nests, found warblers in the hedges, pipits dug into the sand, tanagers settled comfortably in the forked branches of trees. Swallows I especially loved: they were so graceful, so free in their swoops through the sky, their unlikely, unexpected aerial courtships! Several times I scrambled up a bluff to visit the cliff swallows in their precarious abodes of mud high above the valley floor.

One day, halfway up a steep climb, I stopped to catch my breath and watch the bird, with its red throat and white blaze above the beak, flash back and forth across the face of the cliff. Abruptly the knob I had chosen as a handhold gave way, and I fell. Fortunately the cliff was slanted, not sheer, and I skittered down it feetfirst, all the way to the bottom, without any serious damage. My cheek was scraped, and also my hands, from grabbing at the rock on the way down. Standing up shakily, I saw a deep gash just below my right knee. As I brushed the dirt away, the cut gaped open and blood streamed out of the wound and ran down my leg. The knee began to throb.

Though the Serpent had told me about my veins and the fluid that ran through them, carrying nutrients through my body, I had never seen blood before. I leaned over and looked at the cut; I could glimpse white bone at the bottom. I took some of the red stuff on my finger and licked it. It was warm, but I did not like the taste. I felt sick and lay down in the meadow. The sky whirled above me.

Finally the Earth steadied and I managed to get to my feet and hobble home, leaving a red trail in the grass. Several times I was dizzy and stopped to rest against a tree. Looking back along the path, I saw animals sniffing at the blood: a fox, a panther, a bevy of crows. A lioness licked at a puddle but apparently did not like the taste either; she sneezed and began washing her nose with her paw.

The Serpent was coiled before our hut, watching for me, and immediately came to my side. "So you took a tumble, did you?" it said in its usual voice, as if it were asking whether I had found enough hazelnuts for supper. "I wondered what had happened to you. Eve, look at me, in the eyes," and it peered into my face. "You're all right. Pupils the same size. No head injury." With its tail it helped me across the yard. "Come to the stream; we'll wash this gash." It bathed the cut in the fresh running water and found herbs that it applied to the wound, binding it up with vines. In a short time I was lying on a mat with my leg up while the Serpent bustled about. "A light supper will make you feel better," it said. "A pity I wasn't there. I'm afraid you'll have a scar—a mark that won't go away. It's a deep cut. If I'd gotten to you sooner, I could have avoided it."

When we had eaten, it sat beside me and once more looked in my eyes. "You're fine," it declared again. "Now tell me what happened." And it listened carefully, without interrupting, as I described the cliff, the swallows and their nests, my fall.

"I know the place," it said. "Eve, you were lucky." It looked off to the western sky. "Intimations of mortality," it murmured.

"What?" I was half-asleep.

"I keep forgetting, here in the Garden, that you are

after all a human and can be hurt, as you were today." It grinned at me. "Eve, my dear, no matter what you feel, you truly aren't invincible. You can't fly, and you *can* fall off cliffs. We must both remember that! You be more cautious; I'll watch you a bit more carefully. Sleep now."

The following morning I could barely move. I ached all over and was covered with black and blue marks; my fingers were scraped and swollen. For several days I stayed home while the Serpent nursed me, making poultices for my leg and bruises, bathing me in the stream, fetching me the sweetest berries. As my fingers healed, it brought me reeds and long grasses: "It's easier to work with than clay and less messy." So I spent the time braiding the stuff and began to experiment with weaving. When I was tired, I lay back and watched the sky, trees, birds, a passing panoply before my eyes. And the Serpent.

The Garden was filled with animals, all of them beautiful, but the Serpent was the most beautiful of all. Its coat had many colors, arranged in patterns that varied from day to day. Sometimes the colors shifted continually, from dark to light and back, dappled like water in a pond. Or the Serpent would stay one color for a time: indigo, purple, ginger from head to toe, with the muscles a-shimmer beneath the skin. One moment it might be sheathed in red-and-white stripes or green-

and-yellow dots; the next, diamonds bordered with thick (or thin) black lines paraded around its body. At times the tones were pale, so pale that from a distance the Serpent looked white. At others they were brilliant.

At night the Serpent made its skin phosphorescent; it slithered through the grass with strips of white dots from head to tail, so I could follow it easily in the dark. Once it turned its body into an astral display; a tiny moon and stars and planets marched down its back the way they moved above us in the sky. For days I begged it to show me the spectacle again, but it refused. "It's a foolish waste of energy," it said firmly, and could not be budged.

The Serpent was one of the larger creatures in the Garden. Stretched out from head to toe, it was longer than an elephant, though it could make itself smaller at will. I rarely noticed its length, because usually it sat coiled, with its body raised. A narrow, tactile neck allowed the Serpent to swivel its head fully around. Its oval face was the color of a chestnut. It had bushy eyebrows and eyes that were emerald, like the green in a peacock's tail. Its ears were feathered and could lie back against its head or lift to fluffy peaks at each side. Its nose, though small, had about it an aura of dignity; its mouth stretched nearly from one ear to the other. When it laughed you could see smooth, round, white teeth very much like mine.

But what fascinated me most was the Serpent's tongue. Shaped like a four-leaf clover and set on a four-sided, mintlike stem, the tongue was light green with delicate white veins, and soft as lamb's quarters. The Serpent could use each leaf separately, to pluck a berry, remove a speck of dust from my eye or a nettle from my hair. It could shape its leaves into a cup to catch milk from the goat, or roll them like a straw, or flatten them to lap water from a pool. When it bathed, the Serpent doused water over its body and then, like a cat, licked itself dry.

The Serpent's skin was smooth and soft to the touch. Pillowing my head on its back, I felt both the softness on the surface and the great strength beneath. The Serpent was able to heat or cool its body at will, and would warm our porridge or cocoa in a gourd with the end of its tail. At night, if the air was chilly, the Serpent heated its entire mass and I lay warm and cozy in its coils. But when the weather was sultry, it cooled its body, and I was cool too.

In the evening we stretched out on the bank of the pond and looked at the stars. When the sun set and I could not see beyond the wall of bushes, the pond held circles of darkness filled with glistening unknown things. The trees spoke in whispers; leaves rustled on windless nights. From the stream voices called, Who are you, who am I. I curled against the Serpent and it twined itself around me, rested its head on my shoulder, and patted its tail on my thigh. Enveloped in its coils, I felt safe.

Many Questions

ONE DAY I ASKED, "Who is God?"

The Serpent raised its brows. "You know about God. God made the heavens and the earth, the sun and the stars. He made—"

"That's not who God is; that's what he's done. Who is he? Where did he come from? What does he look like? You or me? Or an animal?"

"Why not a rock?" said the Serpent. "Or a tree?"

I thought about that, then said slowly, "Trees are the most beautiful of all. But I don't think of trees as making something. What does God look like?"

"More or less like you. Remember, he made you in his image."

I tried to imagine God looking like me. What did I

look like, anyway? I had seen myself only in bits and pieces reflected in pools of water. I decided that God's Creation, the moon and the Earth and all the creatures and plants, interested me more. "How did God make the world?" I asked.

"How?" The Serpent plucked a blueberry from a nearby bush and balanced it on its tongue. "Well." It swallowed the berry. I watched the fat, round shape slide down the Serpent's long throat. The sun glittered, and the colors of the Serpent's skin glistened iridescent— pink, blue, gold, silver, black, green. "It's hard to explain. He did a wondrous thing. No matter how he behaves sometimes, you have to give him that."

"What do you mean, no matter how he behaves?" I asked, surprised. From all the Serpent had told me, I imagined God as perfect: magnificent and great, a Serpent in a different shape with powers of creation.

"Well." The Serpent looked embarrassed. "He *can* be a little impatient and impetuous. But we all behave badly occasionally. As I was saying, God took nothing— wisps of cloud, dust, drops of water—and he pulled it all together and made something extraordinary. It would have been an amazing feat even if it had turned out ugly, but it did not."

"How did he do it?"

"First he had to think. He thought a lot, for days and days. He saw it—his Creation—in his mind, and then he exerted his will on each one of those whirling, mindless atoms and drew them together to make a whole. To make this world. And all of the animals. And you."

"And you too?"

The Serpent was quiet. "No," it said. "Not me." And no matter how much I begged, the Serpent would say no more about itself.

For a few moments we sat and ate berries, while gray clouds covered the sun. "It will rain," said the Serpent. "That's good for the grapes." But I could not get the idea of Creation out of my mind.

"Why did no one try before?" I began again. "Was there anyone *before* God? How did God make the animals? The way I make my little models, with mud and twigs? How did God give them life? What *is* life, anyway?"

"So many questions!" cried the Serpent. "Teaching Adam would have been a lot simpler." It flopped its tail on the grass as if it had no more strength and tucked its head into its coils. Abashed, I watched the great mound of color change its skin to various shades of purple with scarlet trim, and I wondered if my curiosity would ever be satisfied.

"Serpent," I said at last, "I won't ask any more questions. I'll just listen to you."

The Serpent drew its head slowly out of its coils and smiled. "Oh, Eve, you know I love your curiosity. Just be patient and give *me* time to answer, and *you* time to think about what I say."

As soon as I saw the Serpent was not irritated with me, I asked, "Tell me about Adam."

"Well, I told you that Adam is a boy."

"And I'm a girl."

"Yes. And we've discussed the animals, how each animal has a mate: the cow and the bull, the ewe and the ram, the hen and the rooster."

"Yes."

"What are they called?"

"Females and males. They're each other's mates."

"That's right. Well, Adam is the mate for Eve."

"The mate for Eve? For me?"

"Yes."

"What's he like? Does he look like me?"

"In many ways he does, but he is a male animal, and you're a female."

"Where did he come from?"

"Where everything else came from. God made him."

"From what?"

"From earth."

"Did God make me the same way? Did I come from earth too?"

"Well, there are two stories about that. You remember the words: 'God created man in his own image, in the image of God created he him; male and female created he them.' Not very well put, but the meaning is clear."

"And the other story?"

"The other story says God made you from Adam's rib."

"What!" I cried. "That's impossible! Adam's rib?" I poked my chest; I could feel the solid ridges of bone. "How could he make me from Adam's rib? Anyway, why would he want to? It's stupid."

"Foolish, not stupid," said the Serpent absentmindedly. "Find a better word." The Serpent never forgot its responsibility as a tutor.

"Ridiculous," I said. "Why a used bone? And why leave Adam with one less rib?" I shook my head. The idea seemed preposterous. "Anyway," I went on after a moment, "how is Adam different from me?"

"Like all male mammals, Adam has a penis and testicles."

"What for?"

"Eve, you know that: to procreate—to make babies."

"But who does he procreate with?"

"Eve, my dear." The Serpent peered into my face. "With his mate. With you."

I leaned over and rested my forehead in my hands. I had seen animals mating: the bull climbing on the heifer, heavy on her back, straddling it while the cow turned big, startled eyes on me as if it wanted me to help. "I don't think I like that much," I said. "And will I have babies, like the sheep?"

"Human babies like you and Adam."

"And I'll be their mother?"

"And Adam their father."

"Adam and I don't have a father or a mother."

"No, as you know, God created you; you are the first humans on Earth. But from now on all creatures will have parents: fathers and mothers." I sat still, twisting a blade of grass around my thumb. "What is it, Eve?" the Serpent asked.

"I don't like the idea of Adam . . . on top of me . . . like the animals . . . ."

The Serpent patted my arm gently with its tail. "I understand that, my dear," it said. "With the animals, it is not a gentle act. With humans it will be different. This is one of the things God has done really well. He very much wants men and women to have children, and he has made the making of babies a joy." The Serpent smiled. "It hasn't happened yet, but when a man and a woman love one another and make love, it will be one of the most beautiful things that can happen on Earth. You'll see, when the time comes you'll find it a great joy and a great beauty." The Serpent took a hibiscus leaf in its mouth and wiped my cheeks. I hadn't been aware that I was crying.

"Eve," continued the Serpent, "I've had you in my care since you came alive, and still I don't know you. I don't know why you're crying now, or where you find the thoughts that are in your head. You're an enigma."

"An enigma?"

"The unknown, a puzzle. When I started with you, I thought I could form you completely, make you into anything I wanted. But I can't."

"Does that bother you?"

"Not at all. On the contrary, it's far more interesting this way." The Serpent hesitated. "But it does raise questions, even for me. Wherever did you get all these ideas, and these emotions?" It peered into my face as if it had never seen me before. "Where *do* they come from?"

"I don't know. They just pop up in my head. What about Adam, doesn't he think and feel the way I do?"

"I haven't seen Adam for a long time, but from the few words I've had with God about him, he seems to be a different type altogether."

"Would you really rather teach Adam than me?" I

37

asked. Even to myself, my voice sounded small and strained.

The Serpent opened its mouth wide and laughed, a great belly laugh that shook its entire body. "Oh, Eve!" it cried. "I wouldn't exchange you for all the world."

Meeting God

"WELL," SAID THE SERPENT a few days later when it returned from its stroll, "you'll meet God and Adam tomorrow. We've been invited to come for a visit."

"Where does God live?" I asked. "What will I say to him? How do I behave?"

The Serpent wagged its ears as it did when it was amused. "I keep forgetting how young you are. You behave with God, and with Adam, just the way you do with me. God may ask you questions about what you do and what you've learned. He'll be interested in that."

"What do I say?"

The Serpent grinned. "What *have* you learned? Think about it, and give him your answer."

Early the next morning we climbed a long rise to an area of the Garden where I had never been. The trees were big with thick, long branches and heavy leaves, and not much sun reached the ground. Pine needles covered the path, which was soft as moss. Strawberries grew in clumps, flowers and fruit and leaves reaching out to one another as if they were carrying on a conversation. The berries were full and sweet.

At the top of a bend in the trail, we emerged suddenly into a clearing. A creature towered on the edge of a cliff, etched in profile against the sky. He was looking toward the distant plains and did not see us.

"Is that God?" I whispered to the Serpent.

"It is indeed."

I stared. A massive body, a head topped with white hair, broad shoulders, long arms. All these I could recognize from my own form. But below the waist he was shaped like a tree trunk, a white birch with feet instead of roots protruding from the bottom. The bark of the tree quivered in the wind.

"What a strange creature!" I breathed, afraid that God would hear. "The top of him is human, but then he turns into a tree. A tree with feet. And his skin ripples."

The Serpent's face turned red and its body heaved; I knew it was laughing, but I could not see that I had said anything funny. Finally it gasped, "Oh, Eve! You're wonderful! God doesn't turn into a tree, and it's not his skin rippling. It just looks that way, because he has a big piece of cloth wrapped around his waist, and the cloth covers his legs."

"What's cloth?" I asked.

"Material made from certain plants. You make bits of cloth when you weave. Come, let's say hello."

As we got closer, I could see God more clearly. He was tall—much taller than I—as tall as the Serpent when it raised itself on its tail. Every muscle was tensed, the veins taut in his neck. There was nothing soft about him. I was no longer sure I wanted to meet him.

God remained focused on the valley and still did not notice us. "Where is that boy?" he muttered. "Where has he gotten to now?"

Then he whistled. I had made endless attempts to whistle; I had practiced and blown until my lips were sore, but I could produce only a meager trill, no louder than the smallest birds. God's whistle was magnificent, and God whistling was magnificent to behold. He cupped his hands, hooked one finger in each side of his mouth to pull back the corners, drew in a breath, and blew.

Forgetting my fear, I ran up to him. "Oh, God!" I cried. "That's wonderful! How did you do it?"

God turned and glowered at me. He lowered his

brows over his eyes, and his face flushed. "Eve," he said. "You can't just appear like that and interrupt what I'm doing! Is that any way to greet your Maker?"

The Serpent came up behind me, coughing—I knew it was trying not to laugh. "Eve is a lively child," it said. "You did a fine job when you created her. I've tried to give her a good education, and I'm pleased with the results."

"Well, you haven't done much for her manners." God studied me, and his face softened. "Lively—and lovely! To imagine such beauty could come from Adam's rib! How are you, Eve?" he said kindly, and held out his hand. I looked at the Serpent.

"Put your hand in his, Eve, and squeeze." The Serpent looked down at its lithe body. "I haven't been able to teach her that."

I placed my hand in God's and squeezed. He put his other hand over mine and patted it.

"So you *did* make me from Adam's rib?" I asked.

"Of course. Didn't the Serpent tell you?"

"Yes, but—"

"God, that's the first time I've ever heard you whistle," interrupted the Serpent. "I wish I could do as well."

God patted my shoulder. "Let's go to the hut and get something to drink. That boy of mine has gone off somewhere. I did tell him you were coming, but he must have forgotten. He'll be back soon, no doubt. Come." And he led us up the path.

God's hut, like ours, was a lean-to open at the front, built of wood. Trees had been cut and placed solidly upright in the ground. The roof was thatched like ours, bundles of straw bound together with vines laid side by side across fat bamboo stalks. Someone had taken the trouble to carve designs on the posts: animals with claws and fat stomachs, blackberry bushes, all kinds of trees covered with leaves, nuts ready to fall from the tips of branches. Birds held flowers in their claws or opened their beaks to sing. The Serpent raised itself high and examined every carving. "Nice work," it said. "The boy's talented."

"Yes, he *is* quite good at that," said God. "It's amazing," he went on, "how humans want to make a nest for themselves, just like birds. No sooner had Adam come to life than he began putting up shelters, very simple at first, but now—look at it! Mind you, it's comfortable for me, too. But it surprises me, because it wasn't something I planned."

A bench, protected from the sun by a grape arbor— or pergola, as God called it—ran along the front of the hut. Soft pine branches provided a backrest. God and the Serpent settled together like old friends. "Sit here, Eve, next to me," God ordered, patting the bench, and I lay back against the boughs and watched and listened.

I had, of course, never met anything that resembled a human before, and I could not take my eyes off God. He had a large, rather square face, and a broad mouth that turned easily up or down. His eyes were oval shaped and dark brown, with heavy brows that almost touched when he frowned. Everything about him was accentuated, as if he had been made with precise corners and then someone had gone around him with a black pencil, outlining the edges. His white hair curled over his shoulders, and a beard hid the lower part of his face and his neck. His chest was covered with frizzy hair so thick the nipples barely showed through. A wide band of white material was tucked around his waist and fell to his ankles. It resembled nothing I had ever seen. I reached out and rubbed the stuff between my fingers. It felt soft and smooth.

"God, what is this wrapped around your waist?" I asked without thinking.

God, who was describing Adam to the Serpent, stopped suddenly. "Oh!" he cried crossly. "More interruptions!"

I pulled my hand away and put it in my lap. "But it's beautiful!" I cried.

God peered at the cloth as if he had never noticed it before and rubbed his fingers through the folds. "It *is* beautiful, isn't it?" He looked down at me and spoke more gently. "I'm glad you like it. It's linen, Eve, a piece of linen cloth."

"How did you make it?" I asked.

"Oh, I just waved a finger." God turned back to the Serpent. "What a boy," he said, raising both hands in the air. "Not very bright, mind you, but that's not important. He's the first, you know, my first try, so he's not perfect. But he's beautiful—you must see him run—and he's a nice boy, kindhearted, and good with his hands. I *have* had fun with him; you can't imagine."

"I can," said the Serpent, glancing at me. But I was watching God. God who was able to create cloth simply by waving a finger in the air; what power he must have! I shivered.

"But it's very tiring," God went on. "He takes a long time with his lessons and seems to have trouble remembering names, and he doesn't always pay attention. And for some reason I can't fix him by waving a finger." The Serpent coughed. God frowned. "What's the matter with you? You're always coughing. You never did *that* before."

"Just a little dust in my throat," said the Serpent. "Go on."

"The boy can't sit still, either. He wiggles his toes and

45

plays with his hair until it drives me crazy."

"Mmph," said the Serpent thoughtfully.

"And his balls," said God.

"What?" said the Serpent.

"His balls. He plays with his balls."

The Serpent lifted the front of its body into the air. "What does he do with *them*?"

"He plays with them all the time. All the time. Bounces them about!"

The Serpent raised its head farther and widened its eyes. "That's quite a trick. How does he do it?"

"From hand to hand, back and forth, to and fro, while I'm trying to explain things like the solar system."

"Well," said the Serpent, blinking. "He sounds like quite an accomplished and original young man."

"Yes, he's good with his hands," God repeated. "Look at this woodwork!" God waved at the porch with its carved columns. "And he loves to make those balls I told you about. I must admit it's difficult work, with his big hands. But he makes lots of them, small ones, large ones. He weaves reeds together for the cover and stuffs them with bits of wool or seeds. They *are* wonderful balls, and they bounce very well. He's fascinated by them. I only wish he'd put as much time and interest into learning."

"Oh. Of course," said the Serpent. It sank into its coils, coughing.

"There you go again," said God. "You should take something for it; try honey. Anyway," he continued, "when I ask Adam questions, he acts as if he's never heard the subject before. 'What?' he'll say. 'A planet? Nine planets? What's a planet?' as if we hadn't been talking and eating and sleeping planets for days."

"It must be trying for you," said the Serpent sympathetically.

"I can't tell you how difficult it's been, just getting the simplest ideas through his head." God mopped his brow. "All that Creation and then education on top of it!"

"Yes," said the Serpent. "It must be exhausting."

"Indeed," said God, and he leaned against the boughs.

The balsam needles gave out a strong bittersweet scent that was new to me. *I must get some and take them home for a pillow*, I thought. God closed his eyes, and we were all quiet. I watched an eagle circle in the sky. I knew it was looking for elderberries, its favorite fruit. The Serpent told me it could spot them from a mile high. It could even see the shadow of each berry on the ground. Songbirds sang to each other all around us. I was almost asleep when God spoke.

"But boys will be boys. We can't expect them to sit still and listen all the time."

"I suppose not," said the Serpent, and it winked at me. A rush of love flooded my heart.

Adam

WE HAD BEEN SITTING together for quite a while—the sun was a quarter of the way up the sky—when we heard the sound of singing. It was a wild song, a tale of wind and clouds and trees, of spotted animals that sprang through spotted fronds, of fish that gleamed in many-colored coats as they leaped radiantly from ponds and seas. The voice was stronger than mine, though not as high; it filled the space around me and hit each note precisely. The music rose and fell, and I wanted to leap up and tap my feet and bend my body and fling my arms about. God stood and scowled into the sun. "Ah, here he is at last. It's about time!" he grunted. The Serpent listened with its head tilted, ears raised. And then the boy appeared.

At first I saw only gold. He climbed the hill from the east with the sun low behind him. A halo of gold shimmered round his head and bounced with each step. Gold outlined his body. Even his shadow, which settled and resettled on the splendid, shiny blades of grass, seemed touched with gold. He was tall and looked solid. If you pushed him, you knew he would not budge; it would be like trying to shove an elm tree to one side, and yet he moved with grace. He was indeed, as God said, a joy to behold.

"Adam!" cried God sharply, and the boy stopped, one foot in the air, a final note still quivering in our ears.

"Oh!" he said, as he caught sight of us standing in the shadow of the grape arbor. "Oh, dear. I forgot."

God drew a breath and swelled his chest, his face red. "How could you forget?" he shouted. "I reminded you last night!"

Adam twisted his big toe in the dust and looked embarrassed.

"Adam, speak up!" cried God again. "Look at me!"

Adam glanced up quickly and then stared again at his toe. "Well, I didn't really forget. I mean, I remembered this morning when I woke up, but it was so beautiful, and it was really early, and I thought I'd get some of those roses that grow way off, on the ridge, you know, we noticed them the other day . . . and I saw the roebuck and ran after them. . . ." His voice trailed off. He looked at God, and then at the Serpent and me, and sighed. "Oh, dear," he said again.

For a few moments God stood breathing hard and tapping his foot on the ground. Finally he chuckled and threw an arm across the boy's shoulders. "Adam, you're incorrigible!" he said, but there was a note of pride in his voice, the same tone I heard when the Serpent said to me: "Eve, you're an artist!"—a mixture of surprise and joy.

"But I did get some flowers. For Eve." Adam fumbled at a vine tied awkwardly around his waist and stepped toward me. "Eve, here, these are for you." He held out a few scraggly roses. They were a lovely shade of yellow, like the early sun on a shallow pool, but it was obvious that they had been ripped quickly from the plant. The stems were bent and some of the leaves and blossoms torn.

"Eve, take them," the Serpent murmured in my ear. "And thank Adam."

"Oh. Adam. It was nice of you. . . ." I could not bring myself to say thank you. My heart wept for the roses; they must have been so filled with life and beauty only an hour or so before. Once I had them in my hands, I did not know what to do with them.

"Put them down on the bank," the Serpent said softly, then brushed past me, raising its body to its full height.

"Adam, I'm glad to see you."

"Serpent, hello," said Adam. "I'm glad to see you, too. You haven't been around in ages."

"I've been busy," the Serpent said. "With Eve."

God stepped forward. "And Adam, you must meet Eve properly. You've given her flowers, but you haven't been introduced. Here." God reached out and took my hand. "Eve, this is Adam. Adam, this is Eve." And he placed my hand in Adam's.

Adam put his other hand over mine. "Hello, Eve," he said.

"Hello, Adam," I replied, and we smiled at each other.

Adam's face was not like God's at all. It was round, and his cheeks looked soft like a fawn's. He had no facial hair whatever and very little on his chest, which gleamed with sweat; tiny hairs curled from smooth, unblemished skin. How can it be so smooth, I thought. I leaned forward to look more closely. Adam shifted his feet.

"Eve," said the Serpent. "You're making Adam uncomfortable."

"Oh, I'm sorry," I said absently, reaching out my hand to part the small, golden hairs around his ribs.

"What on Earth are you doing?" cried God.

"Where's his scar?" I asked, grasping Adam's arm to keep him from moving while I palpated his chest.

"Scar!" cried God. "What scar? He doesn't have a scar. Why on Earth would he have a scar? He's perfect!" Adam looked surprised. Behind me the Serpent coughed.

"But the Serpent said you made me from Adam's rib. You put him to sleep and removed one of his ribs and turned it into me. You just told me that too. So he *must* have a scar. Like mine where I fell on my knee."

God lowered his brows and turned to the Serpent, but the Serpent was admiring the view. "How lovely it is here," it murmured. "Very calm, very peaceful."

I poked Adam's stomach. Perhaps boys had their ribs lower down. "Stop," he giggled. "That tickles."

"What happened to his scar?" I bent my knee and ran my fingers over the raised line where the rock had gashed open my leg.

"Well," said God. "There's not always a scar."

"Oh, yes there is. The Serpent told me." I peered into God's face, and his eyes shifted to the horizon. "And why did you make me from Adam's rib, anyway? It seems so unnecessary. Why not make me from dust the way you did Adam?"

"There were reasons." God frowned and nodded as if the reasons weighed heavily on his mind.

"What reasons?"

"Serious reasons, quite beyond your understanding."

God tugged at his beard and glared at me. "Eve, it's not your business to question my decisions!"

"But you *did* make me from Adam's rib, didn't you?"

God fixed his eyes on a fly at his feet. A crab apple lay on the ground, and the fly was investigating it with its proboscis. The hair around God's brow was damp, and a drop of sweat rolled down his cheek. Suddenly he threw back his head like a lion teased by gnats on a hot afternoon. "Oh, stop!" he cried. "You pester me!" He stamped his foot—the fly took off hurriedly—and stomped into the house.

Adam shrugged. "He doesn't like so many questions." Again he made a circle in the dust with his toe, as if that was his defense against a cantankerous god. "It's a good question, though," he added. "I don't see how you could be made from a rib of mine. I have all my ribs. And no scar." He shook his head. "Serpent, perhaps you and Eve could walk around a bit and look at the view while I see if God needs anything. He'll calm down soon."

The Serpent and I strolled to the clearing and gazed at the plain. "Nice boy," the Serpent said. "More to him than first appears." For a moment it paused, then went on. "He's right about God. Try not to ask him so many questions; he's not used to it. Sooner or later the answers will come. You don't need to have them all today."

"Have I done wrong, Serpent? Are you disappointed in me?"

The Serpent tipped its head to one side. "Disappointed? Why should I be disappointed? On the contrary. You've done very well. I'm proud of you." It started to glide toward the house, then paused and glanced back at me over its long, fluid body. "The important thing is: Are you disappointed in yourself?"

I thought. "No," I said.

"Good," said the Serpent.

Back at the porch we found God sitting on the bench with his feet resting on a log. "Ah, there you are," he said. "Come sit down." He motioned the Serpent to coil itself beside him. Adam and I perched opposite them on a second bench, with our backs to the view.

"Adam and Eve," God began. "Up until now you have each received an education apart. You've learned a certain amount about the world, some basic facts the Serpent has taught you, Eve, and that I have taught Adam. You've also learned a bit—not much, of course, but some—from observing things on your own. It's time for you to learn the truly important things, and those *I* will teach you."

"Oh!" I interrupted. "Won't I have my lessons with the Serpent anymore?"

"Yes, yes, of course you will, in the mornings. But

then you'll come here and study with Adam, so I can give you a common view of the world."

"What *are* the important things?" I asked. It seemed to me that everything I had learned was important.

God frowned. "Eve, you must learn not to interrupt! Serpent, I'm surprised you allow it!"

"I find the interruptions are often the most productive moments," said the Serpent.

God hunched his shoulders as if he found the idea incomprehensible, and turned back to me. "Eve, in the next few weeks I will teach you the correct view of the world and the correct view of *me*. You must learn to appreciate what it means, that I created the world and all the animals and the birds and the fish, all the insects, everything!" God waved his hands at the landscape behind us, which Adam and I could not see. A wasp circled around his head, and he waved it away. "*I* created *you*, both of you! Adam and Eve!"

"And the linen," I said.

"Yes, and the linen. And endless other things as well."

"But we know that."

God glowered at me. "Well, you need to appreciate what it means. Quite obviously you don't, as you keep interrupting." The wasp had settled on God's shoulder, and he shrugged it off. "You need to learn to worship me in the proper words and in the proper form. You've done enough running wild." I thought of the hours I had spent motionless, watching a butterfly break free of its chrysalis, a rosebud burgeon into flower. How little God knew of my life.

"Now," continued God, "I will teach you the poetry of worship. Listen carefully." He closed his eyes, drew a deep breath, and words flowed from his mouth. His voice was deep and full, the lines rang out: "He has made the Earth by his power, he has established the world by his wisdom. . . ." Though I understood very little—what was power? What was wisdom? Was God speaking of himself?—I listened, transfixed. The sound was magical.

At first Adam sat still with his eyes on God's face. Then slowly he began to move. From the corner of my eye, I could see his toe reach under the bench. A round globe appeared, green and made of tightly woven grasses. Adam pushed it back and forth between his feet, used his toes like fingers, brushed the surface, gave the ball a twist as he sent it off to the other foot. Then he lifted it and sent it spinning into the air, from ankle to ankle, knee to knee. Rhythmically it leaped and fell, flew to his shoulder and back to his ankle again. Three times on the ankle, bounce, bounce, bounce, shoulder, ankle, left wrist, right wrist, shoulder, ankle, ankle, wrist, all to the rhythm of God's words. The ball was a part of Adam, attached to him, perhaps by webs visible only by moonlight. It had a spirit of its own, but the spirit was subject to Adam's will. The movements of ball and boy were beautiful, transcendent. Here was perfection. I wept.

"The wolf also shall dwell with the lamb," chanted God. Then, suddenly, silence: God had opened his eyes. "Adam!" he shouted. Adam dropped the ball.

"Oh, God, that was so wonderful!" the Serpent and I cried together. I drew my hands across my wet cheeks.

"Look," said the Serpent, "you've moved Eve to tears." God looked less angry.

"I just can't keep still when you speak like that," Adam said. "It's like music. It makes me want to stamp my feet! Do go on."

God seemed mollified. "All right. Now where was I?"

"The wolf also shall dwell with the lamb," said the Serpent.

"Oh, yes . . ." said God, and again he began to speak. Adam twined his fingers together in his lap and sat still. The verses rolled on, and now that Adam was not distracting me, I could hear their beauty: "The voice of my beloved! Look, he comes, leaping upon the mountains, bounding over the hills. My beloved is like a gazelle or a young stag." I thought of Adam's arrival that morning. Now God was tapping his foot to the beat. He was wearing sandals made from a type of green grass I had never seen, woven in an intricate twist, attached to soles of wood. I wondered if I could make some myself.

"God," I interrupted. "How did you make those sandals?"

God stopped in the middle of a sentence. "I didn't," he said. "Adam did. No doubt he can show you how." He frowned at the Serpent. "What was I saying?" Then he glared at me. "When will you learn *not* to interrupt your betters."

"Betters?" I said. "What are they?"

"People who are older than you and have more experience with life, more knowledge and education and wisdom."

"But why does that make you better than I? I'm not sure it makes you always right. Or more honest." I was thinking of Adam's rib.

God opened his mouth to draw breath. The Serpent spoke quickly. "Come, my friend. Yesterday Eve and I picked avocados and tomatoes and cucumbers, or rather I helped her find them, and she picked them and carried them home. She mixed them with basil leaves and olives and covered them with olive oil, and before we left she set them out in the sun. They'll be just right now, soft and warm, and delicious with the new wine. Come and have lunch with us."

"New wine?" said God. "And avocados? So early in the year? How did you do it?" And he and the Serpent started together down the path, with Adam and me trailing behind. Adam said nothing but kept looking at me when he thought I was not aware of it.

"How did you make those sandals?" I asked. "And the ball? You must be very good with your hands."

"Oh, I am," said Adam, stretching his arms in front of him. The rest of him was thick and solid, and big knobs of muscles swelled in his legs, but his hands were fine. Though his fingers were square at the end, they were long and thin; the sun made the tips glow pink. It reminded me of the day I awoke and reached my hands to the sky, and the sun shone through me.

"Tell me," I said, and Adam talked about making sandals and balls, how he cut the grasses early in the morning and found soft wood from a tree that grew only on the northern hills.

"Yes, yes," I said, but I was barely listening. Ahead of us God and the Serpent were deep in conversation; God's voice boomed out, interspersed with the Serpent's soft replies.

I heard the Serpent say, "He's a nice boy. Kind."

God grunted. "Not much brain, though."

"He probably has more than he shows. He may not be interested in the things you want to teach him."

"Well, he should be," said God. "Anyway, he'll be good for strong bodies, for brawn. Eve has the brain." He placed his hand on the Serpent's brilliant, quivering neck. "Oh, Serpent, I can hardly wait to see if it works between them the way I've planned!"

The Serpent looked alarmed. "But it's much too soon! They're barely more than children. Give them time; let them come to it themselves. Otherwise you'll risk ruining the whole thing."

What could they be talking about? I thought.

God turned his head toward the Serpent and pulled at his lip. "I suppose you're right," he said reluctantly. He looked back at Adam and me. "She's a beauty. A truly lovely creature."

"Yes," replied the Serpent. "And funny and bright and good to boot."

God's Parade

THE FOLLOWING MORNING we were again on the path to God's house. The sun was barely up, but God had asked us to come early and stay for lunch. "I have a surprise for you," he had told us as we took our leave the evening before.

"Why does God wear clothes?" I asked the Serpent. "No other creature does."

"Well, bears have fur, birds have feathers. Those are clothes in a way."

"Adam and I don't have feathers or fur, and we don't wear clothes."

"You have skin and hair. You don't need anything else."

"God has skin and hair too."

"Why don't you ask *him* why he wears clothes," the Serpent suggested.

I considered that. "I'm not sure I dare. He doesn't like my questions."

"You had no trouble asking questions yesterday," said the Serpent dryly.

"I was so curious I forgot to be scared. But thinking it over later . . . he's pretty scary. He's so big, and his voice is big too."

The Serpent glanced at me. "I've never known you to be frightened of any creature, Eve."

"I'm not really frightened. I'm just . . ."

"I know what you mean. You're in awe of him."

"Awe?"

"Fear and wonder combined. It's a good emotion. There's nothing wrong with being in awe of God."

I spotted a blackberry bramble at the side of the path and bent to pick the fruit. Awe. A combination of fear and wonder. "I am in awe of God," I said to myself.

Did any other creature give me the same feeling? The elephants were bigger than God. When they ran, the ground thundered beneath their feet, and my heart pounded. The swallows darting and swooping at full speed in a narrow canyon: how beautiful they were, how brave. As I watched them, my heart fluttered in my chest. But it was admiration and wonder I felt, not fear.

And the Serpent: I was never afraid of the Serpent.

On the path again, my thoughts turned to the coming visit. "Why has God decided he wants to teach me as well as Adam?" I asked. "I didn't think he particularly cared about me. He's never come to visit us. Even yesterday he talked a lot more about Adam and wasn't very interested in my life at all."

"Well, he *is* interested in you. That's why he asked me to take care of you," replied the Serpent.

"You said he gave me to you."

The Serpent looked abashed. "It was silly of me to say that," it said. "That was before I got to know you. No one person can be given to another, even by God."

I plucked a four-leaf clover from the tall grass and brushed it against my chin. The Serpent continued, "I've tried to teach you some basic information about the world. A lot you would have found out for yourself, eventually; it just saved time for me to tell you. Now you'll have a chance to hear God's view of the world and to discuss ideas and impressions with someone other than me, with Adam, who's your own age."

"Will you come too?"

"Yes, of course. I like to listen to God's lessons, and it's useful for me to know what he's teaching you. That way if you have any questions, we can discuss them."

The Serpent swished its tail through the grass. "God thinks you'll be a good influence on the boy," he said. "He hopes Adam will want to be more like you."

"Adam's fine."

"Yes, but God wants him to take more interest in his lessons and spend less time running around with the animals." The Serpent chuckled. "God doesn't know you very well. I think he's in for a surprise!"

"You don't think I'll be a good influence on Adam?" The whole idea seemed foolish.

"I'm sure you will, Eve, but not in the way God expects. You may give him some of your curiosity." I frowned. "What is it, Eve? What's bothering you?"

"I don't see why God should be telling us what to do."

The Serpent turned its head and looked at me. "Would you rather not go?"

I shrugged. "No, I don't mind. I'll like it, I guess. As long as you're there, and we still have our lessons, and I can go off by myself sometimes."

When we arrived at God's house, Adam was waiting for us. "Come this way," he said, and led us to a promontory perched above a broad valley. There God stood, planted squarely on a rock, a hand shading his eyes, peering out across the plain.

"Good, good!" he exclaimed when he saw us. "You're here! I have a surprise for you. Stand just there, next to me." He cupped his hands and blew into them. A piercing whistle filled the air and reverberated from the cliffs across the valley. He whistled again and again until my ears rang and tingled. I raised my hands to cover them, but the Serpent frowned at me and shook its head.

Suddenly, from all directions, animals came rushing into the valley below: all the large animals of the Garden. Horses came galloping, and giraffes, moving their necks back and forth as I had when I imitated them. Cows trotted awkwardly with their milk-filled bags banging against their legs, kangaroos leaped and sprang, rhinos hunkered along, their noses weighted down by heavy horns. Dogs loped, ears up, tongues wagging in open mouths. Cats, tails raised disdainfully, stalked in as if they'd been called away from some important mission. Birds flocked over our heads, or flapped in two forked lines behind a leader. Every animal clamored in its own voice: a babel of bleats, whinnies, yowls, and trumpeting, and all the chatter of the birds above. Never had I heard such commotion in the Garden.

God raised his arms above his head. The animals stopped; the clamor ceased. Not a pony pawed the ground; not a cat sat down to lick its paws. They stood like statues on the plain. Even the birds hung motionless in the air.

God waved his right hand, and all the animals moved together in a great ring to the right. God raised his left hand, and the animals whirled and circled to the left; the birds changed direction like a school of minnows in the lake. God dropped his hands. Every animal on the plain lay down, and the birds fluttered to the ground. Another signal from God and they scrambled to their feet; the birds spread their wings and flew. God swayed his hands back and forth, and the animals began to waltz; the birds danced in the air. From the east an eagle appeared, wings stretched wide, balanced on the wind. I could see the great white head with a golden eye, the white tail, the immense golden beak, the curved golden talons with sharp black claws. I thought: it can see the grain of wheat caught in my hair.

God shouted to the eagle, "Ah, there you are at last! Come, lead them all! Fly, my eagle, fly!"

The eagle lay suspended in the air above God's head.

"Go! Go! See, they need a leader." God pointed to the plain. The animals had stopped and were watching him, waiting for his next order. "Eagle! Off you go! Lead them!"

The eagle flapped its wings and climbed into the sky, moving toward the east.

"Eagle, come back!" God thundered. But the eagle disappeared into the sun.

"What a glorious creature!" I cried.

"Ugly, evil beast," God muttered angrily through his teeth. He frowned, then waved his arms, and the animals circled again. Finally God flapped his hands and lowered his arms. The animals stopped, the birds settled; all began moving off. In a few moments the plain lay empty before us.

After the parade we trudged back to the hut, God striding ahead with the Serpent flowing gracefully behind. Adam and I straggled at the back. I felt quite exhausted, as if it had been I who had marched back and forth or swooped through the sky. I wanted to go home and bathe in our pond, and talk to the Serpent about all that had happened, and ask about the eagle.

But when we reached the hut, God turned to the Serpent. "I need to rest," he said. "Why don't you have a nap there, my friend, under the butternut tree, and later we'll have some food and chat." He lay down on the bench and closed his eyes. "Oh, dear," he said, after a moment, raising his head and opening his eyes. "I forgot about you two. Go off somewhere and find some berries for lunch," and he waved us away.

Once we were alone, Adam seemed not to know what to do with me. "Where shall we go?" he asked. "We could swim . . . ."

I shook my head. I loved to swim, loved the feel of

the water on my body, of moving through it. Alone. Adam splashing beside me would ruin it.

"Let's just sit by the river. It's cool under the willows."

So we sat on the riverbank and watched each other out of the corners of our eyes.

Adam was taller than I by half a head. He reminded me of the big cats: his legs were long, made for running. His skin was slightly darker than mine, the color of a walnut, but his hair, like mine, was gold. He had a wide mouth, with full lips that turned up at the corners in a little hook. When he thought something was funny, he narrowed his eyes and pressed his lips together as if laughter were bundled up in his throat, tickling to get out. I came to believe he was trying to hide it because God did not like to be laughed at.

"How did you like the parade?" he asked after a while.

"It was all right. I really like it better when the animals run around on their own. It's a bit stiff the way God does it."

"Oh, I'd love to be able to control the animals that way. Someday I will."

I stared at him. "Why on Earth would you want to?"

"God gave me the animals; he gave me everything on the planet. I can do what I want with them!"

"He did not!" I cried.

"He did. He told me so. He said 'Fill the earth and subdue it; have dominion over the fish of the sea, over the birds of the air, and over every living thing that moves on the Earth.'"

I plucked a blade of grass and tickled my lips with the soft tassel. "That's just a myth. The Serpent says we're all equal, us and the creatures and the plants and the land. We all have the same right to live and to use the things around us."

"That's silly," said Adam. "Obviously you have more right to eat the blackberries than a bear does."

"Why?" I asked. "The bear and I, we're both alive, we both enjoy them, we both have to eat."

"And if you want to build a hut, you can't cut a tree?"

"Of course I can, as long as it doesn't damage the forest. I can take one or two trees, but if I took them all, it would be wrong. *And* stupid, because then all the trees would be gone."

Adam shrugged. "I'll use what I want and leave the rest. There's plenty here." He flapped his hand at the pond and the stream and the meadow and wood.

For a while we were silent. "Tell me about the Serpent," he said at last. "It's amazing to look at."

"It's amazing in every way," I said, and began telling

stories about the Serpent, how it moved with such grace, far faster than I, and could sing underwater and, at night, could run lines of phosphorescent light down its body. I glanced at Adam and saw that he had his eyes squeezed shut, his hands over his ears. I stopped speaking.

"Go on," he said.

"What are you doing that for?" I asked.

"What?"

"Closing your eyes and covering your ears."

"I'm listening; I'm trying to see what you're saying." Adam opened his eyes. "Don't you do that when you listen?"

"Of course not."

"Well, if I don't, the world gets in my eyes and those frogs and the grass that's moving there in the wind, they invade my head and nothing else can get in."

"You don't do that when we're with God."

Adam shrugged his shoulders. "He won't let me. That's why I can't listen when he talks."

"But how can you hear with your ears covered?"

"I don't cover them completely. I can still hear voices nearby; it's just all the stuff out there that gets muffled." He closed his eyes and brought his hands to his ears again. "I always hear you. Your voice is very clear. Go on."

"I've told you everything I can about the Serpent," I said. "Tell me, why does God wear that cloth around his waist? None of the rest of us has clothes."

"I've asked him that; I wondered too," Adam replied slowly. "He told me he likes the feel of the linen against his skin. Also, it sets him apart. All the creatures can see him, no matter how small they are, or how far away, even at night. I don't understand it; I wouldn't like to have a piece of cloth hanging around me, covering my legs. How could you run?" Adam stood up. "Aren't you hungry?" he asked. "I am. Come on, I have some nuts in my bag, and there are blueberries just up the hill." And we went off to pick our lunch and eat it before going back to God and the Serpent.

That evening after supper I told the Serpent about Adam's explanation of God's clothes. "That makes sense," it said.

"But Adam says God gave him the animals and everything on the planet. That can't be true, can it?"

The Serpent sighed. "I'm afraid it can. That *is* the way God sees things. Foolish, and so unfortunate. It won't work in the long run." The Serpent folded the white feathers against its neck, the way a horse will flatten its ears at the first sign of danger. "We can only hope Adam will be more sensible. You can help him see things differently, Eve, and so can I, if he spends more time with us."

Dark was falling. "Look, there's the evening star!" I cried. "I love seeing it come out." We lay in silence, looking at the heavens and the stars. "They make me feel so small," I whispered. "Me and the Earth and the Garden." But if the Serpent heard me, it made no sign.

"How did you like the parade, Eve?" asked the Serpent after a while.

"It was fun to see the animals all trotting along and turning together. Especially the birds, though they often fly that way by themselves."

"What did you like best?"

"The eagle. But God didn't like the eagle at all. He said it was evil. What's evil?"

"Evil is bad: the opposite of good."

"Why is the eagle evil? Because it refused to fly the way God commanded?"

"God thinks the eagle is evil because it disobeyed him."

"That's what evil means? Disobeying God?"

"Well." The Serpent sighed. "It's one definition."

I closed my eyes and again saw the animals running and pivoting and lying on their backs as God signaled them to do, and the birds darting as one, to and fro.

Then the eagle appearing from the west, soaring above, around and around, and disappearing into the sun. "But what the eagle did, it was so fine, so free! How could God not like it? Why couldn't he see how grand it was?"

"I think," the Serpent said softly to the blackening skies, "that God has a different view of the world than you and I."

God's Lessons

🍎

$\mathcal{A}$FTER THAT WE VISITED God nearly every day. I came to feel at home in the hut, which was comfortable and pleasant, with its broad pergola covered in grape vines. While God could be short-tempered, he was often amusing and interesting. His view of the world was indeed quite different from the Serpent's: he had no interest in any opinions but his own and did not like us to think for ourselves. When I interrupted he got angry—we *must* listen to him; we were *not* to ask questions—and he would go back to describing how he had created the world.

God's voice was deep and vibrant, his language beautiful. I sat holding my breath and watched his great hands rise and fall as he spoke: "The earth was without form. . . ." He wiggled his fingers, palms down. "Then God . . . divided the waters from the waters. . . ." His right hand descended through the airs and I could hear the waters dividing, up and down, above the firmament and below. I longed to ask "Why did you do it, why?"— but I did not dare.

God was visibly pleased with our lessons; the Serpent reported that he was delighted with me. Even Adam was less easily distracted when I was there. Every day, as soon as he saw me, God opened his arms and gave me a hug, sometimes swinging me around so my legs dangled in the air. Often he would ask me to sit at his feet; he would stroke my hair and pull on my long tresses much as I tugged absently at the ears of the dog when, after a swim, it lay by my side on a rock in the sun. He insisted on a hug when we left as well.

"Why does God always want to hug me?" I asked the Serpent.

"It's a sign of affection," the Serpent replied. "A way of welcoming you to his house and showing you he likes you. It's a little like shaking hands, only more friendly."

"Why doesn't God hug *you*? He certainly likes you."

The Serpent laughed. "I'm not very huggable," it said.

Usually we got to the hut soon after lunch, and God had a lesson prepared for Adam and me: poems, a story, a song. We would listen and recite and answer questions on what we were taught. Finally God would yawn and say it was time for us to go off and get some exercise, so that he and the Serpent could discuss serious things and maybe have a little nap. "Be sure to be back before the sun touches the trees," he warned, raising his finger to the sky as Adam and I scampered off into the Garden.

During those long afternoons Adam taught me how to carve wood, and I taught him to cook and weave and helped him finish naming the creatures. "I don't like words," he said. "They get me confused." But he knew all about the animals, even more than I. He spent hours watching them, whenever he could get away from God. He knew how they moved and what they ate, how often they drank, where they could be found at any hour of the day or night. His eyes shone as he described them: "When the stags spring, they have all four feet off the ground, like this." He curved his arms in front like a leaping deer. "Oh, Eve, they're so beautiful."

Adam was passionate about one other thing: making balls and playing with them. He could twirl a ball on the end of his nose or juggle eight at once. He taught me to kick and throw and keep my eye always on the hard, round object that whizzed unpredictably through the air. We played endlessly, trying to kick a ball between two rocks or toss it into an empty nest in the notch of a tree or hit it as far as we could with a stick. The games were fun, and I got to be quite good at them, but I was never as good as Adam. He was a genius at it, and he cared.

Adam was always talking about racing the gazelles, and I begged him to take me with him. After a good deal of coaxing, he finally agreed. "Though it's dusty, you know, Eve. It'll make you cough. Meet me by the chestnut tree, at dawn, just as the sun rises."

When I explained the plan to the Serpent, it laughed and shook its head. "You're in for a surprise, Eve, but go ahead."

The following day when I arrived, Adam was watching a herd of spotted deer grazing on a knoll. "See those bushes?" Adam pointed. "Go down there, and when I shout, start running as fast as you can."

"Why can't I stay with you?"

"You're not used to running with them, Eve. I'll give you a head start. Don't forget, as soon as you hear me shout, take off." I trotted to the clump of bushes. *I'll show him!* I thought.

"Eve, go!" yelled Adam, and I sprinted, arms pumping, legs pounding, alone on the plain with the wide prairie stretching ahead. Then came the muffled thud of galloping hooves behind me, the smell of hide damp with sweat, and for a moment I was swept along in the herd. Adam shot past and shouted, "Go, Eve, go!" and they were gone, a hundred white tails bobbing up and down. All else was lost in the dust. At the end a fawn, barely a day old, toddled by; I caught it in my arms and held it until the mother came bleating back for it.

Adam returned an hour later, flushed and happy. "What a morning," he cried, throwing himself down on the grass. "Oh, Eve, I'm so sorry you couldn't keep up. If you'd just made it to the ridge—they don't keep galloping, you know; after a few minutes they stop to graze. In that valley turkey eggs were just hatching. It's so funny to see the babies poking out from under the hens. When they first come out they have no feathers at all. . . ." Adam stopped and looked at me. "Eve, what's the matter?"

I stamped my foot on the ground, and a cloud of dust rose and made me sneeze. "I hate it!" I cried. "I hate it that I can't keep up." I pounded my fist against my knee. "Why can't I run as fast as you can?"

"Well, you're a girl," said Adam. "You're not meant to run so fast."

"Why not? Why shouldn't I? Why should you have all the fun of running with the herds?"

Adam shrugged. "God made you that way," he said.

"Why didn't he make me able to run as fast as you?" I cried. "It's not fair!"

Adam shook his head. "I don't think things *are* fair, a lot of the time," he said. "That's just the way they are."

I stared at him. "Of course things are fair. The Serpent's always fair."

"Well, God isn't, that's for sure," said Adam. "And it's not worth getting upset about."

I snorted and turned away.

"Eve, listen. I can't run as fast as the cheetah, and it doesn't bother me."

"But the cheetah's another kind of animal. I'm human, just like you."

"But you're a girl. A woman. I guess God thought a man *should* run faster," Adam said, taking me gently by the arm. "Sit on this rock. I'll get us some berries."

"I don't want berries. I don't want to sit down." I shook off his hand.

"Okay, then, stay here," said Adam. "And wait for me."

In a few minutes he returned, carrying blackberries in a large leaf. "Look how good these are; they're so ripe and juicy," he said, handing them to me.

"I told you, I don't want any," I cried, and flung the fruit at Adam's head. The berries scattered across the ground; a few caught in Adam's hair. "Don't treat me the way you treat God! I can't be bought off with berries!"

Adam stared at me in amazement. "Eve," he said slowly. "What *is* the matter with you? You're behaving the way God does when he gets angry."

"I'm not!"

"Well, I've never seen you act this way before." Adam's palms were stained, and there was a black spot on his cheek. He seemed stunned. "Eve, what do you want me to do?" I thought he might cry.

Suddenly my anger was gone. Laughing, I pushed back my hair and bent to pick up Adam's offering. We gathered all the berries we could find and ate them together.

"I'm sorry," I mumbled at last, wiping the black juice from my chin. "But it still makes me mad, not being able to run as fast as you!"

Occasionally God chanted the psalms or prayers, but it was Adam and I who discovered music. We began by mimicking the birds, vying to see which of us could most precisely reproduce the canary or the mockingbird. Then we took to singing as we walked, stamping our feet, accompanying ourselves by tapping sticks together or pounding on hollow logs or gourds. We were swept up in a noise-making mania. For days we could think of nothing else. We stretched vines taut in the forks of branches, poked holes in reeds, and blew and pounded and plucked, and, finally, we made music.

Each day we brought our inventions back to God and the Serpent, who continued their habit of spending the afternoon together. To our surprise—"At last he approves of something I do," said Adam—God loved to hear us play and sing.

One afternoon, swept away by the rhythm, we stood and marched forward, back, sideways, twirled around, pounding our drums and piping our flutes. God was delighted.

"Wonderful!" he cried, clapping his hands. "Dance on! It's good for the body and for the mind!" From then on God often danced with us, moving slowly to the left, to the right, bowing his head, clapping his hands. Sometimes he and the Serpent danced together, circling and weaving and bending. God lifted his arms above his head and stamped his feet, first heel, then toe, then heel again, and swayed his shoulders back and forth to the rhythm of the song, and turned and bowed and turned again. The Serpent swept its feathered ears above its head and back onto its neck, and spiraled and spun and tapped its tail to the beat of the tom-tom. There was something reverential in their dance: joy, yes, but also grace, and solemnity. Adam and I beat our drums and sang as we watched, enraptured.

Finally God sank into his seat and said, "Enough, children, enough. To work," and we plunked quite happily into our seats on the bench. We had run and leaped and danced through the afternoon, and we were tired.

It was at this lesson, late in the day, that God told his stories: about Coyote and his tricks, the crow who lost his cheese to a fox, the tortoise who raced the hare and won. ("Impossible!" cried Adam, outraged.)

"Once upon a time," God began, "Anansi the Spider lived in a great, dark forest. By day he played with his shadow in the sun and was happy. But at night, after the sun went down, the forest was black and Anansi could no longer play. He decided he would steal a little bit of the sun. . . ."

"He can't do that," said Adam, frowning.

"Wait and see," said God. "So Anansi built his web into the sky, higher and higher until he reached the sun."

"Silly," muttered Adam.

"Anansi said to the sun, 'Oh, Sun, you're so beautiful, and all day you make the Earth beautiful. But at night when you are gone, everything is dark and we cannot see. Please won't you give me a little bit of your light to take home with me?'

"The sun was flattered, and it gave Anansi a nice fat piece of itself to take back to Earth. And Anansi carried it back in a pot and set it in the middle of a clearing. And all the animals were happy, and every night they came to dance around the sun.

"But after a while, Anansi thought: 'It was *I* who went to the trouble of climbing into the sky. Why should all the other animals enjoy my piece of sun?' And Anansi took the pot that held the bit of sun and hid it in a cave, and every night he went by himself and sat in front of it, and laughed at all the other animals who were left in the dark.

"But the sun looked down and saw what had happened. 'That Spider is a selfish creature!' it said to itself. 'It does not deserve my light.' And the sun sent the wind to blow through the cave and snuff out the sunlight. So Anansi the Spider was left in the dark with all the other animals."

Before the story ended, I was trying to design a pot that would hold even a small piece of sun. But Adam could not keep still. "How can a spider weave its web into the sky to reach the sun?" he whispered, wiggling his toes in the dust.

"It's make-believe," I replied.

One day God announced that he was going to teach us some prayers and hymns. "From now on you'll recite them at the end of each afternoon lesson. Sit along the wall there." He stood in front of us; behind him we could see the valley curving down to the river and the animals wading in to drink. The sun was already low in the sky, and their shadows stretched long behind them.

"Serpent," I called, and patted the bench at my side. "Come sit next to us."

"No, no," cried God. "Don't bother the Serpent." The Serpent waved its feathers at me. Its skin had turned white, the color of a calla lily, and a line of red crosses ran down each side.

"Now repeat this prayer after me!"

"What are prayers?" I asked.

"Eve, do stop interrupting!" God snapped.

"Well," the Serpent suggested. "It might be useful to tell them what they're about to learn."

"I suppose you're right." God pulled at his beard. "Well, hymns and prayers are ways of showing how much you adore the Lord."

"Who's the Lord?" I asked.

God frowned. "*I* am the Lord."

At the edge of the terrace, the Serpent shifted its weight.

"Hymns are sung," God went on, "like songs, and prayers are recited. Both songs and hymns praise the Lord: *me*, that is. You can also use a prayer to ask the Lord to give you something you especially want."

"Something I want?" asked Adam. "Like what?"

"If I prayed for it, would I be able to run as fast as Adam?" I asked.

"No, no, not silly things like that." God frowned and

tapped his fingers together. "Enough of these foolish questions. Listen." He raised both arms and spread his fingers. "Rejoice in the Lord, for he is King! Repeat it!"

"'Rejoice in the Lord, for he is King,'" we chanted.

God went on: "The Lord is in his holy temple: let all the Earth keep silence before him."

"What's a temple?"

God planted himself in front of me, arms crossed, and glared down. "Eve, this is not a lesson in vocabulary! If you don't know what something means, ask the Serpent later! Don't interrupt me anymore! Again, repeat what I say: The Lord is in his holy temple: let all the Earth keep silence before him."

"'The Lord is in his holy temple: let all the Earth keep silence before him,'" Adam and I intoned.

"Don't sound so mournful about it," said God. "This is a hymn of praise. You're supposed to be happy." He raised his hands, palms out. I thought he might call the animals again, but he just continued.

"O come let us sing unto the Lord."

"'O come let us sing unto the Lord.'"

"For the Lord is a great God, and a great King above all gods."

"'For the Lord is a great God, and a great King above all gods.'"

"Good, good. Keep going: In his hand are all the

corners of the earth, and the strength of the hills is his also. The sea is his, for he made it; and his hands prepared the dry land. O come, let us worship and fall down, and kneel before the Lord our Maker! For he is the Lord our God and we are the people of his pasture, and the sheep of his hand. O worship the Lord in the beauty of holiness; let the whole Earth stand in awe of him."

"'In awe of him,'" we finished.

"Now my children, I want you to remember these verses, and recite them to me when you come tomorrow." God cupped his hands; I expected him to whistle, but instead he clapped them together. "That was quite good for the first time," he said. "Serpent, Eve, I'll see you tomorrow. Adam, you can walk part of the way with them." God opened his arms. "Eve, come give me a hug before you go." And I obeyed, though his beard tickled against my ear.

"All I remember is 'let's sing,'" Adam said gloomily as we walked down the path. "How am I going to recite it tomorrow?"

"I'll teach you," I said. "I remember it. We'll sing it, it'll be easier that way." So Adam beat on a hollow log with a stick, and we marched through the Garden shouting, "O *come*, let us *sing* on-to-the *Lord*!" Once or twice, when Adam and I paused to catch our breath, I heard the Serpent coughing behind us, but I was too caught up in rejoicing to note whether it was laughing or choking in the dust we raised.

In the evening I asked the Serpent: "What do you think of those prayers? And why don't *you* have to sing praises to God?"

"Well, God and I are old friends," said the Serpent. "What do *you* think of the prayers?"

"I don't know that I like the idea of gods and kings lording it over everyone else."

"A revolutionary," murmured the Serpent.

"What's a revolutionary?"

The Serpent blew out its breath in a whoosh. "That's a complicated question," it replied. "But briefly, it's someone who's not totally content with the way things are and wants to change them."

"I don't think I really want to change much. But why does God need to be adored all the time? We know he made the sea and the dry land and all the rest. Why does he have to hear it over and over?"

A Special Treat

I HAVE NO IDEA how long we lived in the Garden. It was nearly impossible to mark the passing of time. Seasons changed, but the changes were very slight: leaves turned red and yellow and gold, and the leaves fell. Buds formed and opened to leaves again immediately, so the trees were never bare. Some periods were cooler, others hot, but nothing extreme.

I had time to discover how to shape stones and turn them into tools: knives and hammers and pestles to pound the grains of wheat and oat and millet into flour. I had time to discover the uses of flax and cotton, how to twine their flowers into thread and weave the threads into cloth. I learned to stuff pockets of cloth with the down of geese and ducks and make comforters, and to comb the sheep (they were always shedding clumps of wool) and twist the thick, oily stuff into yarn, then knit it into shawls and blankets. I learned to thatch a roof, to place sweet milk in an urn and let it turn and clot, and with it shape round wheels of cheese. I learned the uses of all the fruits, the vegetables that grew rooted in the ground, the beans that wound their way up the trunks of trees. Red tomatoes, black eggplant, cucumbers, lettuce, squash—green, yellow, round or long.

When it was really chilly, the Serpent would put the tip of its tail into a pot of water or milk and heat it, and we would have a warm meal. But I did not like to ask the Serpent to do this often, and after a while I found I could heat food nearly as well by setting it on a flat rock in the sun. I lined a hollow in the rock with clay, built up the sides, and made a cover to close it in. I pounded grain to powder, added nuts and herbs and water, and shaped it all into a loaf. An afternoon in my oven produced a crusty flatbread. This we ate with cheese or dipped in olive oil. The bread kept well; I was able to carry it in my bag and have it for lunch on the other side of the Garden. One day I brought some to God. He ate it greedily, smacking his lips. "What a grand invention, Eve!" he cried, and from then on I had to bring a loaf to God every day.

But best of all, I learned to crush the cacao bean into

a powder and mix it with milk and honey to make chocolate.

One afternoon after our lessons, God took my hand and patted it. "Eve," he said slowly, "tomorrow I want you to come early, right after breakfast." There was an edge to his voice; it was an order rather than an invitation. I looked at him in surprise. "I have a special treat for you and Adam." He then turned to the Serpent. "Is that all right by you? You can have the morning to relax, without these young ones to worry you."

"A special treat?" the Serpent asked, raising its brows. "Another parade?"

"No, no, just a little idea I have," said God. "A young people's party." He shifted his feet in the dust; he appeared to be waiting anxiously for the Serpent's answer. I drew a circle on the ground, trying to make it perfectly round, like the moon when it is full. I did not want to come alone the next day. I had never visited God and Adam by myself, and now God had the same look on his face I'd noticed when he spoke of Adam's rib. I hoped the Serpent would say no. But the Serpent nodded and said, "Shall I come by for her in the afternoon?"

God looked discomfited. "Oh, well, maybe. Yes, do." He patted my hand again. "Adam and I will see you in the morning, Eve. Give me a hug before you go!" And I obeyed.

As soon as we were out of earshot, I asked the Serpent why it had accepted God's invitation without asking me first. "I'm sorry, Eve," it said. "I wouldn't have, but I can't see any harm in it. If you'd refused, it would have upset God, and Adam even more. Adam's very fond of you—" The Serpent stopped and peered into my face. "Eve. Tell me, what's making you nervous?"

I leaned over and scratched the scar on my knee. "I don't know," I said. "I . . . I feel there's something odd going on."

"With Adam?"

"No, not with Adam. Adam's all right. It's . . . it's God. He sounded strange."

For some time the Serpent was silent. Finally it said, "I don't believe God would do you any harm. At most a little teasing, a touch of embarrassment. Nothing you can't handle."

The Betrayal

THE NEXT DAY WHEN I arrived, God was standing as he had been on my first visit, gazing over the valley. He looked even larger than usual. There was a breeze, and his hair flamed around his head in the sun. "Hello, Eve, how are you?" he said. He made no move to hug me, but continued staring at the plain below. "Adam's gone off again. What a bother." He began pacing back and forth without asking me to sit down. "He's out racing the gazelles and the cheetah. A foolish pastime, if you ask me. But I'm not human, and I'm not a boy."

It was some time before Adam appeared. He came up the hill with the sun all gold behind him, but today he was not singing. Though it was still cool, his hair was plastered wet on his forehead, and sweat made rivulets through the dust on his face. He was panting, and he threw himself down on the bench immediately, trying to catch his breath. "Wow!" he said between gasps. "Those gazelles! They're fast! I raced every animal on the plain."

"Adam," said God sternly. "You haven't even said hello to Eve. She's been here for quite a while waiting for you."

"Oh, I forgot," said Adam, and pulled a fistful of grass to mop his face. "I'm sorry."

"It's not something to take lightly," scolded God. "I told you I've planned something special for the two of you. That's why I invited Eve to come so early."

"I thought we were just going to spend the day together and learn some new songs. But I'll do whatever you want now, though I'm awfully tired."

"Adam can take a nap and I'll stay with you, God," I offered. "I don't mind."

"No. I have other plans. A treat for you both."

"But Adam's so tired."

"No, no," cried God. "I won't hear of it. I've arranged the day around you two, and I won't change my plans just because he ran off and exhausted himself. Sit there, both of you."

Adam and I sat on the bench where we usually had our lessons, and God began pacing up and down the terrace with his hands clasped behind his back. I thought he had a new story or poem to tell us. But he coughed and stopped pacing and stood still in front of us. His eyes glittered under his thick brows. "Life," he said, "is not all games. It is not about singing and racing gazelles and carving birds into wooden posts. You were put on Earth—by me—for a reason. Do you know what that reason is?"

Adam and I looked at each other.

"That reason is," God continued, raising his voice, "procreation!"

"Procreation?" said Adam.

"Reproduction. Babies," I explained in a low voice.

"You created us just to have babies?" asked Adam, his voice rising in disbelief.

God looked taken aback. "Well, not only. I wanted company in the Garden, something amusing to have around, someone who would listen to me, and talk. Something to do, someone to watch. . . ." He trailed off. "But having babies is the most important." He stared across the valley. "Yes, one of the biggest reasons I created you is so you can reproduce, so the Earth shall be filled with humankind." He lifted his right hand and pointed his index finger to the sky, "And now is the time!"

"It doesn't sound like much fun," muttered Adam.

"The Serpent told me it was nice," I said.

"It *is* nice," said God. "I gave it a lot of thought. I wanted to make sure it was pleasurable. Very pleasurable. It's one of the things I'm most proud of."

"Hasn't God told you about it?" I whispered to Adam.

"A little. Not much." Adam leaned his head against the pergola and closed his eyes.

"I designed it beautifully," God went on. "But of course it hasn't been tried yet." He planted himself in front of the bench and looked down at us. His eyes shone. "I hadn't planned to do it so soon, but now that I've seen you together, getting along so well, obviously made for each other, I can't wait any longer. You'll be the first—think of that!—the first of all mankind to love each other, the first to know the joys of physical love! And in so doing you'll prove that, like everything I've made, this too is perfect!"

"Why do we have to prove it? Aren't you sure?" I asked, thinking of the cow and its pleading eyes.

God frowned. "Of course I'm sure, of course it's perfect! How could it not be? It's just that—I want to see it happen, so I *know* it works! All right, you two. Stand up." We stood.

"Come over here to the meadow and lie down. Both of you." Adam stretched himself on the grass and closed his eyes. "Eve, lie beside him." Reluctantly I lay next to

Adam, on my back, arms folded. Far above in the sky an eagle soared.

If only I had wings, I thought, watching the great bird float in and out among the clouds. In the middle of my stomach, just above where the Serpent had sat that first day, I felt a knot I had never known before. I remembered the Serpent's voice: "it will be one of the most beautiful things that can happen on Earth."

"Adam, you're going to make love to Eve," I heard God say.

Adam opened his eyes. "What!" he said. "How do I do that?"

"You know very well; I told you about it."

Adam closed his eyes again. "I ran too much today; I'm too tired."

"Adam!" God waved both fists in the air. "What did I do to have such a son? Eve, move closer to him, put your arms around him. Caress him!"

I stared at God, amazed. Since that first day when I had run my hands down the Serpent's neck, I had petted many animals: massaged the trunks of elephants, combed the long silken hair of colobus monkeys, kneaded the sharp ears of foxes in their dens. Always, every creature enjoyed my caress; even the great cats closed their eyes and purred. But never had I come close to the genitals; without being told, I knew that part of the body was not mine to touch. Now, God was urging me . . .

"Caress him?" I stuttered.

"Why do you keep repeating my words?" shouted God. "You heard what I said!"

"I can't!" I cried, and rolled away from Adam, onto my stomach. God glared at me, then shrugged.

"Adam, you'll have to do it yourself. Go on, go on!"

I closed my eyes and covered my ears with my hands. Adam was making little groans; from the corner of my eye, I could see him moving his hips in the grass.

"Eve," ordered God. "Turn over."

The knot in my stomach expanded and gripped my chest. "No!" I cried, and scrambled to my feet. Quickly God stood in front of me and put his hand gently on my shoulder.

"My dear Eve, I'm so sorry," he said softly. "I'm afraid I've frightened you. It will be beautiful, just as the Serpent said. Take a breath, relax, remember the Serpent's words." He smoothed the grass. "Here," he said. "Lie here." Again I heard the Serpent's voice: "It's something God has done really well." Warily I settled on the ground next to Adam. "Now Adam, make love to her."

Adam rolled over carefully and covered my body with his. He was heavy. "Enter her," ordered God.

"I don't like this," I muttered. I was suffocating

under Adam's weight.

"Don't be silly," said God. "It's beautiful!"

"Oh, oh!" I cried as Adam entered my body. "Stop! It hurts!" Adam stopped.

"Go on, Adam, go on!" shouted God.

"She says it hurts," said Adam. "I don't want to hurt her."

"You're not hurting her. Eve, you're just imagining things. There is no pain in Eden."

I screamed, "It hurts, it hurts!"

"It doesn't hurt," said God. "It's *got* to be nice! Keep on, Adam."

Adam began to move. I screamed again. I could feel my insides rip. The world settled, a burning blade of pain between my legs. I grabbed Adam's hair and tried to shove him away.

"Stop being silly, Eve!" commanded God. "Adam, go on, go on!"

But by now Adam was beyond any command. His whole body bore down on mine, all his force behind his passion. "Uh—uh—uh," he cried. "Oh . . . " Two more thrusts and he lay still across my body. Sweat flowed from his face, his arms, his buttocks, and mixed with my tears.

God leaned over us and smiled. "Good," he said. "It's done. It works." Adam was limp. His hand dropped heavy from my thigh to the ground. Warm liquid seeped between my legs. I wept.

A voice. Low, shaking. A voice I barely recognized, with enormous power behind it. "What is this?" it growled. I opened my eyes. The Serpent loomed over me. "Oh, God—what have you done!" Its tail came round like a whip; Adam rolled off me to the ground. I saw a gash on his shoulder. "He'll have a scar from that!" said the Serpent through its teeth.

God came forward, his hand out. "Serpent, Serpent, my friend," he said. "I was just trying to see how it would work. A little experiment. There's no harm done."

"No harm done!" The Serpent stood on its tail and God drew back. "No harm done! He as good as raped her! With your encouragement! Eve will never forget it." The Serpent turned to me and its face softened. "How wrong I was, my dear. I'm so sorry." It took grass in its mouth and wiped my face. "Come. I'll take you home."

I stood up shakily. God reached out to help me, and I pulled away. "Don't touch me," I cried, and shivered.

"God!" The word came out sharp, and God flinched as though he had been struck. The Serpent drew breath. When it spoke its voice was low, but God trembled. "You have done terrible damage to this child today. You will be fortunate if she ever wants to see you again, you or Adam. You have betrayed her."

"But . . . " said God.

"There are no buts," replied the Serpent. "Some things can never be undone."

As the Serpent led me down the path, I had a glimpse of Adam asleep in the meadow, mouth open, arms akimbo, God hovering behind. I began to shake. "I never want to see him again," I sobbed. "I never want to see either of them!"

"I know," said the Serpent. "Eve, come. I'm with you now; I'll take care of you. All will be well."

Nightmares

I DO NOT KNOW HOW we got to the cave that was to be our home for the next weeks. I remember stumbling along a trail I had never seen, the Serpent looping its tail around my waist and half-carrying me. Then I lay in a pool of warm water that bubbled from the ground, and the Serpent bathed me tenderly, carefully, cooing to me all the while, "It's all right, Eve. Cry, cry, let it go. . . ." Later I lay on a mat, covered with quilts. The Serpent brought me a bowl of tea, and I slept.

It cannot have been long before God appeared. The Serpent had left for a moment, perhaps to get me another drink. There was a rustle at my shoulder; I opened my eyes and shut them again. God was standing by my bed looking down at me, his hands clasped over his stomach and a pained look on his face. I lay as still as I could, forcing myself to breathe as though I were asleep, and peered out through partly closed lashes. In a flash the Serpent was back. "What are you doing here?" it whispered, but its voice had the force of thunder. "Have you not done enough harm to this child today?"

"Harm?" said God. "How could I? They were supposed to enjoy it—I planned it that way. It can't have been anything but good." The Serpent tapped its tail angrily and God hesitated. "Truly, Serpent," he said, his voice rising, "I just wanted to see if it would work the way I expected."

The Serpent, black with rage, glared from the full height of its body, its nose an inch from the top of God's head. "God," it spat out, "you're a fool—"

"I'm not!" God cried.

"—and blind!" The Serpent lashed its tail. "You have no conception of the damage you've done!"

"I didn't—" God began, but the Serpent went on as though God did not exist.

"I told you they were too young! I warned you to let it happen naturally, in time, as it would have! But you couldn't wait. You made Adam force himself on her!"

"He didn't force himself on her! I explained it to them, and Eve herself told Adam it must be beautiful, because *you* said it was."

The Serpent groaned. "She may never believe me again. I *did* tell her it was beautiful, as it will be—when it is done with love!—not as an experiment to see if the parts work as they should! God, you are so obtuse!"

God glowered at the Serpent, his face flushed. "How dare you criticize me this way!" he shouted. "I do as I like!"

"That may be," replied the Serpent dryly, "but even the Great Creator cannot escape the consequences of his actions."

"Consequences!" God stamped his foot. "You're making a fuss over nothing. Eve is a child. Adam went too fast and frightened her, that's all. She'll forget it in a few days."

The Serpent stared at God in disbelief. "How can you not see what you have done?" it said slowly. "Until today Eve has felt—no, known—that the world was good. She trusted everything around her: the trees and cliffs and lakes, all the creatures, you, Adam, me. You, God—*you!*—have destroyed that faith. From now on Eve will never believe in you as a benevolent god. Nor will she trust Adam—or, perhaps any other man, now and to the ends of time."

"Nonsense," muttered God, but he looked worried.

"*You* used her to your purpose, to prove that you have created well. Adam used her to bring pleasure to his body, as if she were an accessory, a quilt, perhaps—one of those quilts she makes so well—though Adam did not understand what he was doing."

"But it was just in fun! Eve, listen to me," God cried, and stepped toward me, arms out, as if he wanted to give me a hug. I held my breath and lay still on the mat.

The Serpent twined itself in a circle, opened its mouth, and dropped its fangs. They were sharp and pointed like the jaguar's, white as a lily and slightly curved at the ends. I had never seen them before. "Keep away," it said softly, tightening its coils.

God's jaw dropped open and he stepped back. "Serpent," he growled. "Don't try to intimidate me! *I am God!*"

The Serpent sheathed its fangs. "I know very well who you are," it replied. "I also know your place in the universe, and mine! *You* appear to have forgotten your role; you have overreached your domain." Again the Serpent whipped its tail, raised its ears, and stretched itself to the sky. "Let *me* remind *you*, God: *I* am the Serpent. Do you recall my other names?"

God scowled. "Nachash," he snapped.

"Yes, Nachash. But I am known by others as well. Wisdom. Reason. Justice." The Serpent spoke quietly. It paused. I could hear the wind hum through the aspen trees and the plunk of water in the stream. The Serpent went on, every word it spoke weighted. "My role on Earth: to counterbalance the excesses of a jealous god. *I* will defend Eve against any evil that comes her way." It looked at me and its voice softened. "And do my best to heal her body and her soul." A great sigh came from the depths of its body. "If Eve's pain does not upset you, God, reflect on this: If I do not do something magical to heal this child, she will never have anything to do with Adam—or with you—again."

God looked aghast. He ran his fingers through his hair; his hands were shaking. "Will you make her well, Serpent?" he asked in a low voice. "For the good of humankind?"

"For the good of humankind or to satisfy the whims of God?" The Serpent narrowed its eyes. "I will heal her not for your sake but for hers. Now you must leave. I don't want you to come near Eve until the moon has filled and faded six times. You, or that foolish misguided boy."

"Six times!" cried God. "That's too long!"

"Six moons," said the Serpent firmly.

God turned to me—all the while I had been lying still with my eyes nearly closed—and spoke quickly. "Good-bye, Eve. I *am* sorry. I had no idea this would happen. I thought it would be nice for you."

"You *thought*," said the Serpent. "You *thought* of

your pretty experiment, not of Eve. Now go!"

God left, and the Serpent came to my side and looked at me. "Eve, are you awake?" it asked softly. I lay quiet; I could not talk, even to the Serpent. "I think you are," the Serpent said, "but you are wise. Far better that you sleep. Drink this." It held a bowl of tea to my lips and, eyes squeezed shut, I drank.

I slept and woke and slept on and off for a long time. I woke and it was night and the moon quivered through the falling water; it was midday and puddles steamed in the sun; it was dawn and a pink sky lightened to my left, but to the right stars blazed in a black void.

In the black of night came dreams.

> *I was pinned against a cliff. The stone, cold and sharp, dug into my spine. Adam pressed his weight against me and thrust. Each lunge forced the breath from my body.*
>
> *"Stop!" I cried.*
>
> *Adam's eyes brimmed with tears. I felt his lashes wet against my cheek. "I don't want to hurt you," he said. "But God told me to do this, and I must do what God says."*
>
> *"Stop!" I cried again.*

I woke. The Serpent was shaking me.

"Eve, Eve! It's only a dream. You're safe." I wept until I slept again.

> I was in a wood, walking through an orchard of apple trees in full bloom. The way seemed easy and the trail clear. Then the path narrowed and the sweet trees grew closer and pressed their branches against my face and shoulders and caught at my legs as if they were trying to turn me back. But a voice was calling, "Come, Eve, come," and I had to make my way to the center of the forest.
>
> I heard a great sigh—"Alas," moaned the trees—and the path opened before me, pleasant underfoot, thick with pine needles. Black hemlocks replaced the fruit trees. Sharp-needled branches drew away to let me pass. And still I heard the call: "Come, Eve, come."
>
> There was a harsh cry in the thicket, and a creature leaped in front of me and barred my way. It was the wolf that lived not far from our hut; I often played with its pups. Now its lips were drawn back and its fangs gleamed sharp and white; the hair on its neck stood up in a ruff. Its head was low to the ground and it advanced on me, snarling.
>
> "Wolf, Wolf, it's Eve!" I called. But it contin-

ued moving toward me and snapped its jaws at the hand I held out. A spasm of fear clutched my stomach. I ran until I could run no more.

I was in a glade. The sun was slanting through the trees, and it was calm. I sat on a rock to catch my breath. Nearby a bee gathered pollen from a wild rose. It turned and, for a moment, balanced itself in flight. Then it flew directly at me, landed on my arm, and stung me. I saw the stinger pierce the flesh. I cried and shook my arm to get rid of it. It tumbled into the air and flew around my head. My wrist swelled red. Other bees appeared. Again I ran.

I came around a corner and there was God, sitting on a log looking away from me at a stream below. "Oh, God," I cried. "I'm so glad you're here. Such dreadful things are happening. The wolf growled at me and the bee stung me."

"Eve," said God, "I've been calling you." But he did not turn around.

"Look, God. My legs are all scratched and my arm is red and has a big bump on it and it hurts."

"Ah well," said God. "These things happen." And still he did not turn around.

"God, please!" I cried. "Please help me!"

Then he turned his head, and I saw that his face was very red as if he had just run a long way. He looked me over from the top of my head to my toes, so intensely that I felt he must see the wax in my ears and the dirt on the soles of my feet. He scowled. "You're dirty," he said. "Come here."

Again I felt the grip of fear. I backed away. "No," I said. "No."

God's face changed from red to purple. "Come here," he shouted. Then he lowered his voice and took a breath. "Eve," he said, and stretched a hand to me, as though he were enticing a lamb with clover. "Come. I have something for you." He stood and turned to face me. In his arms he held a long, straight horn that twisted on itself and spiraled to a sharp point. I had never seen one like it. God cradled it lovingly in his arms and began to stroke it. "It's the horn of the narwhal that swims in the northern sea. It's beautiful, is it not?" He smiled at me. "I have it for you," he said. "That's why I was calling you."

"That's very kind of you," I said.

"Yes," he said. "I'm going to run it through your navel. Then I can lead you around on a rope. Don't make a fuss; it won't hurt at all." He raised

*the horn shoulder high and started to walk
toward me.*

I screamed and backed away from him.

"Hush," said the Serpent. "Eve, wake up. There's
nothing to fear. I'm with you. Wake now. It was another
dream. Be calm, be calm. It's not real."

"The bee," I cried. "It stung me! And the wolf
growled! And God wanted to run a horn through my
stomach. Keep him away from me, Serpent, don't let
him near me!"

"He won't come near you," said the Serpent. "Not
within five valleys, for a long time."

"I never want to see him again."

"Of course you don't," said the Serpent. "Here,
drink this, my dear," and it brought me clear water from
the stream, mixed with herbs. I drank thirstily. "It will
help you sleep," it said, "without dreams. When you
wake, you'll feel better. And then we'll swim and walk
and lie in the sun. And someday, we'll talk about your
dreams." The Serpent coiled itself behind me as a pillow,
and I slept.

Healing

WHEN I WOKE, the sun was rising over the hills to the east. The Serpent was gone. The sun touched my shoulders; as I stretched, my shadow played on the back wall of the cave and curved above me on the ceiling. Little by little it came back to me, the horror and the pain. But the Serpent's potion had done its work; the menace of God and Adam and my dreams had receded as behind a haze. For the moment I could move ahead with the day.

The Serpent appeared, carrying a basket awkwardly in its mouth. "Ah," it said, dropping the basket. "You're awake. Good. I've been doing all the work. It's hard to lug this around with no arms and legs." It stretched out flat on the sand and panted.

"How long have I been asleep?" I asked.

The Serpent shrugged. "Two days," it said. "Long enough for the strawberries to ripen. They're delicious. I'd better wash my face." It passed its clover-shaped tongue over its mouth; its nose and chin were red with juice. "I couldn't wait," it added sheepishly.

For half a moon we did not move from the area around the cave. I bathed in the warm bubbles of the pool and sat under the falls, letting the pellets of water bounce on my skin and watching the stream cascade over the rocks. I dozed on and off during the day but slept poorly at night (though there were no more dreams), waking frequently with my heart pounding in my chest.

Then one day the Serpent drew itself, glistening, from the pond, and shook the water from its ears. "Enough lying around," it said. "We're getting lazy. Let's have a picnic."

Our favorite picnic spot was a meadow ringed with mulberry trees, half a morning's walk from home. We had gone there often in the past, before God's lessons had begun. The meadow, on a round-backed hill, over-looked a valley and, beyond, a mountain covered in cloud. The field was always a riot of colors: poppies, daisies, cornflowers. Suddenly, more than anything else on Earth, I wanted to race through that meadow, smell those flowers. Quickly I climbed from the pool and began tying back my hair.

"Let's go," I said. "We'll find avocados along the way, and mulberries by the field. I hope they're ripe."

At first my body was stiff and I walked slowly, but I soon felt the blood rise and my arms and legs limber up. It was good to move, to walk, to stretch, to feel the dust between my toes and the breeze on my cheeks. My body was strong; I was strong. The Serpent looked at me and smiled.

The mulberries were black and ripe; we filled the basket with them and settled among the flowers. When we had eaten, the Serpent turned to me. "Eve," it said. "The night we came to the cave, you had a bad dream— you were shouting, 'Stop!' and when I tried to wake you, you pushed me away. Was it Adam in your dream?"

I clutched my knees to my chest. "I don't want to talk about it," I cried.

"You must," said the Serpent firmly. "We haven't talked at all about what happened to you, or about your dreams, and until we do they'll haunt you."

"Serpent, leave me alone! I can't think about it now."

The Serpent persisted. "Eve, tell me, what was Adam doing?" I clenched my fists. "Eve," the Serpent repeated in a tone I had to obey.

"He had me pinned against a cliff," I faltered. "He

was—doing it to me. He said he had to, God had told him to. He was crying." I rolled over and buried my head in the grass. "Oh, Serpent, I can't bear it," I wailed.

The Serpent continued calmly, "And in the second dream, there was a wolf and a bee and God wanted to run a horn through you?"

"Through my navel, so there'd be a big hole and he could lead me around on a rope," I sobbed. "And the wolf growled at me and the bee stung me." My entire body was shaking.

"What did God say?" asked the Serpent inexorably.

"He said it wouldn't hurt, so I shouldn't make a fuss." I curled myself into a ball and covered my head with my arms.

"All right." The Serpent sighed. "Those were dreadful dreams, Eve. But they are gone."

It twined itself into a circle at my side and heated its body. It did not touch me—at that moment I could not have borne to be touched by anything at all, even a feather—but little by little I stopped shaking, and my sobs changed gradually to hiccups. "Eve," the Serpent said at last. "Sit up and have something more to eat. Look at the view; it's exceptionally lovely in this light."

I sat up; the sun had started its downward sweep to the west, and the valley at our feet was dappled with light and shadow. The Serpent settled by the basket of food we had collected along the path and pushed an avocado toward me. "Have one," it said. "You only had mulberries for lunch." Suddenly I was hungry.

"Feel better?" the Serpent inquired as I finished my third avocado.

I nodded.

"Eve, my dear," it said. "It's very hard, forcing you to talk about such horror. But I had to do it. You *must* listen to your dreams."

"Why?" I asked. "Why can't I forget them?"

"You can't forget them, because they tell you your deepest feelings and fears," the Serpent replied slowly, as though it wanted each word to sink into my mind. "Now that you've talked about them, the terror behind them will begin to fade."

"Why did they come?" I asked, shivering.

The Serpent began giving hard little taps to my back with its tail. "Don't start shaking again; you're done with that. The dreams came because you couldn't bear to think about the violence that was done to you, or face the fears, and those fears came to life in your dreams."

"I've never had dreams like that before."

"There has never before been anything in your life to give you such dreams." For a moment the Serpent frowned and its head grew black. "I never believed God would be so selfish and so blind," it muttered. It took a breath, and gradually the color of its head faded to blue.

"What did they mean?" I asked in spite of myself. I had nearly stopped shivering, but the Serpent continued its firm taps on my back.

"The first dream grew from your horror at Adam's act. The second came from your fear that God himself will attack you—not your body, but your innermost being—and come to control you, mind and soul," the Serpent said.

I tried to think about that. I wanted to ask about the soul, but I could not focus on it. The Serpent lowered its eyebrows and looked hard at me with its emerald eyes. "Is there anything more you want to ask?" it inquired. I shook my head. "Then we'll let it go for now. How calm it is here," it added. "There are flamingos in the lake; you can just make them out."

I looked across the valley. I had forgotten how wide it was, and how lovely the view. Far away a mountain grew out of the forest. From a mound of powdery green trees it rose, up and up, much higher than any of the hills around us. Sun gleamed on its sides, slashed by shadows. The top was hidden in cloud.

"Can we climb that mountain?" I asked.

The Serpent glanced at me in surprise. "It's a long way away—well outside the Garden, and it's a steep climb once we get there."

Outside the Garden? Of course the Garden did not cover all the Earth; I knew that. Once I had asked what it was like outside, and the Serpent had answered, "More or less the same, though not as lush." I had hardly thought of it since. There was our hut and God's house, the plains and rivers, and hills and canyons around. Plenty of room to roam and endless varieties of birds and trees, fruits, rocks, vegetables, animals, insects, to examine and explore. But I had never been to the edges of the Garden. I had no idea where they were. Now, suddenly, I wanted to find out for myself what was there, outside the Garden.

"Why do you want to go, Eve?" the Serpent asked.

"I want to see what it's like, and what kind of mountain it is. You can't tell from here. The base is hidden in the jungle, and a cloud is always sitting on top. Do you know what the top is like?"

"It has an odd summit," said the Serpent.

"What do you mean?" I asked.

"Well," said the Serpent, "a long time ago the top blew off."

"In the wind?"

The Serpent laughed. "No, in an explosion. It's hard to explain. If you want to go, Eve, we'll go. But we'll need to prepare for it. It will take several days to get there, and we won't find much to eat near the volcano."

"Not much to eat?" It was impossible to imagine not having food everywhere at hand, hanging from trees, sprouting from the ground. "There's always something to eat!"

"Not on that mountain. When the volcano exploded—we say *erupted*—it left ash and lava all over the ground, so almost nothing grows there. I'll tell you about it when we're there; it will be easier to understand."

As soon as we got back to the cave, I began planning for our journey. At the Serpent's urging I gathered nuts and small fruits and piled them on a rock. "Will that be enough?" I asked anxiously. "How will I carry them?"

"You'll come up with something," the Serpent replied absently. "I'm going off for a while; we'll leave first thing in the morning." It slid quickly away through the trees.

I need a container like the bag I hang around my neck but bigger, for food, I thought, and after a bit of fiddling found a way to attach vines to a basket, which I then slung over my shoulders. It was not very comfortable—it rubbed against my back—but it carried food enough for two or three days.

"Look," I said proudly when the Serpent returned. "I'm ready to go."

"Well done," the Serpent replied. And the following morning our journey began.

The Volcano

🍎

FOR A DAY WE traveled through parts of the Garden I knew so well I could run through them on nights when the moon hid its light. But in the afternoon of the second day, the path descended into an area where I had never been. Pools awash in water lilies lay on each side. Big flies with hairy legs waving behind them, tiny black gnats, and many other insects drifted around our faces and brushed our eyelashes with their wings. Then we could go no farther. Several trees had fallen and lay in a jumble of branches and brambles across the way.

"Is this the end of the path?" I asked.

"It is," the Serpent replied. "This is the edge of the Garden. The animals rarely go outside, so there are no paths there. That won't be a problem; it's quite open land. But it's not going to be easy to get through the barricade. Especially for you." The Serpent craned its neck right and left to look at the mass of twisted branches. "It seems that someone wants to keep us from leaving the Garden. Trees don't often come down." In fact, though occasionally we found broken branches in the Garden, this was the first fallen tree I had ever seen.

It took me an hour to get through the barricade. The Serpent slid gracefully under logs and around the roots of brambles and pointed out the best route, but I had to scramble through the scrub and climb over and under the trees. When we finally reached the other side, it was nearly dark. I collapsed on a bank of moss. Sweat ran down my temples and neck and between my breasts. In front of us a hill rose gently, covered with a grove of fir trees.

The Serpent coiled itself next to me. "We'll spend the night here. That was quite a workout for you. A pity you're encumbered with all those legs and arms and hair. It's much easier to get around on your stomach." I kicked a foot weakly in its direction. It looked at me kindly and laughed. "Get some water over there," it said, nodding at a stream than ran nearby. "Then we'll eat, and you'll feel better. We can sleep under this pine."

In the morning I was so stiff I could barely get up. My legs and arms were covered with scratches, and my

fingernails were torn from scrambling through the barricade. There was no path, but the ground was soft underfoot and it was cool under the pines. The Serpent was
very quiet. Occasionally it shook its head and frowned.
"A bad sign," it muttered, but would not elaborate.

We left the lowlands and moved through fields filled
with wildflowers. It was pretty enough, though the blossoms were not as large as those in the Garden, and the
colors were muted. That night we slept in a hollow
under a crab apple and ate its sour fruit for our evening
meal. The next day we followed a long canyon with steep
sides, and the volcano was hidden from sight. We spent
the night under a brier, brushing its yellow petals into a
pile to make a mat. The brier had no fruit, and we for-
aged until we found some small wrinkled mushrooms,
which we ate with the few grapes and bread left in my
bag.

"What will we eat tomorrow?" I asked, shaking the
crumbs into my palm.

"We may be able to find some nuts and a few more
mushrooms."

"How much farther is it?" I asked wearily as I
stretched out under the bush.

"We're nearly there. We'll start climbing as soon as
the sun is up." The Serpent smiled at me. "Tired of our
trip? Want to turn around?" I was too sleepy to reply.

The sun was barely up as we set out in the morning. When we emerged from the canyon, the mountain loomed above us. We began to climb. The way grew steeper, far steeper than any hill in the Garden: I had to use my hands for balance, and dig my toes into the black earth to keep from sliding back down the slope. Short gorse replaced the flowers, and little twisted black trees bent away from the wind. Then there were only rocks covered with splotches of gray-green lichen. The cloud that hid the mountaintop lay before us like a curtain, fluffy, suffocating. We entered its gray and silent world and moved through black dust and scarred and pitted stones—lava, said the Serpent, and ash from the volcano. I could see only my feet and a small area around us. The ash lifted and settled around my ankles as I climbed, following the Serpent's sinuous curve. *This is a dream*, I thought. *It can't be real.*

The ground leveled off a little, though it was still steep. Rock replaced the dust; my feet slipped and skidded on small, round stones. "Be careful," said the Serpent. "Go slow." Then, "Stop! We're here."

"Where? I can't see anything!" I said.

"Look carefully." I peered ahead. Under my toes a void appeared and disappeared in the cloud. "The volcano," said the Serpent.

Hurriedly I backed away from the rim. "We've come

all this way to see a cloud?" I groaned, and plunked myself on a rock. "I'm thirsty."

The Serpent waved its feathers toward a crevice a short distance away. "There's a pool there." I drank greedily and sloshed the cold, black water over my face.

"Feel better?" asked the Serpent.

I shook my head. All around was cloud, damp and chill. "I still don't know what the top of the mountain looks like."

"Wait," said the Serpent. It stood on its tail and whistled, every bit as loud as God had.

"I didn't know you could do that!" I exclaimed.

The Serpent looked abashed. "Sometimes it's better not to exhibit all your talents at once," it said. "Listen now."

At first I heard nothing and felt only the silent weight of cloud. Then came a moan, a song, a boom, a shriek. Wind slapped my cheeks, swirled around us—and the cloud lifted.

We were standing at the top of the mountain, with the world spread out below. To the east, low hills dotted with shrubs and small trees. To the south, rolling plains of grass and, beyond, a band of yellow. To the north, white mountain peaks. "Snow," explained the Serpent. To the west the Garden and, far in the distance, an expanse of blue. "That," said the Serpent, "is the ocean.

And this is the cauldron of the volcano."

We peered into the chasm. The sides were steep—one careless step would have sent me straight to the bottom. All around giant fissures ran jaggedly down the cliff. In some places ridges of ash had built up from the base. Far below something shimmered among the rocks, the way sunlight dances at the bottom of a pool; but here it was red, and glittered and flared. A curious fog seemed to come from it, bearing an odor I had never known. From time to time there was a crack, a burst of sound, and bright points of light flew in all directions. "Sparks," murmured the Serpent.

"What is it? I've never seen anything like it."

"It's fire, and this is the only place in the world you can find it." Deep in the cauldron mounds of red mud churned and popped and tumbled. "Magma," the Serpent explained. "The inside of the Earth. It's much more turbulent than when I last saw it."

I stared into the depths; my head whirled. I felt myself stagger forward, felt the Serpent's tail whip around my waist and draw me back. "Come, Eve," it said quietly. "Sit here." It settled me behind a boulder. "You need some food."

"There's no food left," I said. "We've eaten it."

"It's all right," said the Serpent. "I thought we might run out, so I asked the eagle to deliver a few provisions for us. They're over there." Sure enough, on a flat stone nearby lay a packet of nuts and pears and tomatoes wrapped in a grape leaf. "Don't move!" the Serpent ordered as it went to fetch the food. And there behind the boulder at the top of the world we had our meal.

"What have you learned this morning?" asked the Serpent, grinning at me.

"Lots of things," I muttered through a mouthful of nuts.

"Don't talk with your mouth full," the Serpent said mildly. "It's rude and unattractive."

"Sorry," I said.

"You did learn many things, but what was the one crucial lesson?"

"Oh! Not to look into the cauldron of a volcano!" I exclaimed.

"Unless you're holding on to something solid or tied firmly to a rock."

"Or have the Serpent next to you," I said. "Thank you, Serpent. I wouldn't have liked to fall in."

"No. I wouldn't have liked it either, especially on an empty stomach. Not good for the appetite, chasing Eve into the cauldron."

"If I had fallen in, what would have happened to me?"

The Serpent shook its head. "I'm not sure. In the

Garden you're totally safe, but here, outside . . . I'm glad we didn't have to deal with that problem."

"What's magma?" I asked, finishing the last of the pear.

"As you know, the middle of the Earth is hot, made of molten rock—magma. In the volcano that liquid center is near the surface and bubbles out; when it mixes with air, the gases burn. That's fire. It's very hot and will hurt you badly if it touches you."

"There's no other fire on Earth but what we see here?"

"No, but if you know how, you can make it."

"Make fire? How?"

"I'll show you someday."

"Why would we want to make it? What use would it be?"

"You can use it to heat food, cook grains and vegetables. Warm porridge and cocoa if my tail isn't available."

I giggled. "I can do that with the sun," I said.

"Not at night or on a rainy day. With fire you can cook at any time. And a fire is very comforting on a cold evening."

"But it's never cold in the Garden."

"Well, it gets chilly at night; we do use a blanket occasionally."

I closed my eyes and thought of the cauldron. "Does

all that mud just stay there and bubble like that and burn?"

"Not always, but it's been this way for a long time. Sometimes the volcano erupts; the gases and magma inside explode and overflow and run down the mountain. That's the lava we saw on the way up. All this black rock around us is lava that has hardened."

I looked across the hole that had been a mountain. It was clear that the summit was missing. I could nearly see the peak it once had been. "It must have been enormous," I said. "What happened to it?"

"The top blew off." The Serpent grinned at me.

"Oh, Serpent, don't tease me! You told me that. But how? When? What did it look like?"

So the Serpent told me how the pressure had built up in the Earth until the thin skin could no longer contain it, and the uppermost part of the mountain exploded and the molten lava gushed red from the hole and flowed like a river down the sides. And the Earth heaved and split and burned. An apocalypse.

"But the animals, the birds?"

"There were no animals or birds."

"The trees, the flowers, the ears of corn?"

"There was nothing on the Earth."

"And God? Where was God?"

"It was before God."

"Before God? I thought God was here always."

"No. Not always. This happened before God came."

"And you?"

The Serpent squinted into the sun and licked its tail. "Me?" it said.

"Yes, you. You must have been here. How could you describe it so well otherwise? How would you know how it happened?"

"You're right," the Serpent said. "I was very small, hardly as big as the nail on your little finger. I was hiding in a rock on the other side of the valley. Even so, I could only look out occasionally when the explosions slowed and the heat was less intense." The Serpent seemed to have gone into a reverie. Its eyes closed to narrow slits; its tail lifted and traced circles in the ash. The fine, black powder lay in splotches on its back and darkened the brilliant blues and greens and reds of its coat. After a while it said quietly, "Then the Earth shook and shouted for a long time. Great bolts of lightning screamed up and down and sideways and hit the peaks on every side."

"Peaks?" I looked around. "What peaks?"

"They're gone now. At the time this mountain was in the middle of a big range, surrounded by peaks just as high. The others were destroyed."

"And?"

"Otherwise it was dark. Black, black. No light at all.

The Earth was wrapped in cloud, but I couldn't see even the cloud—except when the lightning blazed. There was no sun, no stars. No sky."

"Horrible," I said. The sun was hot, but I shivered.

"Yes," said the Serpent. "But beautiful as well. And simple."

"Simple?"

"Yes. Life at its simplest. Black, silver, black. Silence, tumult, silence."

"Weren't you afraid?"

"What was there to be afraid of? I was thirsty. And after a few days, hungry. At first it was a great spectacle, but then it got boring." It sighed. "I slept. Then it rained. I drank and drank. But it kept on raining and the water rose all around me and swept me away."

"What did you do?"

The Serpent laughed. "I learned to swim. Finally the rain stopped, and I was on dry land again. Grass grew, and flowers and trees, and I ate."

"Then what happened?"

"I thought: God must be around. Only *he* could cause this chaos. So I went looking for him."

"Where was he?"

"Just about where he is now, in the Garden, playing with his toys."

"Toys?"

"Earth and rocks and water and so on. Thunder and lightning: he'd discovered how to make electricity. He was creating things, playing with them." The Serpent stretched. "No more questions now. Time for a nap."

But I was too excited to rest, and while the Serpent relaxed in the sun, I explored the area, staying well away from the rim. We were atop a field of rock that was pitted with holes, small holes and large ones. Most were rough and pocked, but one was absolutely smooth, as if it had been polished. I caught the image of my face slightly distorted on the bottom. There, in the middle of my reflected eye, lay a tiny white bead. When I picked it up, it was hard, with a slight give. I dropped it into the pouch of woven grasses I carried around my neck.

When the Serpent joined me a short time later, I was dribbling a handful of black ash through my fingers. The ash was soft and silky, but there was a grittiness at its core.

"You like that?" asked the Serpent. I nodded. There was something especially satisfying about the stuff. It was so black, so uncompromising, so much itself. But I could not find words to describe my feelings. I scooped some ash into the palm of my hand and shook it into the pouch.

"It's time to go," said the Serpent. "Do you want to look into the volcano once more before we leave?" I nodded, and we went again to the rim. Cautiously, with one hand on the Serpent's neck, I peered into the cauldron. The lava was boiling harder than before, sending chunks of flaming rock into the air.

"We must go," said the Serpent. "Hurry."

The Earth jolted; I staggered and the Serpent clasped me in a coil. On the opposite flank of the cauldron a split appeared in the rock; half the mountain fell away. I saw the molten lava burst through, pushing aside massive sections of cliff, and pour like a torrent down the eastern slope, devouring shrubs and trees. At the front edge of the flow, boulders bounced as if they were the balls Adam made, flying from his hands.

I stood, mesmerized, on the very edge. The Serpent pulled me away. "Run!" it said. "As fast as you can!" And it followed close behind as I raced down the mountain, tripping on rocks and loose stones, while the volcano heaved and thundered under my feet and poured out its heart of flaming muck above.

Somehow, gasping for breath, I reached the bottom of the mountain, the Serpent at my heels. "Stop here, Eve," it cried above the tumult. "We're safe now." I threw myself to the ground; ash puffed up around my body. The Serpent coiled itself beside me. "Well, now *you've* seen a volcano in action!" it said. "A real show. I certainly didn't expect it. We're lucky; it was the other side that cracked, and the lava flowed east." It twisted its head and blew the ash from its body while I dusted myself off with my hands.

I felt a clutch of fear in my chest. "Do you think it's God? Do you think he found out we left the Garden?"

"No," the Serpent said. "God takes no interest in what goes on outside the Garden. He won't even notice the smoke and ash; the wind is blowing them to the east." The Serpent glanced at the sun. "It's past midday," it said. "We must go."

The Serpent refused to stop for the night until we had put a range of mountains between the volcano and ourselves—"You never know with this sort of natural upheaval," it said—and it was dark before we slept. It took us two more days to get to the barrier. There was no rush; we walked slowly, admiring the trees and discovering tiny black grapes and nuts and mushrooms I had not seen before. When we came to the fields we rested, and I made daisy chains, which I hung around the Serpent's neck. In the late afternoon we passed through a grove of pine trees, and there ahead of us stood the barrier, dark and forbidding. I stopped and stared at it; my heart pounded in my chest. I expected God to appear behind it, waving his arms.

"Eve," the Serpent said softly. "Stop worrying. God's not here. We won't see him tonight, or for many moons to come. He doesn't wander about in the evening, certainly not this far from home."

"But couldn't he hear we've left? From an animal or a bird?"

"It's very unlikely."

"If he did find out, he'd be furious, wouldn't he?"

"I think so. He obviously put that barrier there to keep all creatures inside the Garden, and he wouldn't be pleased if he knew we'd been out."

"But he didn't tell us we couldn't go! It's not as if we'd disobeyed him."

"No. But as you know, God is not always rational."

To the South

WE SPENT THE NIGHT outside the barrier. The next morning I scrambled through it without too much trouble, and we took the path toward home. After the gray silence of the volcano, the Garden seemed flamboyant: sunflowers flared yellow; meadows flashed their varied, vibrant greens; birds shouted in the trees. We reached the cave on the second afternoon. I was asleep before the sun went down and slept late into the morning. When at last I crawled from my mat, I was stiff and my muscles ached; even the Serpent admitted to a certain soreness in its coils.

"We can go back to the hut today," the Serpent said as we finished breakfast. Drops of water from the waterfall spattered on its skin, creating dark dots on a sky blue background. "We don't need the cave anymore."

"I'm glad," I said, and we packed up our few belongings and carried them home. But when I saw the familiar pond and the stream and the terrace, suddenly I was afraid.

"Won't God come to see us here?"

The Serpent shook its head. "I told you, Eve. You needn't worry about God."

My heart thumped. "What about Adam?" I asked.

"Neither of them will come near us for another five moons."

"Are you sure?"

"Absolutely."

I stared at the Serpent, wondering if I could believe what it said. I no longer trusted it as completely as before: it had been wrong about God's plans for me.

"Eve," the Serpent said. "I know I was mistaken once. I was too relaxed; I did not see into God's mind. Now I'm on my guard, and I will *not* be mistaken again." It put its tail gently on my hand. "You can trust me, my dear, in this and in all things." And I knew that was true.

It was good to be at the hut again, with our quilts and clay cups, and the terrace outside, and the stream gurgling into the pond. However, though I was tired and needed rest, I could not settle to anything. I wandered aimlessly around the terrace, or slept, or lay in the sun. Each night we watched the moon grow—from a sliver to a half moon to a full round orb that made shadows on the ground.

"What we need," the Serpent announced as the moon began to wane, "is a soak in the hot springs." So we made our way to the next valley, where steaming liquid bubbled from the bottom of a pool, and lowered ourselves carefully into the water. Fronds of bright green weeds grew on the rocks and waved serenely back and forth in the current. When I touched them with my toes, tiny green fish swam out from between the leaves.

"Eve, tell me, what did you think of our journey? We've been back nearly a moon and we haven't really talked about it."

"It was wonderful!"

"*What* was wonderful?"

Wonderful was not a word I used very often, and I was surprised it had popped out that way. In fact, not everything about the trip *had* been wonderful, or even pleasant. The long walk and the climb through the ash were hard work, and I had been weary, and bored when there was nothing but mist to see. When the volcano erupted, I had been terrified. "A lot wasn't especially nice," I began slowly. "I was so tired, and we couldn't see anything. But when we got there, the volcano, and the magma boiling way down inside: it was so . . . impressive. And your story—the ring of mountains that have disappeared . . . the *idea* of all those great peaks exploding, and just gone. And then when the volcano blew up, and the lava flowed . . . " Again I saw the burning stream crawling inexorably over shrubs and trees, with the boulders crashing ahead. I paused. "I was scared."

"So was I," said the Serpent. I stared at it, dumbfounded; I could not imagine the Serpent frightened. Even when the Earth was young and the mountains were blowing apart all around it, the Serpent had not been afraid. Now it looked at me. "I *am* afraid, Eve. Occasionally. Not for myself, but for you."

But my mind had jumped to God. God, who had organized all that chaos, playing, as the Serpent had said, with his toys.

"God must know about the volcano," I said. "He knows everything."

"Of course God knows the volcano is there; he made it. I'm not sure he realizes it's still active; for years there was not a rumble from it. It's certainly come to life again."

"But how could it, without God knowing?"

"As I told you, God has lost interest in the world outside the Garden." For a moment the Serpent was quiet and closed its eyes, but it soon spoke again. "Eve, what did *you* learn?"

"So much! About what it was like in the beginning, and magma and lava, and the volcano erupting. But mostly—" I drew in my breath sharply, the idea had just come to me—"I learned there's a world outside the Garden."

"You've always known that. I told you from the start."

"But I never really understood what it meant. I thought 'outside the Garden' was just the same as the Garden, only farther away. And it's not. It's as different as . . . as night from day. Only that's not quite right either: it looks a lot like the Garden, but it *feels* different."

Again the Serpent was silent. "Anything else?"

"Well, I found out that God doesn't want us to leave the Garden."

"Yes," said the Serpent quietly. "That was a surprise for us both."

I thought of the barrier, how hard it had been to get through, and I saw the God of my dream, angry and shouting and waving his fists. "Will God know we've been out?" I asked in a sudden panic.

"I think if he knew, he'd be down here by now," the Serpent answered, making a little whirlpool in the water with its tail.

"Will he know when he sees us? Some of those hymns and prayers say he knows everything. Does he?"

"God knows many things. But have you ever had reason to believe he can read your mind?"

I opened and shut my fingers in the water, watching the tiny bubbles on my skin. "When I'm with him, I often think things about him he wouldn't like, like how I hate it when he shouts and how silly all those prayers are . . . and he never seems to be aware of it."

The Serpent nodded.

"But why can't he read my mind, if he's omnipotent?"

"I don't know," the Serpent replied.

"Can *you*?" I asked. At times the Serpent seemed to sense my thoughts before I knew them myself.

The Serpent laughed and wobbled its ears, sending droplets of water over both of us. "I often have a pretty good idea of what's going on in your head. But that's because I know you so well, not because I'm reading your mind."

I lay back in the water and gazed at the treetops. Now that I was sure my thoughts were safe from God, I felt more secure. "When's our next trip?" I said after a while.

"I want to visit the other places we saw from the volcano."

"I wonder if all the exits will be barred," the Serpent murmured to itself.

"Do you suppose God has put a fence all around the Garden?" I asked.

"Interesting question. We could go across country, not on a trail, and see."

I stood and shrugged the water from my shoulders. The drops made little rings that expanded to the edges of the pool; the fronds stirred and quivered. "When?" I asked.

"And where?" said the Serpent. "Where do you want to go?" It stretched its neck onto a rock and elegantly drew its great body out of the water. Today it was sheathed in white fleur-de-lis against a glowing emerald ground. I watched the tiny silvery flowers on its skin expand and shrink as it moved.

"To the plains and the desert first," I said. "Then I'd like to see the mountains and the snow. And then the ocean. Can't you tell me about the ocean?"

"You'll see it for yourself; that's much better than hearing about it."

I groaned and climbed out of the pool. "Let's get started."

"Eve, we can't just leave. We need to prepare for our journey. We'll need to take water with us."

"Water? There's water everywhere. There was even water on the volcano."

"That's because it rains there. There's no water in the desert."

I couldn't imagine a land without water. "How do things grow?" I asked.

"Not many things do," the Serpent replied.

I cupped my hands and dipped them in the pool, watching the water run out the sides. "How can I bring water with us? It's impossible."

"You make bowls and jugs."

"But they're not very big, and how would I carry them? I can't hold them all the time; I need my hands free. And they break so easily."

"I'm sure you'll come up with something," the Serpent said. "Let me know when you're ready to go."

For two days I tried unsuccessfully to make a large bowl with high sides that could be covered at the top. "I'm so sick of this," I cried as the fourth one broke in my hands. I flung the pieces on the ground. "There must be some other way to carry water!" Suddenly I thought of the gourds Adam and I used as drums. "How foolish I am," I muttered to myself, and ran into the meadows to find one.

The following day we started on our way to the desert, walking cautiously through the woods, heading south. I had improved on the basket I had made for our trip to the volcano. This one was larger and woven of soft grasses that did not prickle. In it I packed bread and olives and apricots, and a fat yellow gourd filled with water, its mouth stuffed shut with a sunflower.

Avoiding the animal paths that crisscrossed the Garden, we pushed through the underbrush. Tall, splendid trees grew thick against one another. Giant cats lay languid along the branches; their tails curled and tapped over our heads, and their pelts glowed black, or yellow.

After two days we came to a glade that passed like a broad river between the trees. Again the way was barred, this time by a solid wall of bramble, raspberries and blackberries and roses that climbed twice as high as my head and extended on each side as far as I could see. "I can go under quite easily," the Serpent said. "But you certainly won't get through with any skin left."

On the inside of the bramble, immense trees marched east and west into the distance. I had never seen trees so large: trunks as wide as the Serpent was long, branches reaching far out in every direction, heads towering into the sky. Monkeys flew back and forth above us, clinging casually to vines.

I peered at the monkeys. "I can go over the top of

this barrier," I said. "I'll climb one of these trees and come down the other side." I frowned at the branches, high above my head. "If I can reach that limb."

The Serpent chuckled. "I'll give you a tail up." It leaned against the tree and wound its body back and forth up the trunk until only its tail touched the ground and its shining coils made a stepping ladder for me. "There you go," it said, and I climbed easily to the lowest branch. "Hold on tight," it called as it lowered itself to the ground. "You're not a monkey."

I scrambled into the tree until the branches grew too small to hold me, then settled myself in a crook and looked down. On every side there were monkeys, chattering and waving their tails and tweaking my hair with their fingers. Far below the Serpent craned its head; it looked no bigger than one of the red worms that came out of the mud after a rain, but I thought it better not to say so. The Serpent had taught me, and surely believed, that each creature was as fine and worthy as every other. Nevertheless a worm is a worm, and I suspected that the Serpent was proud of its brilliant skin and feathered ears.

When it reached the far side of the barrier, the Serpent called me, and I clambered down to the lowest branch where again it offered the gleaming spiral of its tail as a stairway. We walked south, while the monkeys and the parrots chattered at our backs and the cats stared, amazed. "Why don't they follow us?" I asked.

"They won't leave the Garden," replied the Serpent. "Didn't you notice on the trip to the volcano that there were no animals or birds?" I'd been too busy noticing other things, but now I realized that after the barricade we had not seen any living creature.

"Except the eagle," I said, remembering our meal on the mountaintop. "The eagle carried our lunch to us."

"Yes, it did. The birds are different, freer in the air . . . and the eagle is the greatest of them all, lord of the skies."

"Why don't the animals leave?"

"Why should they? They have everything they want there, life is very comfortable, lots to eat, lovely surroundings."

I walked for a while without speaking. The ground had turned sandy, and I kicked it with my toes. "But that's not all there is," I said.

"No?" said the Serpent. It grinned at me. "What else do you want?"

I shrugged. What else *did* I want? I loved the Garden, its beauty, its animals, its fruits and flowers, the expanse of valleys, the trees. Until the day of betrayal, I'd loved my talks and games with Adam, and enjoyed listening to God's stories, his conversations with the

Serpent. What was missing?

The forest had given way to a broad plain covered with shrubs and stubby, wind-blown trees. Ahead lay prairie, not unlike the plains where Adam raced the gazelle. The grass stood stiff; its short yellow stalks held bristling golden crowns. But here there were no gazelle, no rabbits, no pheasant. In all the world around us, the only sound was the dry scritch of the grain as the wind brushed through. I bent my head against the sun and trudged on.

"Eve!" cried the Serpent sharply.

I looked up. In the distance clouds were beginning to form, clouds unlike any I had seen before. They were black, and from them sheets of gray rain fell in straight lines to the earth below. A funnel came out of the sky and roared across the land, swirling bushes and trees and clods of dirt and grit into the air. The Serpent threw its coils around me and pulled me to the ground. I was crushed in the sand, entirely covered with its body. "Lie still," it shouted. The world screamed and blasted around us.

At last the Serpent rolled its body away. I sat panting on the ground while the air reeled with dust and debris. "What on Earth was that?"

"We'll call it a tornado," said the Serpent. "As far as I know, it's the first that's ever been." It looked me over carefully. "You're all right?" I nodded. "We'll sit here a moment while you catch your breath. One advantage of the Garden," it continued, "is that we don't have tornadoes."

"Did God make it?" I asked.

"I don't think so," said the Serpent. "It must be one of the things that got away from him."

"*Got away from him?* How do you mean? I thought God can do what he wants. He *made* the volcano and the thunderstorms."

"Yes, but that was in the beginning, when he was first creating the world. Somehow when they get outside the Garden, the things he's created begin to change. They grow into something different, something he never intended, or even imagined."

"How does he feel about that?" I asked.

"I'm not sure he knows yet. He hasn't left the Garden in ages, and I don't think he realizes what's going on. I've only just realized it myself. Drink some water, Eve, and we'll go on; we haven't seen the desert yet."

But the basket with its food and water gourd was nowhere to be found, though we searched everywhere. "I'm afraid the tornado carried it off," the Serpent said. My throat was parched, but I did not say so for fear the Serpent would insist on turning back. Instead it looked at me and laughed. "You *are* bedraggled," it said. "We'll find something to drink farther on."

We soon left the prairie behind. Sand stretched to the horizon in great drifts that folded over one another and rolled into the distance. Wind lifted sprays of sand from the summits of the dunes and spread them in the sun. The Serpent slithered beside me with its usual grace, leaving lovely symmetrical half-curves in the sand. I tried not to walk on the design. The idea of God losing control of the world was terrible—but there was something exciting about it too. My breath came fast, and my heart pounded beneath my ribs.

All at once I was overcome with exhaustion. I was desperately thirsty and hungry. I stopped walking. "Well, I've seen the desert," I said. "We can go back."

The Serpent chortled. "We haven't seen everything yet," it said. "A little farther."

We plodded along. In front of us a pool of water spread across the sand. I began to run toward it. "Eve, it's not real. It's a mirage," said the Serpent. A bush: "Another." A long way away I saw a tree.

"Another mirage," I said.

"No," said the Serpent. "Keep looking."

Sure enough, we came to a tall plant standing rigid in the sand. Branches protruded stiffly from its sides, looking like arms bent at the elbows. Under the plant was a patch of shade. "We can eat here," said the Serpent, "and drink." It opened its mouth wide and dropped its fangs into the trunk. Water dripped from the gash. "Cup your hands, Eve," it said, "and catch the water." So we sat under the cactus and drank its juice and ate the sweet pink fruit that grew in the folds of its branches.

"Now we'll rest. We can't walk in this heat." Using its nose and tail, the Serpent pushed sand into a pile behind my back. "Lean against that. You've had a long morning."

I wriggled about until the sand shifted into a seat that fit me perfectly. "This is so comfortable," I said. "Serpent, you're brilliant!"

The Serpent grinned. In the last moments it had changed its colors and was outfitted in gleaming white from nose to tail. "It's too hot to be brilliant," it said. We were quiet. I thought of the tornado, and of God.

"Serpent?"

"Eve."

"How long has it been since . . . since . . ."

"Since Adam raped you?"

Abruptly I sat up. "Why do you say it that way?"

"Not to upset you, Eve. But you must see it for what it was. It's not something you should forget."

"Why?" I cried. "Why should I remember it? Why can't you just leave me alone?" I kicked my foot into the sand; some scattered across the Serpent's back. "Why do you bring it up now, in this beautiful place, when we're so peaceful? I hate you!" I stopped, horrified. The Serpent laughed.

"Oh, Eve, I love it when you get mad! You get all red in the face."

"It's the sun," I said grumpily.

"Well, it's very becoming.

"Eve," the Serpent continued quietly, "I'm not the one who brought it up—you did. And I'm glad. You must remember that day in all its horror and pain. Only when you do will you be able to put it away for good. We've spoken of it once, and that was mostly about your dreams." It turned its body in the sand. "And Eve, to answer your question, two moons have passed since that day. I told God he couldn't see you for six, so we have four to go."

The sun, moving across the sky, reached under the cactus and shone into the Serpent's eyes. It raised its ears and spread its white feathers like a parasol over its head. I reached out and touched one of the spines of the cactus. It was long, pointed at the end, and surprisingly cool to the touch.

"When I had those dreams, you said I wouldn't have to see God again, ever, if I didn't want to."

"I did. And you don't. I don't say such things lightly,

and I will never go back on my word."

"What would God say?"

"God would be angry. Very angry and very upset. Adam would be upset too. Even more than he already is. I suspect poor Adam is having a pretty rough time."

"How can you say '*poor* Adam'!"

"Eve, my dear, Adam had no intention of forcing himself on you. It was God who made him do it. The last thing Adam wanted was to hurt you. He cares a great deal about you."

I closed my eyes and thought about it—the way Adam looked at me, and brought me berries, and lifted the hair out of my eyes. Did I care so much for him? No. Even before, though I had liked him well enough, I had not cared for him the way he did for me. I clenched my fists. Now I never could. Never.

"He could have said no. He had a choice," I said.

"And *you*? Did *you* have a choice?"

I stared at the Serpent, appalled. "I had no idea what I was getting into!"

"Neither did Adam."

"And you told me it was *good*! The nicest thing on Earth!"

"Perhaps God told Adam the same thing."

I gasped, remembering. "*I* told Adam that. He was so tired, he really wanted to sleep, and God kept on about how he'd planned this marvelous special treat for us. I was sure it was all right. You said God wouldn't do anything to hurt me."

"I told you what I believed to be true." The Serpent's voice shook. "Eve, I'm so sorry this happened to you." It broke off and was silent for a long time. I looked up and stared, aghast. The Serpent was weeping. Tears filled its eyes, rolled down its cheeks, and fell to the ground where they lay in the sun, round, shimmering with all the colors of a prism, before melting into the sand.

Awkwardly I struggled to get up from my soft, slippery seat. "Oh, Serpent, don't cry! I'm all right, I'm fine. Truly!"

"No, Eve, stay there." The Serpent shifted its body to lie more fully in the shade. "The Serpent's tears," it said, as if to itself. "Never shed before. In fact, I had no idea I *could* cry."

"But why are you crying? Because of me?"

"Eve, you've brought—you and Adam—such joy to the world. But with that joy comes sorrow. Grief."

"Grief?"

"Grief—the sadness you feel when someone you love disappears from your life. You miss them. You *grieve* for them."

"Are you grieving now? But why? No one has left.

I'm here. Adam's in the Garden."

"I weep for you both. I weep for the world, for every living thing, now and in the time to come."

For a long time we were silent. I gazed at the desert. When I had first looked at it, everything seemed the same, a great expanse of yellow sand. But it was not so; I could see squiggly lines, stains of gray and brown, tiny ridges and wrinkles in the sand. It was the hottest time of day, the sun shone scorching hot above; the wind had died and all the world was still. The dunes rose and stretched before us, roiling and rolling, falling over onto themselves, one side smooth and even with no shadow to be seen, the other in deep shade.

"Next week there will be a different landscape," the Serpent said, following my eyes. "The desert is always changing." As it talked a breeze came up, and minute particles of sand skimmed across the surface, skittering to and fro. "Those bits of sand come from one hill and will make another, somewhere else."

A single drop of juice bubbled from the cactus and crept slowly down its side. "What happens to the cactus?" I asked. "Does it get buried?"

"No. The cactus is in a spot where there's not much wind, so the hills don't form here. Otherwise it never would have grown in the first place." The Serpent stirred. "Other questions, Eve, before we go?"

With an effort I pulled my thoughts together. "Why does God care so much about my seeing Adam again? What's so important about it?"

The Serpent hesitated. "I'm afraid," it said at last, "the answer will distress you. You are, my dear, in God's plan, the mother of all human beings, and Adam is the father."

I looked up in horror.

"I said you wouldn't like it."

"The mother of all . . . what does that *mean*?"

"Eve, I've told you this before." I shut my eyes. The Serpent was right; I knew God's plan. I had pushed it to the back of my mind.

"You and Adam are the first and thus far the only people on Earth," the Serpent went on. "You will, or should, have children, who will themselves have children, and so on, until the world is full of men and women, babies, and boys and girls."

"And the way you make babies is by . . . by . . ."

"As you know."

"What Adam did to me?"

"Yes. Sex. Making love. Which is why God is so worried."

"Oh." I buried my head in my hands. "It's *so* awful! You said it was one of the most beautiful things that can happen. How could you *say* that?"

The Serpent shook its head. "Eve, I never lie to you. When a man and a woman come together with love, and sex is the fulfilment of their love, it is filled with beauty, wonder, and ecstasy. I hope someday you'll know such love." Its voice hardening, the Serpent went on: "But, beautiful as it is, love, especially its physical aspect, has a dark side. When it's done as it was to you—with force and against your will—it's one of the most dreadful outrages a man can commit, and one of the most dreadful harms a woman can suffer."

The memory of that day in the field flashed across my mind. My stomach churned, and bile rose in my throat. And it was *God* who wanted me to do it again, with Adam, to have babies to populate *his* world!

"Nobody asked *me* if I wanted to be the mother of all those people! And I don't!" I shuddered. "You can't be right, you *can't* be right, Serpent! It's awful; it's disgusting! I don't want to have anything to do with Adam again!" Tears, mixed with sand, ran down my cheeks.

The Serpent touched my hand gently with its tail. "Eve. I promise you, if you don't want to see them again, either one, God or Adam, no one will make you do so. You have my word."

"But what will God say? And *do*? What about my children, and all those other children waiting to be born, who won't be unless I . . ."

"That's a problem, Eve. But it is my unshakable belief that every creature on Earth—man and woman, chickadee and eagle, spider and ant, cheetah, wombat and kangaroo, snake, even the blind worm at the bottom of its hole—is an individual, unique, with its own soul, its own view of the world, and its own right to choose the life it wants." The Serpent settled back in its coils.

"That doesn't seem to be the way God sees it."

"No, I'm afraid it isn't. God sees the world and its creatures as an extension of himself. He's not able to imagine anything having a will or a spirit or a soul that's not connected to him."

"Soul?"

"A soul is the very essence of being. It's what goes on in your head and in your heart, that knows the difference between right and wrong, that has wants and needs and desires. It is the soul that reflects, the soul that perceives the beauty of the world, that loves and feels. The soul is who you are."

Tipping its head to one side, the Serpent smiled at me. "Can you understand that, Eve?"

For a moment I was silent. When I run, my body stretches and my heart pounds. When I swim, my arms reach out and my legs kick. Sitting still to watch the pollywog, my body doesn't move at all. But all the time, whatever my body is doing, something is turning in my head, moving in my heart, that other heart, not the one that pounds from running, but the one that flips over sometimes when I see a lily white against the sky, a dove, a rainbow. Or when the Serpent smiles at me, and I'm overwhelmed with love.

"Eve?"

"Yes, I do understand," I said. "It makes perfect sense." I placed my palms against each other and folded the fingers over the backs of my hands. It always surprised me, how well my hands fit together. I remembered God clasping his great hands in just the same way, the day we first met, to whistle.

"As for the other," the Serpent continued, "the problem of you as the mother of humankind. Well, that *is* important. But it's not as important as your freedom. So if you decide you don't want anything to do with Adam again, you don't have to."

"And God?"

Chuckling, the Serpent raised itself and began carving its body over the cooling sand. "God will just have to make other arrangements," it said. "Come, Eve, it's high time we started home."

As we left I scooped a handful of grit and one of the cactus flowers into the pouch, which still hung around my neck.

To the North

OUR TRIP BACK TO the Garden was uneventful. The Serpent helped me into the tree as it had before, and again there was no sign that God had noticed our absence.

Before we went to bed, while we were watching the stars, I said to the Serpent, "I'm sorry I said that, about hating you. I don't hate you."

The Serpent's body heaved in the disconcerting way it had when it laughed. "I know that, Eve," it said.

"I think I might be willing to see Adam and God again. Some time."

"I hope so. You won't really be over this until you do."

"And I might even be able to have Adam as a friend again."

"Good."

"But"—I trembled—"nothing else. Ever."

"All right, Eve." The Serpent coiled itself carefully by my mat, and I slept.

Even though we were less weary than after our trip to the volcano, for the next days we did little but sleep and swim lazily in the river by the hut, absorbed in our thoughts. The Serpent lay absolutely flat and still on the shore with its ears folded down and its eyes half-closed. Occasionally it passed its tongue around the edge of its mouth as if its lips were dry, or grumbled deep in its throat.

"What's the matter?" I asked.

"Nothing, Eve. Go back to sleep."

But I was not sleeping. In my mind I went over each moment of our journeys. I saw the volcano, smelled the acrid, pungent odor of its smoke, heard the crackle of flames consuming the air. I felt the sand hot between my toes and tasted on my lips the cool, sweet liquid of the cactus. I laughed again at the monkeys and saw the heavy faces of the leopards and lions as they watched us walk into the desert. Why did they not follow? What were they thinking behind those shaggy manes and freckled yellow eyes? How could they live on the edge of the Garden and not want to know what was beyond?

The tornado howled and twisted into my vision; its funnel, greedy and treacherous, moved across the Earth. No mind propelled it or controlled it—it went without purpose. I looked at the great trees, the river, rocks, clouds, my own fingers, the nails with tiny white half-moons—God had created all this, so fine, in such detail. And yet he did not know about the tornado?

I saw God as he had been that last day in the field, angry, impassioned, shouting at Adam to go on, go on.

I sat up and pulled my hair over my face and watched the sun shine through it. The Serpent lay motionless on the bank. The Serpent could tell me about the stars and how God made the Earth. It could keep me safe in a tornado and guide me through the outer world. It could protect me from God's whims and excesses, at least to some extent. But I was not the Serpent: I was Eve, and in that moment I knew that someday, somehow, I would have to deal with God on my own.

At the end of the second afternoon, the Serpent stretched and yawned. "I'm hungry," it said. I watched it wind its way in one smooth movement up the tree that grew by the stream, so much more graceful, and easier, than my tree scrambling. "Eve, would you like an apple?" it asked. I shook my head. I had gorged myself on figs and felt bloated.

"Well," the Serpent said. "If you want to make other journeys, we should start preparing for the next trip. We have three and a half moons before us. Do you still want to visit the North first?"

I closed my eyes and saw the white peaks on the northern horizon and the thin line of blue to the west. "Yes. I'd like to save the sea for last; I have a feeling it's the best of all."

The Serpent nodded. "Fine. But if you want to go north, we have to figure out how to keep you warm. It's cold, very cold, and windy. You'll be walking in snow—you can't go barefoot or naked."

"What's naked?"

The Serpent laughed. "Naked is as you are, with nothing to cover your body. In the Garden you don't need clothes. The temperature doesn't change much."

I tried to imagine being cold, really cold. Sometimes at night I felt chilly, after supper, when I first curled into the Serpent's coils. On the volcano it had been damp in the fog, and I had shivered. But really *cold*? "Your feet will turn purple," the Serpent had told me when it first described the North, "and your nose and fingers." I rubbed my fingers between my toes; even the little grains of sand that had settled there felt warm. *Cold* was almost impossible to imagine.

The Serpent uncoiled itself and moved toward the path, shaking its head as if to clear away the past days' lethargy. "I'm going to the northern edge of the Garden to find the best route. Think about how to keep warm. We'll talk about it when I get back."

How to keep warm? I thought of all the warm things in the Garden: the soft, fluffy down shed by the geese; the round balls of white cotton that grew in the fields; the thick, wool coats of the sheep. I had learned to make cloth from cotton or wool, and comforters stuffed with goose down, but I could hardly walk to the far North trailing a blanket behind me. I needed to find a way to shape those warm covers and keep them on. I began to draw pictures in the dirt.

When I had decided on what I would need, I set out to collect the materials. The sheep, grazing in the meadow where the sunflowers grew, came running as soon as they saw me, curious in the way of sheep, bleating with their chins in the air, their long, heavy tails bobbing behind. I sat by one and rubbed its neck and shoulders with my left hand and ran a comb of thorns down its back. The ewe stood, a bemused expression on its face—I've always found sheep rather silly—sweet, but silly—and moved its fat body in rhythm as I brushed. The other sheep watched, jostling to be next in line. I brushed all twenty-six of them, and when I was done I had a heap of thick white wool. Using long strands of ivy, I tied the wool into bundles and lashed the bundles together into one large packet. I strung the vines over my shoulders and began to pull. One of the dogs followed behind, sniffing at the bits of wool left in the path.

It did not take me long to realize I would never be able to get my burden back to the hut. I had gone only a short distance; I was panting and my arms ached. The wool was heavy, the ground bumpy, and there were occasional puddles of mud. I thumped to the ground with my head in my arms. I would have to undo the load and make several trips. I sighed. I was a long way from home.

The dog lay down beside me and licked my hand with its rough tongue. It was a favorite of mine: one ear was white and the other brown, which gave it a humorous air. It was big; it stood higher than my waist, with strong legs and shoulders and smooth black hair all over except around the neck, where the ruff was thick and bushy. "Good dog," I said, and it rolled onto its back, paws in the air. I rubbed its stomach, and one of its hind legs twitched rhythmically. "If only you could help!" I whispered, and the dog curled out its tongue and touched my nose, as if it knew just what I meant.

I need to find some way it can help me pull, I thought, and I began stringing vines around its body. *That's it!* "Don't move," I said, lifting the dog's head carefully from my lap. I cut more vines from the edge of the path, braided them and, through trial and error, managed to fit a harness to the dog's shoulders and secure it with straps tied under its stomach. The animal got to its feet and turned as I asked it to, but lazy with the heat, it flopped to the ground as soon as I had finished.

When the dog's harness was securely fastened, I fashioned a second one for myself, so that the dog and I could pull together, and tied on the packets of wool. "Get up!" I cried, drawing the thongs over my shoulders. The dog barely lifted the end of its tail. "Dog, come. Please. We have to get these bundles home." I tugged at the straps. The dog stood and shook itself, first its head, then its thick ruff, its back, rear, tail. The dust whirled from its coat into the air. When it had given its entire body a good shake, it raised its head and licked my hand.

I knelt and hugged it, then threw my weight against the halter and started up the hill. After a moment's hesitation the dog followed, and the packet bounced behind us. Startled, the dog scuttled forward. I put my hand on its head. "It's all right," I said. "Don't be frightened." It looked at me and wagged its tail again. We both leaned into the harness and pulled.

An hour later we arrived home. It had been far less difficult than I expected. "Look, Serpent!" I cried.

"Look what we did, the dog and I! It's so easy to pull things this way."

The Serpent sat up and grinned. "Good work," it said, leaning over to examine the harness. "Well done, well thought out. I congratulate you, Eve." The blood rose to my cheeks; the Serpent did not often bestow such praise.

In the next days we scoured the Garden for other materials. We gathered goose down from under the goslings as they squawked openmouthed in their nests, combed thick strands of wool from long-haired goats, and picked balls of cotton in the fields. In all this finding and gathering and hauling home the Serpent was very useful, but once I began making the clothes it could do nothing to help. "How practical those hands are!" it mused, watching me as I sat cross-legged on the terrace, twining tufts of wool into strands. "The way the fingers are articulated, and the thumbs. Very well designed. God really knows what he's doing when it comes to hands." Then, shaking its head: "Pity he often has such poor judgment about other things. And a temper." It began to move toward the path. "There's not much more I can do for you, Eve, until you finish the clothes. I'll only distract you. I'm going to explore our route again."

From then on I barely saw the Serpent. It left early in the morning and returned late, reporting to me briefly about a cliff, a crack in the rock, a ridge—none of which made sense to me.

I set to work. I had often made rugs and blankets and linen sheets. Now I wove the wool into cloth and cut the cloth with my sharpest knife into loosely shaped pieces. These I sewed together with cotton thread and a needle I carved out of soft wood. I made a tunic with sleeves, and pants tied at the waist and ankles with cord, and a long jacket with a lining, which I stuffed with down. In the swamp the Serpent had found broad-leafed reeds; these I pounded with a stone until they were supple and soft, then plaited them together to make a waterproof jacket. I made boots of the same material and lined them with wool. They were awkward to walk in, but they were very warm. At the end of six days, I had a serviceable wardrobe. I lifted each garment and shook it hard. Nothing fell apart, only a few feathers poked out between the seams.

For the first time in days the Serpent was home, having finally found a route out of the Garden. I could hardly wait to show off my clothes. I put on everything: the pants, which I tied around the waist with a vine, the tunic and coat over the top, and the boots. "Serpent, come see!" I cried, bursting with pride. "Will these be all right?"

The Serpent spiraled from its tree, coiled itself beside

me, and cocked its head to the left, then to the right, then back again to the left, eyes wide.

"Well, what do you think?" I asked impatiently.

"I think," said the Serpent, and coughed. I looked at it with concern. Its voice sounded strange, its eyes were closed, and tears squeezed from their corners.

"Serpent, what's the matter?" I cried.

"Oh, Eve!" sputtered the Serpent. "Eve, you look so funny!" and it collapsed on the ground and heaved with laughter.

"Oh! You're awful!" I cried. "I hate you! How can you be so mean! I've worked so hard!"

"My dear Eve," said the Serpent, straining to stifle its laughter. "I know you have. I know, my dear. I'm sorry. I'm behaving very badly indeed. But I'm used to seeing you with nothing on, you know, your beautiful body, the way you move, and now here you are all covered up. And it's all so thick and nubbly. It just looks so funny." Again it dissolved in laughter.

I was somewhat appeased. I liked hearing I was beautiful, though I wasn't sure what it meant. When I caught a glimpse of myself in a pool of water, I saw a wobbly image shimmering upside down, with limbs that looked like the trunk of a young aspen, but crooked, bending the way no aspen would ever bend. Could *that* be beautiful? But the voice of the Serpent, or Adam, or God, always took on a special tone when they spoke of my beauty.

"Well," I told the Serpent. "You're the one who said I should make clothes. I never would have had the idea myself."

"You'll need them," said the Serpent. "We couldn't go to the North if you didn't have clothes to keep warm. Let me look again." And it had me turn around and sit down and raise my knees and stretch my arms to make sure I was able to move freely, and it nodded and said good, good, well done, nice stitching, how clever you are, until I was nearly ready to forgive it for its laughter.

The Cliff

THE FOLLOWING MORNING we started before sunrise, the Serpent, the dog, and I, heavily laden. For the dog I had fashioned a sledge from young birch boughs and loaded it with the bulky packets of clothing. I carried supplies of cheese and fruit, and unleavened cakes of bread.

The Serpent had told me to cut long vines from the trees by the pond—vines I had so often used as swings. "They'll be useful when we climb the cliffs," it said, and I looped them over my shoulders.

At first we walked through the rising hills I knew, but on the second day we reached wilder, steeper slopes, where rocks were heaped haphazardly on the ground. It became harder for the dog to draw its load, even with the Serpent pushing from behind. By the third day the dog could no longer pull the sledge, and we had to remove the clothes. I tied as many packets as I could to the dog's harness and carried the rest, going back and forth several times to transport the lot. The sledge we dragged, empty, as best we could over the rough terrain.

"Why wasn't I made with hooks?" the Serpent cried, shoving a packet with its nose. "Think how useful they would be!"

I leaned against a boulder and laughed. "Hooks!" I snorted. "Hooks? Where would they *go*? How could you ever glide?"

"Well," said the Serpent huffily, "you may laugh, but it's not easy for me to watch you and the dog doing all this work, and not be able to help." It whipped its tail against a packet of clothing. The vines that tied it together parted, and my parka slid sideways down the hill and disappeared into a gorse thicket. The dog ran after it, waving its tail and barking.

"Serpent," I said, stifling my laughter, "you've been infinitely valuable to us in this journey, as in all things. You're just not very good at carrying things. It's not . . ." I searched for the right words. "It's just not in your nature to carry."

The Serpent looked at me. "You're a kind child," it said. "Thank you. The route starts just around the bend;

I'll wait for you there." It swept gracefully out of sight.

I watched the dog drag my parka up the hill; bits of white goose down clung to every stone in its trail. After tying the packets together again, we crept painfully through the boulders and found the Serpent beyond the next turn, coiled at the base of the rock face. A thin fracture split the cliff bottom to top. "That's the path we'll take," said the Serpent.

I looked at the crack. "I won't climb that cliff." I sat down firmly. The rough ground felt solid and supportive. The dog plunked itself beside me and licked its toes.

"It's the only possible way," said the Serpent. "I've searched this cliff from east to west. At each end there's a ravine that's impassable."

"But we can't get up there," I said. "I'm not sure even you can." I glared at the rock above me. "The dog certainly can't. And I don't want to try. Look, the cliff actually bulges out. Ugh." I shivered.

"That's why we brought the vines," said the Serpent. "I know it looks impossible, but I'm sure we can do it. I wouldn't suggest it otherwise."

"What if we fall?" My stomach churned.

"If I fall, nothing. Anyway, I won't. If you fall, a few bruises and cuts, which I'll patch up. Nothing worse can happen. We're still in the Garden."

I thought of how I had felt after falling down the

rock face, and again when Adam raped me. "It won't be like that," said the Serpent, as though it had read my mind. "And you won't fall. We'll spend the night here, and go up in the morning."

We sat down for a meal of bread and cheese and oranges, and peered at the cliff. It began to seem less impossible; I could see knobs of rock I could use as footholds and finger-holds.

The following day I tied the strongest vines together into a long rope, and the short ones into a sling to hold the dog and the packages. The Serpent took the end of the rope in its mouth and moved to the cleft. "Good luck!" I said. The Serpent grinned at me; bits of leaves curled up around its nose. Rising high on its tail, it inserted itself into the crack, thinned and elongated its body to twice its usual length, and wedged between the rock faces, drew itself upward. From time to time it looked down at the dog and me and waved its ears.

When it reached the top, the Serpent coiled and peered down at us. "You should be able to do it without too much trouble, Eve." The vine slithered down the cliff. "Tie the sledge onto the vine and I'll haul it up. I have my end secured to a rock behind me."

The sledge bumped easily up the cliff. "Now the dog," said the Serpent. I attached the vine to the sling and checked each knot carefully. The dog watched warily. I had packed the sling with my clothes to make a safe, comfortable nest. "Come, my friend," I called, and snapped my fingers in the basket. "Come, climb on, and we'll get you up the cliff. See, the Serpent's there already." The dog lifted its ears and turned its head to the side, whined, and backed away. Finally it clambered in reluctantly and lay in the bottom of the sling, looking at me with sad eyes, its paws hanging over the edge, tail tapping against the side. "Poor dog," I said. "You'll be all right."

The Serpent reappeared at the top of the cliff with the rope clasped in its tail. "I'm going to start pulling. Yell if there's a problem," it called. The sling lifted an inch or so off the ground and began to swing. The dog whimpered. I steadied the sling with my hand as it inched upward at the end of the vine, a foot or so from the rock face. "It's fine," I shouted to the Serpent, "it's going well. Good dog!" In a moment I could see only the tips of the dog's ears, one brown, one white, the fine hairs raised in the breeze. The sling arrived at the top, and I saw the Serpent reach out its tail and lift the terrified creature onto the rock. The animal's nails scraped frantically on the stone; tiny bits of gravel came spitting down. I drew back and brushed the dirt from my hair.

"Good," called the Serpent. "Now you, Eve. I won't be able to pull you; you're too heavy. You'll have to climb. Tie the rope around your waist, and I'll keep hold of the end. It will steady you, and I'll be able to hold you if you slip."

The rope came snaking once more down the face of the cliff. I caught the end—there were still a few long, serrated leaves clinging to it—and knotted it around my waist. I ran my fingers along the fissure in the rock. At the base it was hardly a thumb-width across, though it widened above. I could see the Serpent peering down. "Come along," it cried. I felt the slack tighten on the rope. A gust of air rushed along the cliff. My hair whipped across my face and into my eyes. "Wait," I called, and I bound back the hair with a strand of vine. "I'm ready, I'm coming," I said, and started to climb.

At first it was easier than I expected. I was able to insert my fingers and even my hands into the cracks and find good holds and rest my feet on knobs of stone. As the crevice widened, I put my feet on one side and my body on the other and inched my way up. Later I straddled the crack, with a leg and arm on each side. High on the cliff I nearly put my hand on a pair of snakes; they rattled their tails at me and tasted the air with their black split tongues. Birds, swallows and hawks, and others I had never seen, rested in unexpected places or swooped toward me and away.

I looked down once. I had a foot on each side of the chasm, legs spread wide. I could see my knees—the right one was scraped and bleeding—and my toes braced against the rock. Far, far below was a swirl of blue and black water and leaping, bounding chunks of white. Suddenly I could not move. My heart pounded at my ribs, my arms and legs trembled, rivulets of sweat ran into my eyes.

"It's a river," said the Serpent quietly, above me. "A river from the north, and ice. Isn't it beautiful? Eve, look at me."

I could not take my eyes off the water. The tumbling ice below roared over the whine of the wind. My head whirled.

"Eve!" said the Serpent sharply. "Close your eyes! Close them! Now!"

I willed my eyelids shut.

"Raise your head," ordered the Serpent. "Tip it back; lift your chin." I raised my chin. "Now look at me."

I opened my eyes and saw the Serpent's feathered ears only a short distance above. The Serpent took a deep breath. "Good," it said. "You're doing fine. Keep climbing, you're almost up. There's a good handhold for you to your left. You can reach it easily." I turned my head. "Don't look down, watch that knob you're going for." I put all my weight on my left arm and shifted my right hand to the rock above. "Good, good," cried the Serpent. "Next step." I saw what to do, and swung the left hand to another firm hold and brought my leg across. To my amazement I found a ledge, not wide, but solid beneath my feet. I stood and felt the good rock dig into my soles, and I clung to the knobs with my hands and waited for my heart to calm. "Fine," said the Serpent. "We'll make a mountain climber of you yet."

The Serpent tightened the vine and I used it to steady myself. I needed it; I was tired, my arms and legs ached and my fingers and knees, scraped raw against the stone, stung. After each step I clutched my handholds and rested, forehead against the rock. Its roughness was comforting, assurance that the Earth was still there, dependable, solid, the antithesis of the wind and the void. Another step. I pulled my chest onto the flat rock at the top of the cliff; my legs kicked wildly into the chasm behind. The Serpent reached out its tail and drew me to safety.

I lay panting, exhausted. The dog came and lay next to me, pressing its body against mine. It whimpered softly and licked my neck, but it seemed to sense that this was no time for exuberance. The Serpent pulled me farther from the edge. "No point in having you fall back down after all that effort," it grunted.

By the time I was able to stand, the Serpent and the dog had nearly finished lugging the supplies to a small clump of bushes. "Bring the last packet, Eve," the Serpent called above the wind. "We'll spend the night here. It's too late to go on."

We were on a great ridge that stretched east and west along the top of the cliff as far as I could see. The Serpent had packed some of my clothes into a hollow in the rock sheltered behind some scraggly gorse, and the three of us lay down to sleep in this nest. *This must be how eagles feel*, I thought. There was no moon, but the stars blazed, and we saw all the creatures we knew in the sky.

Snow

THE FOLLOWING MORNING I found myself on top of the world. To the south lay the Garden, green and lush. The air was so clear I could see the fingered leaves of oaks clinging to their branches. Beyond were meadows where animals, tiny dots, grazed by puddles of blue. Here and there I could just make out the fronds of palm trees. Further south, beyond the green wall of forest, was a blur of gold covered by haze. In the east the sun was coming up behind the volcano. A thin cloud of smoke rose from the cauldron; even from here the mountain looked forbidding. To the west lay a vast swamp and, beyond, the blue line of the sea.

To the north, the ridge fell off sharply. At its base, the steppe began to climb into a white wasteland. Far away, peaks rose an unbelievable distance into the sky.

"Are we still in the Garden?" I asked the Serpent. "We haven't seen a barrier."

"I imagine God considers the cliff to be enough of a barrier," replied the Serpent. "But we *are* still in the Garden. It seems to end here where the ridge falls off. Look around us, at the flowers; there are none below." I had not noticed them before; in every crack along the ridge, tiny starlike anemone bloomed. The rock below was bare.

I shivered; the wind was cold.

The Serpent had moved a short way down the slope. "Come here, Eve," it called. "It's out of the wind. You'd better put on your clothes."

But putting on clothes was not easy. I was unused to the straps that had to be tied, and my fingers were stiff. Dog sat on the ground and watched. When I pulled the hood over my hair, the animal leaped back and yelped. "Oh, dear," I said. "Do I look so strange?"

The Serpent laughed. "You're warm, aren't you?"

The slope was steep and slippery. Halfway down my feet flew out from under me, and I slid the rest of the way on the icy rock, out of control, spinning back and forth, my pack catching on the stones. At the bottom I came up short against a stunted tree. Above me the Serpent craned its neck to see if I was all right. The dog crouched on the ridge, barking.

I stood and brushed the pebbles and twigs into the wind. "I'm fine," I called. "It was fun! Serpent, slide. It's the quickest way." But the Serpent spiraled, graceful as ever, down the slope, bracing its body, thick and orange today, carefully against the rock ledges. "I'm too old," it said, "to make a spectacle of myself!"

"You're just scared!" I retorted. The Serpent flapped its ears and continued its dignified descent.

I looked back at the ridge. The dog sat on its haunches, ears raised like a parody of the Serpent. "Here, Dog, come along," I shouted. But the dog backed away from the edge and lay down. "I'll go help it."

The Serpent looked thoughtfully at the dog. "You can try, but don't be disappointed if it won't come."

"Not come? Of course it will come. We can't possibly leave it behind on that ledge—it would be miserable all alone. Besides, we need it to help pull the sledge."

"Remember the other animals," the Serpent warned. "None of them would leave the Garden."

"But they weren't our friends." I started up the slope. "I'm sure the dog will come if I show it the way."

The dog whined and jumped up on me and licked my face, but when I took hold of its ruff and tried to pull it down the slope, it tore itself out of my grasp and ran off. Then it refused to come near me. It lay on its stomach just out of reach, and whined and leaped away when I grabbed at it.

"Eve," shouted the Serpent. "It's no use. The dog won't leave. You'd better slide back down yourself. It's getting late." Reluctantly, I agreed.

"But it can't stay here! What will it eat?"

"I left some food in the hollow where we slept," said the Serpent. "The dog will find it. It will be fine. Come on now."

I put my arms around the dog's neck and whispered in its ear. "Keep well," I said, and reluctantly slid down the slope to join the Serpent.

The dog's refusal to come with us was a blow. We had counted on it to pull a good load on the sledge—at least as much as I could carry. For weeks, ever since it had helped me drag home the wool, the dog had hardly left my side. It had become a companion, friendly and warm, always happy to go for a walk, or swim, or root about in the earth for potatoes and peanuts. When I was weaving or sewing, it lay by my side with its head on my foot, occasionally flopping its tail on the ground.

"I'll miss the dog," I said sadly. "Are you sure it will be all right?"

"Of course it will." The Serpent shook its head. "I should have realized it wouldn't come." We sat on the frozen ground and looked at the pile of bundles we had scattered around us. We could hear the dog whimpering on the ridge.

"How much of this do we really need?" I asked.

"Do *you* need," corrected the Serpent. "I don't need anything."

"You don't?" Every day the Serpent and I had our meals together, and it ate the same things I ate, fruits and grains and nuts. It drank milk and water and wine. It always appeared to be every bit as hungry as I was. "But you eat just as much as I do."

"Yes," replied the Serpent. "And I enjoy it, but I don't need food to live. I can get along perfectly well without it. Whereas you must have regular supplies of food and water or you'll give out. Think carefully about what to bring."

"How long will we be gone?"

The Serpent stretched its neck and squinted its eyes to the north. Its shadow wavered on the rock in the weak sun. "It should take us about a week to get there and back, more if we have a snowstorm," it said. "We should have food for two weeks to be safe."

I couldn't imagine snow falling instead of rain. "What will we do if we get caught in a storm?" I asked.

"Dig in and wait," said the Serpent.

"Dig in? To this rock?"

"No, ninny," the Serpent replied. "To the snow.

You'd better start tying up your bundles or we'll never get off." In the end, we took all our warm coverings and half the food, divided between the basket I carried on my back and the sledge.

Finally we were ready. I lifted the pack to my back, fit the harness around my waist, and stepped forward. Before us the ground rose steadily, and I had to use all my weight to move the sledge, despite the Serpent's help.

"Not too heavy?" it asked.

"No. It's all right." In fact, the sledge and pack were heavier than I had expected, and I wondered how long I could walk.

"They'll get lighter each time you eat," said the Serpent, with its knack of knowing my thoughts almost before I knew them myself.

All day, and the day after, and the day after that, we walked in a world dominated by cold and by wind. I pulled my hood close and swaddled my face with a woollen band. My mind didn't work very well, and to stay awake I counted to one hundred over and over again. The wind howled and screamed. I felt I was again in a dream, being attacked by a tiger with icy claws.

On the third day it began to snow lightly. As night fell, we huddled under the sledge for shelter, with the Serpent coiled around me. I slept fitfully. My body ached and my fingers and feet were swollen. At times the Serpent shifted its body and the air came through, bitter, inimical. I shivered.

"Are you all right, Eve?" the Serpent asked. "I'm afraid I can't make it any warmer. It's just too cold."

"No, I'm all right." I settled further into my clothes. "Only, I feel as if . . ."

"What?"

"As if the storm were alive. Like something in my dream, where all the creatures and God wanted to hurt me." The Serpent raised its ears and a gust of cold air blew into my face. "This storm is *against* me. If you weren't here, I'd be blown away somewhere and never get home."

After a time the Serpent answered, "You remember when we were lugging things to the cliff, you told me it was not in my nature to carry. It's the nature of a storm to blow; it's the nature of wind to get into crannies, the nature of snow to be cold. The storm, the wind, the snow mean you no harm. You've come into their territory; you don't belong here. If you choose to enter it, it's up to you to adjust and survive."

"But I'm not here to hurt the storm."

"That has nothing to do with it. The storm doesn't know you're here; it has no knowledge you exist."

"It certainly doesn't *feel* that way!"

The Serpent's coils heaved and I knew it was laughing,

though I couldn't hear it above the howl of the wind. "It's conceivable that a snowstorm may notice a range of mountains standing in its way, but you? My dear, you're just too *small*."

"That's not nice," I said.

"What's not nice about it? I didn't say you were too foolish or too ugly; I merely said what's true. For a snowstorm, you're only slightly bigger than an ant." It heaved again, and the air came through a crack in its coils.

"Stop laughing, Serpent," I said. "I get colder every time you do."

The Serpent tightened its coils and concentrated on heating the nest. I was almost asleep when it spoke again. "It's very natural to believe that everything is aimed at you: storm, cold, whatever. Most of the time it's not; you just happen to be there when it's happening. If you can believe that, it will make life easier."

"And God," I said. "Was I just in his way? Or was he trying to harm me? Is that his nature?"

The Serpent paused before it replied. "I'm sure God was not *trying* to harm you. He wasn't even aware that what he was doing could hurt."

"Like the storm," I said. "That makes it worse. Because God *isn't* like the storm. He thinks and feels; he knows I'm here."

"I think," said the Serpent, settling more comfortably

in its coils, "we really can't deal with God tonight. It's too late and too noisy." As if to confirm the point, the wind rose to a shriek.

"I don't believe God and I are going to get along very well," I muttered into my blankets.

"I'm afraid you're right," the Serpent replied. "But that may not be a bad thing for either of you."

In the morning it was snowing hard. As the Serpent had said, the snow was beautiful. I raised my face and let the flakes fall on my eyelashes, stretched my arms, caught the fat crystals in my mittened hands. The Serpent stirred its tail in the gourd to heat water for tea. A thumb-depth of snow had accumulated on its back in the night, and tufts of it tumbled off as the tail went round, making little mounds of white powder where it fell. When the water was hot I added mint leaves and lemon rind and a small piece of sugar cane, and the Serpent and I took turns sipping from the gourd and dunking strips of flatbread, now hard as wood, into the hot brew. "Eat well. We have a long day ahead," the Serpent said, looking at the sky. "This is building into quite a storm. I know you like to bring back a bit of earth from each place we go. You'd better take some now before the ground is frozen solid and the snow gets too deep." And it helped me dig up a clod of pebbly brown soil. When I took off my mittens to stuff the clod into my pouch, my fingers stung from the cold.

All day I plodded through the snow in the Serpent's wake. In the late afternoon I stumbled and fell sideways into a drift. "Serpent, I can't take another step," I cried through the storm. "Can't we rest?"

The Serpent hauled me out of the snow. "Poor Eve," it said. "I *am* sorry, but we can't stop here; there's a danger of avalanches. We have to go just a little farther." We trudged on. Finally the Serpent stopped. "Here it's safe, and we're close to the mountains. If it clears we'll see all the peaks."

The Serpent began to spiral, coiling round and round until it had dug a nest in the drifts. When it was satisfied with the size and shape it had made, it began to push the snow that had fallen to the sides into heaps. "Help me pat this solid, Eve."

"What *are* you doing?" I asked. It seemed crazy to begin playing in the snow at this hour, in this weather.

"I'm building a house out of snow," the Serpent explained. "An igloo. We'll be warm tonight. You won't have to worry about cracks or drafts."

It took quite a while to finish the igloo to the Serpent's satisfaction. I piled as much of the deep snow as I could onto the sledge, which I then dragged back to the Serpent, who helped me tip it against the wall it was building. Then we both patted it firm. Little by little the top curved into a roof. When the sloping sides nearly met, I placed one of the sacks that had held our grain across the hole and we covered it with snow. The Serpent stood on its tail and lighted its head so we could see the entire structure.

"That is a fine igloo—" it began, and looked at me. "Oh, Eve, you're frozen. Get inside quickly." But I could see only a white mound, like half a walnut shell, sitting in the snow, and no entrance.

"How?" I asked.

The Serpent came to my side and guided me along the igloo wall. "I've made a crawl space; lie down here." It pointed me down a narrow passage. I lay on my stomach and pulled myself along with my elbows. I came to a corner and twisted around to get through; there was barely space for me to fit. At last the snow no longer pressed against my back, and I rolled over. I had a glimpse of the ceiling curving above me, but the confined space was dark. The Serpent crowded in beside me, pushing our bags. "Take off your clothes, Eve, they're wet. You'll catch your death of cold."

"Death?" I asked. "Of cold?"

"An expression." The Serpent shoved the gourd from the pack, filled it with snow, and began heating it. "Add some grain," it ordered, "and some dried corn. A hot gruel is just what you need." It tugged dry coverings from a bag and spread them on the floor. Its body glowed red and the igloo began to warm. The Serpent looked around the room with pride. "We did a good job," it said. "This will protect us no matter how hard the wind blows. The food's almost ready."

Huddled in blankets, I leaned against the Serpent, warm and comfortable for the first time since leaving the Garden. "How long will it last?" I asked.

"Two or three days . . ."

"We're never going to get to the glacier!" I wailed.

"It won't go on forever," the Serpent said.

I fell asleep with the spoon in my hand and slept the night through, and half the next day.

When at last I woke, I was alone. The igloo glowed white around me, its icy walls curving up to the sack I had placed at the top. I could not tell if it was still snowing, but I could hear the wind screaming. The igloo was warm, so I knew the Serpent had not been gone long.

Conversations in an Igloo

THE SERPENT SOON reappeared, covered with snow. At the entrance it shook itself like a dog. "I've never seen a snowstorm like this," it said. "It deserves a name of its own. We'll call it a blizzard."

"Blizzard," I said, emphasizing the z's. "I like that."

"You can hardly see the igloo, it's snowed so much," the Serpent went on. And there's a terrific wind!" It tipped its head and grinned at me; bits of snow clung to the feathers on its ears. "Slept well, didn't you? You needed it after the last few days. And you found the water I heated. We can have cereal for breakfast."

"Can we go out?" I asked as I rummaged through the pack for the grain. "Can we go up the mountain and see the glacier?"

"We can take a look at the blizzard if you like," the Serpent replied, "though you won't find it easy to manage. We certainly won't be able to go anywhere. Too much wind and too cold."

"So what will we do?" I asked, stirring the oatmeal into the gourd.

"Sleep, eat, talk." The Serpent chuckled. "An igloo in a blizzard is conducive to good conversation."

The cereal had thickened; I poured it into two bowls and handed one to the Serpent. As I lifted my wooden spoon, the Serpent lowered its head and lapped the oatmeal with its tongue while the steam curled around its feathered ears. I ate carefully; the Serpent cared about manners, and I knew this would be as true in an igloo as in the Garden. It always waited for me to start and never dribbled on its chin.

"You and God don't have to be in an igloo to talk," I said when I had swallowed.

"Neither do you and I," replied the Serpent. "We have good conversations."

"You certainly tell me lots of stories and show me how things work."

The Serpent laughed. "That's more a lecture than a conversation. I did that in the beginning, when I was giving you information about everything, explaining all you saw and heard. But now"—the Serpent took another sip of oatmeal—"now you have opinions of your own, and we *discuss* things: ideas, impressions. You've learned a great deal."

"From you."

"Not only from me. Think of all the things you've done, all you've thought about and seen."

"On our journeys."

"On our journeys, yes, but also in the Garden, before you ever imagined going outside—making quilts, weaving, creating useful objects, like cups and bowls from clay. And then going beyond that to make little animals!"

"Little Serpents."

"Indeed." The Serpent chortled. "For this journey you learned to make clothes and boots. You even came up with the idea of a sledge."

"Laziness. I didn't want to have to carry everything on my back."

"Laziness is an excellent reason for inventing something." The Serpent stretched its neck. "Those are big accomplishments, Eve."

"But all those things were in front of me, asking to be used."

"You wonder about things," the Serpent went on, "how they get to be the way they are, how other creatures think, why they behave as they do. There were those weeks when you *were* an elephant, you *were* a heron or a swallow."

"I was playing. It was fun."

"*You* were the one who wanted to leave the Garden, Eve. No one else, animal or human, has ever done that before—not Adam, not wolf or bear, not even a bird, except for the eagle."

"God has."

"Yes, but a long time ago, when he was first creating the universe. He hasn't been outside the Garden for a very long time."

"Why not? I can't imagine making something and then losing interest in it. Never knowing how it's turned out."

"I suspect he thinks he knows. Maybe he can't imagine that anything could change without his permission. Perhaps he can't imagine *change*."

"*You* have been out of the Garden," I said.

"Eve, before these journeys of ours, I hadn't left the Garden for years. And I'm neither animal nor human."

The Serpent was coiled on the mats we had placed on the floor. Its great body, scarlet and orange today, gleamed in the dim white light reflected from the snow. Its emerald eyes, the only thing about it that never changed color, sparkled. It did not look remotely like any plant or creature I had ever seen, including Adam or me or God. For the first time I saw the Serpent as something extraordinary, entirely apart from the rest of the world.

"What *are* you, Serpent?" I asked.

Suddenly the blizzard hushed; the wind was still. "We're at the center of the storm," the Serpent said. Its voice echoed from the ice walls; s*torm, storm, storm.* Then it was silent, eyes closed, ears folded against its head, motionless. I stared at my hands, lying red and swollen in my lap. I felt the afternoon had passed, the day, a moon or two. At the Serpent's ear fluttered a blue feather; a wave of cold swept through the entrance tunnel. The wind took up its keening.

"What *are* you, Serpent?" I repeated.

The Serpent came out of its reverie and looked at me, its eyes glowing in the half-light. "I am many things," it replied slowly. "Teacher, companion, friend. And recently, guide."

"That's what you are to *me*. Not what you are *yourself*."

"Eve, you always surprise me. Of course you're right. But who I am is too complicated to explain."

"Do you have any other names? Does God have other names?"

"Other names? 'Serpent' and 'God' aren't enough for you?"

"Other names the way the animals do. You taught me that a cow is a ruminant and a bovine and a mammal, and sometimes Adam and I give it a name as well. Adam has four names: boy, human being, mammal, Adam. But you, you're the Serpent. God is God. We never call the two of you anything else."

"Well, we do have other names; we just don't use them much."

"What are they?"

"God has several. Yahweh. Allah."

"Nice names. Much softer than God."

The Serpent chuckled. "But the character doesn't change."

"What about you? What other names do you have?"

The Serpent hesitated. I thought this might be another question it left unanswered. Finally it spoke so softly I could barely catch the words above the wind. "Sometimes I am called Nachash."

"Nachash. What a beautiful name."

"And sometimes I am known as Wisdom."

"Wisdom." I had forgotten the Serpent's conversation with God, but now it came back to me in a rush. "Wisdom, Justice, Reason!" I cried.

The Serpent looked at me and raised its brows. "So you heard that! I thought you were awake. I'm amazed you remember."

"Are those really your other names?"

"They're names for some of the things I do."

"Like calling God the 'Creator' because he created the world?"

"Exactly."

"So you make Reason and Justice and Wisdom?"

The Serpent laughed. "Reason and Justice and Wisdom are not things one makes. They are qualities that make life better. I do my best to further those qualities in the world."

"Tell me again what they mean. I remember *Reason*; it's using your mind to figure things out."

"The use of the intellect—the mind—rather than the emotions."

"Justice?"

"Justice is what is fair and right."

"And Wisdom?"

"Wisdom is made up of knowledge, judgment, and insight. Knowledge is what you know; judgment is how you make decisions; insight is being able to feel and understand a situation intuitively, going beyond the facts. When the three are combined, you have wisdom."

"*You* have wisdom."

"Yes. And I should. I have lived a long time and seen many things."

"Will I ever have wisdom?" I asked. As I said it I realized it was an outrageous question. But surely wisdom was the most desirable thing on earth.

The Serpent smiled at me. "You have cereal on your chin." I wiped it hurriedly. "Dear Eve, you're far too young to have acquired wisdom. But you're inquisitive and thoughtful, not to mention adventurous. You possess a wonderful, exciting mind, and you have empathy for others. I have every hope that someday you'll be wise."

Suddenly, the wind resumed its howling. The Serpent raised its feathers and began to uncoil its long body. "If you really want to see the blizzard, finish your breakfast, put on all the clothes you can, and come outside while there's still light. At this time of year in the far North, it gets dark very early."

I scraped the last bit of mush from my bowl and scrambled into my boots and jacket. The Serpent slid down the narrow tunnel in front of me. "Grab onto my neck as soon as you get out," it said. "If you don't, you'll be blown away."

As I pulled myself out of the passage, the wind hit me, nearly knocking me down. I threw my arms around the Serpent's neck. Pellets of snow and ice attacked my face and stung my eyeballs. I could barely breathe. The Serpent's head glowed. In the red light I could see the snow driving toward me, vertically, in long white lines, swirling up and down as gusts of wind came through in little tornadoes. Everything was white; the earth glowed white. No sign of sun or moon or star—the whiteness howled and screamed, dislocating the world. Nothing could stand against it. With the Serpent's coils around me, I watched in horror and ecstasy.

Alpenglow

THE BLIZZARD LASTED two more days. Then in the middle of the night, silence thundered into the igloo and jolted me awake. "Serpent!" I cried. "Are you here? What's happened?"

"The storm is gone," the Serpent said. "It has howled itself away."

"Can we go see the glacier now?" I asked eagerly.

The Serpent laughed. "In the morning. It won't be easy—there's a lot of snow—but we will certainly try."

Before dawn I stuffed some food into my pack, and we scrambled out of our shelter. "We only need one meal," the Serpent told me. "We can't go far—the days are very short, and we don't want to stay out after dark; we'll freeze. It will be much colder today, now that the blizzard's over." The Serpent lifted its head and started ploughing through the drifts, making a path for me. In the half-light we struggled through snow so deep it nearly covered my head. We were climbing, and I kept slipping and falling. "Why are we *doing* this?" I mumbled through a mouthful of snow, but I would never have turned back.

At length we were at the top of a crest of snow. Before us a great pyramid of granite loomed, suspended in the sky. The stone began to glow. First a tinge of pink, then orange, red, as if a fire flared inside the stone. I sank to my knees and stared, fists clenched to my cheeks. Beside me, the Serpent was motionless, alert, feathers raised and flaring, its entire body tinted red.

Gradually the glow in the mountain faded; the sun rose and our shadows stretched before us on the ground.

"Serpent," I said, breathless, "what is it?"

The Serpent's eyes remained fixed on the granite. Finally it replied. "It's alpenglow, Eve, one of the most beautiful sights on earth. It happens on a clear day when the rays of the sun, rising or setting, strike a mountain peak."

"But the whole mountaintop, the whole rock, was on fire."

The Serpent laughed. "It only looks that way." It turned its head from side to side. "Look, Eve, now that it's light, you can see all the peaks." And indeed great peaks towered in a circle around us, some capped with snow, others steep and bare. The mountain that had glowed in the slanted rays of the sun stood taller than all the rest, a great triangle of granite rising perpendicular from fields of snow.

"See the glaciers?" the Serpent went on, pointing with its tail.

"They look like rivers—rivers made of ice."

"That's just what they are. This is a glacier we're walking on. Here, look into this crevasse." The Serpent pointed to a jagged slash in the ice. Balancing against its tail, I peered in. The crevasse was narrow; my body would have just fit into it, but it went down and down. Immense horizontal layers of ice descended toward the center of the Earth; I could not see the bottom.

"It's green," I exclaimed. "Blue-green." Removing a mitten, I knelt in the snow and ran my hand into the gash. "It's so smooth. And cold!" I shook my hand and put my mitten back on. "That hole—"

"Crevasse," said the Serpent.

"That crevasse is awfully deep. I wouldn't want to fall in."

"No chance of that. We'll start back to the igloo. Follow right in my tracks." We threaded our way around crevasses and beneath broken glacial walls. On all sides blue ice gleamed, breaking through snow. Above, the rugged peaks soared into the sky. All was silent, only from time to time an avalanche roared into the valley, sliding, tumbling, sending up showers of fluffy snow.

When we reached the igloo just before dark, I was able to see the surrounding landscape, which had been invisible in the morning darkness. The Serpent had chosen the site well: avalanches had swept by on either side of the little round house, leaving massive chunks of snow and ice. One final time we crept through the narrow passage, had a quick supper of gruel and tea, and slept.

Early the next morning we bundled together our tattered belongings. We had little to carry, only a small bag of food, and we abandoned the sledge under a drift. As I slung my pack over my shoulder, the Serpent squinted at me in the bright light. "Was it worth the climb yesterday, Eve?"

"Yes," I said. "Oh yes."

The return to the ridge was easy. We were going downhill with the wind, steady and strong, behind us. The blizzard had ended in a storm of sleet, and all around the snow glistened and sparkled. Every evening the Serpent used its tail to make a nest under the ice-hard crust, and there, huddled in the Serpent's coils, I slept. On the third day I began to see the outline of the rock at the top of the cliff and the stunted tree halfway down the ledge, then something moving, running back and forth. "Oh, Serpent!" I cried. "It's the dog! It's all right!"

"I knew it would be," the Serpent replied. "It must have caught our scent on the wind."

The animal was leaping and dancing with joy, all four feet off the ground. When we finally reached the ledge, the dog jumped onto my chest and knocked me down, whimpering and licking my face. We rolled together on the ground and hugged each other.

In the morning we entered the Garden. The obstacles we had met on the way out—the cliff, the arduous rocky path—seemed mere anthills now. After lowering the dog in a sling, we descended the rock face easily, as if we were clambering about in an apple tree. From there it was an easy walk, first between the boulders and down the steep hills that had caused us such effort on the way out, then into glades that glowed green, lush, welcoming. In two days we were home: the pool with its pebbles, dappled fish and water lilies, our hut tranquil and serene, with dry grass for bedding stacked carefully against the wall, the sand on the terrace just as I had left it, raked in parallel lines.

To the Sea

○

*B*ACK IN THE GARDEN I felt strangely unsettled. My body and my mind both yearned for rest, for stretching and running, for sleep. I needed time to make everything I had learned a part of myself. But I was restless. By day I was unable to focus: I gathered reeds but could not bring myself to start a basket; the clay I dug lay in clumps along the bank. At night dreams came, not nightmares, just vivid reenactments of my adventures: flaming stone pyramids danced in the snow, blocks of ice bounded beneath my feet, snakes rattled their tails and flicked their black forked tongues. I woke convinced I was in the igloo again and strained to hear the wind.

"Eve," the Serpent said. "Not sleeping?"

"No." Admitting it, I was surprised. I always fell

asleep as soon as I lay down on my mat and woke only with the dawn. "All those places we went, they keep coming into my dreams."

"Understandable," the Serpent said. "So many new things, and so vivid."

"I feel as if I've eaten too much."

The Serpent laughed. "What did you discover about yourself?"

"About *myself*?"

"About the kind of person you are. What happens when you come up against something new, something not as easy as life in the Garden?"

I remembered the cliff, the miles of deep snow, the blizzard, building the igloo. "I guess I discovered that I'm stronger than I thought."

"Physically?"

"No, *inside*, inside myself." I put my hands on my chest. "Here."

The Serpent was quiet. "Eve, you have learned that you are brave," it said at last.

I wasn't sure what that meant, but I knew it was good.

Again we settled into our old routine. The dog had attached itself to us permanently; it ran beside us, swam when we swam, and lay in the sun while we talked. In the evening it went off—to see its friends, the Serpent said, and I imagined it trotting through the woods, touching noses with other dogs, wagging its tail, lifting its leg—but at dawn it was always there again, ready for the day's adventures.

One morning, after the moon had waned and disappeared and grown again to half size, I woke to find the Garden in focus again. "I'm ready!" I shouted to the Serpent as it came up the path.

"For a run?"

"Well, yes. But also for the sea."

While we were eating breakfast—cherries and papayas—I bombarded the Serpent with questions. "What should we take?" I asked. "Will it be cold? Do I need clothes? We won't need water—there's lots in the sea! What about food? How will we get there?"

The Serpent laughed. "Good for you; you're thinking ahead. It won't be cold, but it may rain. And you can't drink the sea."

"Why can't I?"

"The sea has salt in it."

"Salt!" I exclaimed.

"Salt." The Serpent nodded. "That makes it easy to swim, but you can't drink seawater; it will make you sick. There's too much salt—your body can't absorb it."

I opened my mouth to ask another question, but the Serpent raised its tail. "You'll see it in a few days and find out for yourself. Keep to your planning."

"So we need to carry water, like we did to the desert?" I asked. Carry water to the sea? It seemed ridiculous.

"No, we'll find food and fresh water along the way."

"Are you sure we'll find food? There wasn't any going north, and very little on the way to the volcano or in the desert."

"Plants and trees have trouble growing in those places. It's either too dry or too cold, or the ground is covered with lava. Going toward the sea, it's warm and there's plenty of rain, so we'll have our choice of food."

"But once we get there—you said we can't drink the sea?"

"No, but there are springs of fresh water nearby."

"How do we get there?"

The Serpent winked one eye. "What would you suggest, Eve?" it asked.

I looked across the sandy terrace to the pond and tried to visualize the Garden as we had seen it from the volcano. Four cherries lay on the table in front of me. I placed them carefully: "Volcano, east; desert, south; mountains, north. The sea is to the west"—I placed the fourth cherry—"beyond the lake. Adam and I went there once to see if the sun would sink into the water." I giggled. "We were so silly. We knew perfectly well it didn't. We waded around at the end of the lake, but the mud was so deep we could hardly move. And that whole area is overgrown with bushes and vines. Is there another way?"

The Serpent shook its head. "The swamp covers all the land to the west of the Garden. It would take too long to go around."

"How will we get through, then?"

"Go look at the area again. See if you can come up with something," the Serpent said. I knew better than to complain: by now I realized the Serpent's apparent indifference was part of my education.

The western shore of the lake was a solid tangle of reeds and bushes. The dog had trotted along beside me, but when we reached the banks, it lay down with its muzzle on its paws and went to sleep. I clambered about in the mud, shoving aside brambles and twigs, but the morass seemed impassable. Finally, discouraged, I sat on a rock and glared at the water. Minute grains of pollen floated on the surface, golden specks shimmering in the sun.

I put my head in my arms and closed my eyes. Tiny waves slapped the rocks and slurped against the mud. *If we want to go to the sea*, I thought, *we have to go through the swamp. There's no other way. Mud. Worse than snow.* I looked back at the wall of brush.

Again the specks of gold caught my eye. But now they were closer to the shore, wafting lazily toward the west. As I watched, a few grains began to turn, caught in the outer ring of an eddy. Faster and faster they swirled in a diminutive whirlpool and disappeared under a witch hazel bush.

As quickly as I could, I made my way through the mud to the place where the pollen was drawn into the swamp. There was indeed a brook, and when I pulled back the bushes, I found that it widened beyond the first mass of brambles. Disregarding the branches slapping at my face, I waded downstream. The stream grew wider and deeper; finally I had to swim. Ahead of me, winding through the swamp, lay our path to the sea.

I returned triumphant to the Serpent.

"Splendid," it said, after listening to my report. "Are we going to swim?"

"How far is it?" I asked, subdued. I had not thought about how we would navigate the river. I was a strong swimmer, but not as good as the otter or the eels; I could not stay in the water for days, or even for several hours.

"Farther than the volcano or the desert," replied the Serpent.

"I could never swim all that way," I groaned. "I suppose we could rest on the bank when we get tired."

"The shore's not very hospitable."

"What else, then?" I rubbed my hands over my eyes. I remembered ants on twigs floating across the pond, frogs comfortably seated on lily pads unrolling their gummy tongues. "We need a lily pad!" I cried.

The Serpent laughed. "What an idea—you and me on a lily pad! But you're looking in the right direction."

"You know the answer!" I cried indignantly. "Why don't you just *tell* me?"

"Thinking exercises the mind, and your mind needs more exercising than mine."

But I was no longer paying attention. "Something that floats, but big enough to carry us. A log? No, it rolls; you fall off. Maybe a few logs tied together? With vines—I could do that."

So it happened that a few days later, the Serpent and I were navigating the stream on a raft. Dog was not with us; as soon as it had seen us packing our things, it had run off whimpering with its tail between its legs. A few provisions—our drinking gourds and bowls, a couple of baskets, fruit to nibble on while we were under way, straw mats and quilts for sleeping, and some extra vines—were lashed to the deck. Some yards into the swamp, a fallen branch heavy with blooms lay across the way. I fixed it upright at the bow and we sailed proudly downriver, behind a burst of cherry blossoms.

At first we allowed the raft to float freely, limiting our

efforts to pushing off when we got too close to shore. But the current was not strong and progress was very slow, so I cut a long, solid stick and experimented with shoving it against the banks. After trying various approaches, which succeeded in covering us both with mud, I came upon a more efficient method. Standing at the front, I thrust the pole into the riverbed, pushed against it and walked to the rear, propelling the raft forward. The Serpent stretched out on the deck, steering with its tail, while I tramped back and forth.

"*You* look comfortable!" I said, wiping the sweat from my eyes. "I thought we were just going to *float* down the river!"

The Serpent laughed. "I *am* comfortable. It's very relaxing. And the exercise is good for you."

For five days we drifted silently through the swamp. I was constantly hungry—poling was hard work—and when the Serpent spotted an orange tree or a banana plant or coconuts fallen to the ground, I guided our barque ashore and we clambered off with a basket to take on a supply. The fruit was smaller than that in the Garden, and not as sweet, but I quickly developed a taste for it.

To my surprise there were a few warblers in the trees, while in the river crocodiles lay silent, eyes and snouts barely raised above the black water. Hugging a tree, a lemur stared at us with its round, white-rimmed eyes, and a herd of pigs, black and round and short-legged, rooted noisily in the mud on the bank. Two or three times I caught sight of the eagle sailing in the clouds. It was the first time we had seen living animals outside the Garden.

One afternoon I spotted a baby raccoon floating belly up, staring wide eyed at the sky, arms and legs spread eagled in the water. I fished it out; it was stiff in my hands. "Serpent," I cried, dropping my pole. "Something's wrong with this raccoon. It doesn't move! What's the matter with it?"

The Serpent took the animal gently in its jaws and laid it on the deck.

"It's dead," it said. "It must have fallen into the river and drowned."

Dead? Drowned? I shivered, as if a wind from the glacier had reached me on this raft in its journey to the sea.

"Let us lay this baby to rest," the Serpent said. "Then we'll talk about death." It swung the raft to the river-bank, and we wrapped the raccoon in leaves and buried it in the soft mud. When we were again floating on the stream, the Serpent spoke.

"That's the first dead creature we've ever seen on Earth. I'm sorry you found it. One day we would have spoken of death, but not quite yet." The Serpent shifted its tail to bring the raft into the current, then raised itself high. "Eve, you know that in the Garden all creatures are safe. Nothing can seriously harm you. Death does not exist."

"Death?"

"Death occurs when life goes out of a creature and the living being dies. Only the shell—the body—is left."

I could not conceive of a body without life. "But a body *is* life!" I cried. "How can life leave it? You've never told me about that."

"There was no need to," the Serpent said. "There *is* no death in the Garden. But as we've seen, once you step outside the Garden strange things happen. Nature assumes a life of its own. There's danger: tornadoes, volcanoes, blizzards. And now, there is death."

I thought of the little creature stiff in my hands and shivered again. "You said the raccoon drowned. What's that?"

"You know that fish breathe through their gills and have to live in a pool or stream, or in the ocean." I nodded. The Serpent had taught me never to remove a fish from the water. "Animals, on the other hand, can't live *in* the water for long. They have to breathe air, and if they're caught below the surface, their lungs will fill with water and they'll drown. That's what happened to the raccoon; it got water in its lungs, and couldn't breathe anymore."

"But raccoons are good swimmers."

"Yes. For some reason the one you found wasn't able to swim. Maybe it fell out of a tree."

"So it drowned, and it was *dead*?"

"Yes."

"But why was the raccoon stiff, and lying that way with its eyes open?"

"When it died, there was no force left in it to close its eyelids. After death the body gets stiff for a while." The Serpent frowned. "I'm afraid it's a harbinger."

"Harbinger?"

"An omen, a sign of what's ahead."

"You mean death will come even in the Garden?"

"Or perhaps the Garden will no longer exist. It will be emptied of its life."

"Emptied?" I could not imagine such a thing, the Garden with no living creatures. "Where would all the animals go?"

"Outside. Here." The Serpent waved at the riverbanks. "Or to the desert, or to the east or north."

"And you and Adam and I, and God—would we go too?"

The Serpent shook its head. "Eve, who knows? Perhaps it will never happen. It is not decided yet."

"Will it come soon—*death*—to the world?"

"I think not for a long while," replied the Serpent. "Eve, I know it's almost impossible to do, but try to put it aside for now. Look at the live world we're moving through; see how beautiful it is. Later it will be time to speak again of death." The Serpent peered at me and sighed. "There are some things I can't protect you from, my dear. Look, there's a papaya tree; we haven't seen one since we left the Garden. The fruit looks perfect. We'll stop and pick some, and stretch our bodies."

But through the next days, the baby raccoon was never far from my mind.

As we got farther down the river, the brambles and shrubs gave way to giant mangrove trees, their tangled legs spread into the mud. I poled until I was tired; rested, then poled again. Occasionally we swam or beached the raft to pick blueberries or smooth-skinned avocados. On the fourth day we came to a run of rapids but managed to bump and gyrate down the canyon successfully. Even our figurehead gave up only a few blossoms to the white water. From there the stream opened into a river that led through reeds and sandbars to the sea.

I was lying on deck watching the treetops pass above—the last day or two the current had increased and there was no longer any need to pole—when suddenly the trees disappeared. The world around me lightened, lost its tint of green, and turned yellow and bright. To the west a sound peaked and faded, as if the wind, instead of blowing through leaves, was crashing through stones.

"What's happened?" I cried, sitting up quickly. "What *is* that?"

"The ocean," the Serpent said. "We're here." As it spoke the raft rounded a spit of sand. Ahead, there it was—the *sea*.

Water, only water, all the way to the horizon. There were no clouds in the sky. The sea was still, like a great lake, and deep cobalt blue. Occasionally a puff of wind ran over the water, rippling it out of its tranquility, before it grew calm again. Near the shore the water became lighter, azure, and I could make out the sand at the bottom, and all sorts of fish darting about, in shapes and colors I had never seen. The raft rocked calmly in the narrow channel of the stream; on either side, a wide beach extended into the distance.

I stared; my hair whipped in the wind and I hugged it to me. I could not say a word.

"I told you there was no way to describe it," the Serpent said. "Let's push the raft behind that sand spit so it won't get carried out on the tide. Then we'll tie up and go exploring."

A few minutes later I was standing with the Serpent at the edge of the water. Wavelets pushing fringes of white foam raced to shore, tickled my toes, and receded, leaving bubbles in the sand. I waded in up to my knees. The water was as clear as any spring in the Garden. I could see two starfish twitching their serrated legs on the sand. "There's no salt here, Serpent. You're imagining things."

"Taste it," the Serpent said. "Taste the water."

Instead I dove and took several strokes away from the beach. Treading water, I turned to the Serpent on shore. "I will!" I said, and ducked underwater and took a gulp. Salt ran down my throat and up my nose, my eyes stung. I surfaced quickly, sputtering and spitting.

"It's awful! Horrible!"

The Serpent chuckled.

"But it's great to swim in," I shouted. "You're right; the water holds me up. I hardly have to kick at all. Come in!"

"Not now. I'll sit and watch for a while," the Serpent replied. "Eve, I want you to be careful in the sea."

"Why? It's no different from the lake."

"Ah, but it is. Today it's calm, but the waves can be rough, and the coral reefs can give you nasty scrapes. Remember how you cut your knee trying to find the swallow's nest?" The Serpent looked at me sternly. "And," it went on, "be cautious with the creatures of the sea."

"Cautious? Why? The animals always take care of

me." I thought of the monkeys I had met on the way to the desert, high in the trees, teasing and poking but ready to catch me if I lost my hold.

"In the Garden, yes. But outside, we've come upon forces we never expected."

"But that was the tornado and the blizzard. Things that got away from God. Not animals."

"We've never met animals outside the Garden before, Eve. These are the first. We have no idea whether they've gotten away from God as well."

I poked the starfish warily with my toe. "What could they do?"

"Impossible to say. Some of them might bite or sting. Or they may be every bit as kind as the animals you know. We'll just have to see."

But the creatures of the sea were friendly. The jellyfish did not sting; when I brushed my hands through its dangling tentacles, they curled softly around my fingers, while the bulbous diaphanous bell pulsated against my arm. The orcas and sharks grazed the shallows of the shore and swam idly by, trailing ribbons of porphyra or carrageen from their jaws.

I spent most of the day in the water, seeing how long I could float, twisting and turning in the gentle waves, twining long strands of seaweed around my neck. A furry white sea otter floated by, wrapped in fronds of giant kelp. It lay on its back, arms crossed on its chest, completely relaxed as though it were in bed. It turned its black nose in my direction, and I thought it might swim over to investigate. But apparently I was not very interesting, for it sank deeper into its nest, and the current wafted it away.

There was seaweed in all shapes and hues and textures: long, green hairlike strands; fat, rubbery ribbons; brown weeds that branched like shrubs with speckled, swollen tips. Thousands of fish, or so it seemed, brushed against me as I waded and swam, and, though my vision was blurred underwater, the forms and colors and movements were clear. When fish jumped—which they did often—I could see them well. An orange fish, smaller than my hand with fins like the wings of a butterfly, suddenly flung itself out of the water and flew through the air in an arc as high as an elephant's ear! Another fish, yellow as the sun, thin with three white fanlike fins near its tail, stared at me with its big black eye. When I touched it, it puffed itself into a ball three times its size, with spikes sticking out on all sides like a porcupine.

Tiny brown fish with yellow heads and white stripes hid in pink bouquets of sea anemone, peeking at me through the flowers, while other fish swam en masse and turned at lightning speed, one way, then the other, all together, like the animals in God's parade. I tried to follow their turns, but the fish were too fast; they appeared to respond to signals that were beyond my ken.

At the end of the afternoon, I reluctantly dragged myself from the waves. Behind the dunes an open forest ran the length of the shore: coconut and date trees, bananas, pineapple bushes. Fan-shaped fronds had fallen from the trees and carpeted the ground. Here we set up our camp: a lean-to of branches covered with the giant leaves. For supper we had bananas and coconut milk. Before the sun sank into the sea, I was asleep.

The following day there was no wind at all. The water was flat and calm as a pond. The Serpent used its tail and I a giant leaf as paddles, and we propelled the raft far into the ocean until we could barely see the shore. While the craft bobbed on the waves, I swam among the coral reefs, taking care not to scrape my shins or toes, and saw fish of all colors, brilliant fish, and bright and brittle coral. The Serpent told me the coral was alive, and I watched it carefully to see if it would move or grow, but it looked like stone to me.

When I got tired, I lay on the raft and stared deep into the dark interior of the sea. Far below great creatures wafted to and fro; with a flick of a tail they could turn and dart off in a new direction. I yearned to swim with them, as I had yearned to run with the antelope in the Garden.

"Eve, they're far too deep for you," said the Serpent. But dolphins and porpoises came and played with me later in the waves, tumbling and turning as they swam, racing ahead and rushing back to see if I was still there, all the while sending little hiccups back and forth.

"Are they talking to one another?" I asked the Serpent, who was swimming at my side, poking the raft along with its tail.

"Yes. That's their language."

"What are they saying?"

The Serpent laughed. "It's a language I haven't learned."

The wind rose in the night, and by morning the water was rough.

"I'm glad we went to the reefs yesterday," the Serpent said, looking at the sky. "A storm is coming."

Giant swells followed one another across the sea and shattered against the shore. I could hardly wait to throw myself in.

"Eve." The Serpent frowned. "Listen to me. Be careful today. Those waves are strong. They can do a lot of damage. Dive into the trough of the wave as it's breaking— and take special care coming out. It's easy to be knocked down."

"Are you going to swim?"

"No, I'll watch." The Serpent settled comfortably on

the sand, making random designs with its tail. While the sun moved across the sky, I dove again and again through the white water, learning to ride the waves and get back to the beach without being rolled in the surf. Once or twice the Serpent joined me, but most of the time it watched from the beach, amused.

"Come in!" I kept urging.

But the Serpent refused to be tempted. "I'm reserving my strength for hauling you out when you get into trouble," it said.

In the afternoon the wind strengthened and the water grew more turbulent. Finally the Serpent called me in. "Eve, come ashore now. It's too rough."

For the rest of the day we wandered along the beach, peering at conches and abalone, at mussels and clams opening and closing their shells, at tiny red crabs skittering sideways across the sand. The shells smelled of seaweed, sometimes a little rotten, and some of the big ones sang when you held them to your ear. I found two tiny, round cones shaped like miniature volcanoes, with striated sides and smooth, shiny, fluorescent linings, and added them to the collection in my pouch. As we settled under our quilts for the night, great clouds swept across the water, and the wind howled in the palms.

The Eagle's Eye

WE ROSE TO a different world. Violent gusts tore at the trees and whipped whirlpools of sand into the air. On the other side of the dunes, mountains of water threw themselves at the shore.

"It's fantastic!" I said. "I can't wait to go in."

"No swimming today," the Serpent stated firmly. "You'll get crushed. It's too much even for me."

I stared at the tumultuous sea. "It looks so wonderful! I'm sure I could manage it."

"Eve," the Serpent said sternly. "You underestimate those waves. They have tremendous force. Remember how the blizzard could have blown you away? The waves are just as dangerous. You may be able to swim tomorrow; the storm will have passed by then."

"What shall we do?" I asked.

"I was planning to go to the ridge," the Serpent said. "The eagle saw a vine there that doesn't exist in the Garden. I thought you could have a day to rest. Explore the beach; there's a great deal you haven't seen. But keep well back from the water—you don't want to be carried into that sea."

I looked at the waves, which towered over my head. "Can I come with you?" I asked. Spending the day on the beach without being able to swim did not appeal to me.

The Serpent shook its head. "I'm sorry, Eve; it's too far. I can get there and back in a few hours; it would take you days, and we need to start home soon." It looked at me and frowned. "You've gotten too accustomed to company, Eve; you used to go off alone every afternoon, and you loved it. Go on now. At supper we'll talk about the things each of us has discovered." The Serpent started spiraling toward the ridge, but turned just before disappearing among the trees. "Stop being foolish," it called, waving its ears. "And keep away from the sea!"

That was as close to a reprimand as the Serpent ever came, and I was annoyed. I scuffed the sand; the wind seized it and flung it in my face. I looked for shells and mollusks, but the beach was bare.

Perhaps they have holes they hide in when it storms, I

thought, imagining cozy corners deep in the sand where clams slept or lobsters dozed, stretching their claws lazily from time to time. I tried to skip stones, but they were gobbled up immediately by the waves. At last I sat morosely in the sand and watched the wild world around me. The rollers came racing in, trailing white plumes. They rose to great heights before crashing to bits against the shore and then withdrew, dragging with them shells and stones, before the next blow descended.

There was a pattern in the movement of the waves. Immense, they threw themselves at the beach, but there was nothing haphazard about their entrances and departures. Like the dances we performed on God's terrace, all the maneuvers were timed; there was a rhythm to the tumult.

I understand what the water's doing, I thought. *I can master that sea, dive into it and swim, and get out with no trouble at all in spite of what the Serpent says!*

Once I get clear of the surf, it'll be easy; the salt will hold me up.

And without thinking any further, I threw myself in.

It was harder to cut through the breakers than I had expected. Solid mounds of water pounded my face and threatened to fling me back onto the beach. I struggled, sputtering, salt in my eyes and nose and throat, but at last I managed to reach the relative calm beyond the breaking waves, where I could stay afloat fairly easily. For some time I swam, beating against the spume and the gale, reveling in the battle, rejoicing in the feel of my body stretching and reaching in that savage sea. At last, beginning to tire, I looked back at the shore and was startled to see how far I had gone. The beach was a yellow streak broken sporadically by roiling white froth, far, far away.

I had a touch of panic—I was extremely tired—but then I told myself, *It will be easy, just lie in the water and the waves will carry you in.* I lay on my back and headed toward the coast, waving my arms back and forth like the fins of a fish. High above me I thought I glimpsed an eagle, but with the spray in my eyes it was hard to be sure. When I turned to check on my progress, the shore looked even farther away. *Perhaps there's a current out here, like in the river,* I thought. *Just swim hard, you'll get out of it,* and I put my head down and punched my arms vigorously in and out of the sea, kicking as hard as I could, counting my strokes. *That should do it,* I muttered when I reached five hundred, and raised myself in the water to look. But the shore was at an even greater distance than before. I could barely see the yellow strip of sand, and the palm trees were a prickle against the hills.

I tried again two or three times to battle toward land before realizing that I *would not* get back: the waves were too rough, the current too strong. In fact, I was being swept farther and farther out to sea. *Maybe I can reach an island or a sand strip,* I thought, without much hope. I remembered the raccoon stiff in my hands, and sobbed, and the sour, salty water slopped into my mouth. *Stupid,* I said to myself. *Relax.* After that I lay bobbing on the surface, willing my muscles to go limp, my body to rest, occasionally raising my face to gulp a lung-full of air.

Once when I lifted my head to breathe, I found I had sunk well below the water and had to kick energetically to bring myself to the top. Next time I was still farther down; way above I saw the glitter of light on the waves. Struggling to get there no longer seemed worth the effort. I breathed and coughed and breathed again.

Suddenly the world was beautiful, and before my eyes everything was clear. Around me swam fishes of many colors—colors brilliant as those the Serpent wore. *The Serpent, will it miss me?* I thought. A giant tuna with yellow eyes gaped at me; bubbles bobbled upward from its mouth. *Am I drowning? Is this what it is to drown?* I rocked peacefully in the current far beneath the waves.

A shimmer in the green sea a long way away, a swirl of motion. Water rushed by me—no, it was I who rushed through water, raced away from the depths, to the light. Something clasped me at the waist, melded me against a body that slithered and flew through the depths and burst finally into the air. Sky, storm, a flash of feathers in the spray. Upside down, I was pounded and squeezed. Water poured from my mouth and nose. I choked and coughed and, at last, gasped a great breath of air.

"Good," said the Serpent. "You'll live." Holding me above the water with its tail, it waggled its ears at me and laughed. "What a foolish child you are.

"Now," the Serpent continued when I was breathing more or less normally, "we return to land. Get on my back. Wrap your legs around me and hold onto my ears. Hang on tight. It's going to be a rough ride."

The next moment I was rushing through the thundering sea, clinging to the Serpent's ears, knees clutched around its neck. Waves crashed into foam and broke, only to form and break again, as far as I could see.

"We're nearly there," shouted the Serpent. I saw the land ahead, the palm trees waving wildly. The Serpent paused just behind the line of breakers. "I'll choose a good wave and swim straight in, and keep going right over the dunes. Grip your knees as hard as you can and hang onto my ears. Don't let go until we're under the trees." A great mound of water rose beneath us. "Here we go!" the Serpent cried.

All was chaos around us, howling and white: wave crashed on wave, spume shot high in the air. The

Serpent's body twisted and bucked, the ocean pulled at me, trying to tear my legs away, loose my fingers, take me back for itself. Then we were on the sand; the sea launched one last assault against us, one last great wave. The Serpent groaned and heaved itself free, and we were skimming across the beach; a blur of sand sped by, gold, on either side. We were over the dunes, under the trees. The Serpent twisted its body to the side, and I tumbled, limp, onto the ground.

After that I remember nothing until I woke at dawn, in the same spot, covered by a quilt. *Where am I?* I thought, and then it all came back in a rush: the storm, the battle with the waves, the drift to the depths of the sea. The flash of light: the Serpent. I came fully awake and was overwhelmed with shame.

The Serpent found me lying on my stomach, my face half buried in the sand. "Are you all right, Eve?" it asked. When I did not answer, it rolled me over with its tail. "Still breathing, I see. Well, you'd better tell me what's bothering you, so we can have breakfast. I don't know about you, but I'm famished."

I sat up and combed my fingers through my hair, tangled and stiff with salt. "I'm so ashamed," I said. "Serpent, I'm so sorry."

"What are you ashamed about?"

"You told me not to go in, and I did, and I almost

drowned, and you had to come and save me. I'm so stupid!"

"Foolish, Eve, not stupid." The Serpent coiled next to me and gazed into my face. "Foolish not to listen to my advice. I've never kept you from doing anything unless it was truly dangerous. And you should be able to amuse yourself for one day on the beach."

"I tried, I did try. But the water looked so exciting...."

"Well it certainly was *that*!"

"And"—I hesitated, mortified; I could feel my face blazing—"I was furious with you for going off the way you did."

The Serpent laughed. "I know," it said. "But it's not *that* serious. We all have the right to get mad at someone from time to time." For a few moments I could not speak. "Eve, there's no need to cry," it went on.

"Serpent," I said, rubbing my hands across my cheeks. "Thank you. For rescuing me. And being so nice."

The Serpent raised its ears. "You know, I rather enjoyed it. I haven't swum in a stormy sea for ages. It was quite exhilarating. Come, I've picked bananas for breakfast. The wind has died down a bit; we can eat on the beach." As it slithered away it glanced back at me, grinning. "And yes, Eve, I would have missed you."

"I don't know what would have happened if you hadn't appeared," I said when we were settled on the sand. The wind was lighter, and the waves no longer pounded the shore. Even so I had no desire to swim; I tucked my feet under me, away from the water. "How did you know I was in trouble?"

"The eagle told me. It saw you struggling in the waves, so I came as fast as I could. But by the time the eagle got back here, you'd disappeared."

"Was it the eagle in the waves when you pulled me out?"

"So you saw it, did you?"

"I wasn't sure what it was, everything was such a muddle. But how did you find me in all that ocean?" I shuddered, recalling the tug of the riptide and the coast shrinking before me as I swam.

"I know this part of the coast—I was here once, ages ago—and I know there's a strong rip when there's any wind. But it took me longer to reach you than I expected. The current swept you along very fast."

"Was I drowning?" I asked.

"Yes. Undoubtedly you were."

I shut my eyes and saw again the tuna popping its mouth at me. "It was quite pleasant, actually, once I got beyond the choking part," I said. "Lovely colors and friendly fish. If you hadn't gotten there, would I have died?"

For some time the Serpent was silent, turning its tail

in the sand. Finally it answered, "I suspect so. But there may be some protection, even outside the Garden, that could have brought you back to life."

"If I had died, what would have happened to me? Where would I be now?"

Again the Serpent was still. Even its tail stopped making patterns in the sand. "You would be at the bottom of the sea, rocking about with the fish."

"With my eyes open?"

The Serpent sighed. "Yes. With your eyes open."

"And my soul—what would have happened to my soul?"

"When life goes out of the body, the soul disappears."

"Disappears? So when we die, it's as if we'd never lived at all. Everything goes?"

"Not quite. Eve, do you see that wave? It ripples in and ripples away and then comes back again. Each time it runs out, it leaves a bit of itself behind, a few bubbles, an invisible sheen, some part of itself, and that residue changes forever the way the grains of sand lie together all along the length of the beach. After that wave has come and gone, the shore is never the same again. Can you see that?"

I nodded, watching the waves repeat their endless, inexorable rhythm.

"Or when it rains in the night, and a pool of water gathers in a rock. All day the sun beats down and the water evaporates; in the evening if the wind comes it will not ruffle the pool, for the pool is no longer there. The water has become part of the atmosphere, and we cannot see it, but it is still here. And like the sand, that air is changed: it has been enriched—in a sense leavened. It has more to give: to the seeds in the meadow, the acorn under the tree, and all the other pips and spores and embryos lying in wait for life. And so, because of that drop of rain, the world is forever changed." The Serpent turned its head and ran its eyes up and down the shore. "That is what happens to the soul. Because you have lived and reflected on many things, and danced and planted seeds of many kinds, the world is never the same as it was before. In that sense, when you die a part of you—your soul—goes on forever."

The Serpent stirred. "Come, let's see if the crabs have reappeared from their holes."

All day we strolled together on the beach, quiet, not talking much, at peace. As we wandered I added shells and grains of sand, tiny seeds caught in seaweed, lichen I pried from the stones, to my neck basket. In the late afternoon, as the wind abated, I sat for a long time watching a blue and gray and brown rock emerge from the sand on the falling tide.

The Serpent's Bowl

COMING FROM THE Garden, we had floated on the current, raft and river both moving toward the sea. Going back we were navigating upstream, with the current against us. I poled, and the Serpent helped by twining its tail around boulders and trees and pulling. It was hard work. On the second day a wind came up from the west and pushed at my back, and we moved through the water slightly faster.

"If only," I mumbled, looking at the cherry branch still standing at the bow.

"If only what?" said the Serpent.

"I know!" I yelled. "Serpent, put in to shore. Please," I added hastily as the Serpent raised its brows, but it twisted its tail in the water and we bumped into the bank.

"What is it, Eve?"

"I have an idea. Maybe we can use the wind—the way we used the dog."

"To pull the raft?"

"To push it." I looked around the little barque. My sleeping blanket lay on the deck. I had made it for our trip to the North, and it was closely woven. "If we can find some way to tie that blanket to the branch, it might catch the wind."

The Serpent sat on one end to keep the blanket from flapping while I lashed the other edge to the branch, which I fixed more firmly at the front of the raft. When we first shoved back into the stream, the makeshift sail blew about wildly and struck me two or three times in the face, until I tied one corner with a vine. Eventually we were sailing upstream at great speed with the blanket billowing out ahead. I had nothing to do but lie on the deck holding the vine to steady the sail, letting it out or drawing it in as we negotiated the curves in the river, while the Serpent steered the raft with its tail.

"Well done!" the Serpent said.

Now that I could relax, images of the sea danced

before my eyes: whales blowing while their calves, searching for the nipple, bumped against their sides; dolphins calling one another as they sprang through the waves; tiny butterfly fish leaping toward the sky. Hundreds of fish turning as one and turning again, purple feathers streaming from their heads.

"Does God know about the sea?" I asked the Serpent.

"Of course he does. He made it."

"Does he know there are animals in the swamp? About the fish and the whales, and the jellyfish and sponges and coral reefs?"

"He certainly knows about the creatures of the sea. In the beginning it was he who made them. I don't think he realizes how many there are now or how large they've grown. And I doubt he's aware of the animals that have left the Garden."

"What about the storm, the waves, the current, and the riptide?"

"I doubt it."

"So the sea is one more thing that has gotten away from God."

"We can't be sure, Eve. But I believe that's right."

By the time we reached the rapids, the wind had stiffened into a gale. Despite the current, we swept upriver through the white water, jerking and bouncing off rocks.

I used the pole only to keep us from hitting the largest boulders.

As we neared the border of the Garden, the wind died. Even with the current running against us, we had made better time on the return trip, and I hadn't worked nearly as hard. Nevertheless, when we finally pushed our way through the last tangle of bushes onto the lake, I was more than ready for a rest.

For several days we relaxed, walking through the fields to see how the plants had prospered in our absence and to greet the birds and animals. The dog did not appear. "Perhaps it thinks we're making a habit of journeys and doesn't want to risk being dragged along," the Serpent said, but I was sad. I missed our companion. The eagle we glimpsed occasionally, soaring in the clouds.

On the seventh day the Serpent announced early in the morning that it was going to pay a visit to God. I was sitting on my heels at the edge of the pond; I had taken all the bits of earth I had acquired on our journeys and was dribbling them into a large gourd.

"Serpent, look," I said. "This sand, see how white it is—it came from the desert. And the yellow sand comes from the beach." I let the grains trickle through my fingers. "This is the earth we dug up in the North, before the blizzard. It's all gritty. And here's some ash from the volcano." As I poured the black stuff into the gourd, the white bead slithered out and rolled across the ground.

The Serpent raised its ears. "Where did you get that?"

"It was in the bottom of a hole on the volcano." I picked up the bead and rubbed it between my hands. "Isn't it lovely? There's something special about it."

"It *is* special," said the Serpent. "It comes from the very center of the earth. It was formed when the world was new. What will you do with all these treasures?"

I glanced at the Serpent to see if it was laughing at me, but it was quite serious. "Make something." I cupped water in my hands and poured it into the mixture.

"A mud pie?" asked the Serpent, teasing me.

"A bowl," I said, "made of all the places we've been. I'll put you around the rim."

The Serpent looked pleased; it lifted its ears and grinned. "I'll look forward to seeing it when I get back," it said.

"What are you going to say to God?" I asked.

The Serpent frowned. "I'm not sure what I'll say. I want to go to him before he comes to search us out. The sixth moon is waning, and our time is up. I have to find out what's going on in his mind, and whether he's gained the slightest understanding of what he did." He paused.

"Does it worry you to have me see him?"

I rolled the clay around and around in my hands. I had been wondering about that and still wasn't sure how I felt. But suddenly it was clear. "Much less than before," I said. "I'm beginning to feel I can cope with him. And Adam." I applied sharp little slaps to the wet surface of the ball. "In fact, there are times when I think I'm looking forward to seeing God."

When the Serpent returned at midday, the bowl was finished. It was about as large as the palm of my hand, oval, with simple ridges down the sides. Curled round the rim lay the Serpent. The front of its body was raised high, the eyes wide and intense, as though it were watching an eagle high in the sky. The feathers caused me a good deal of trouble, they were so thin and serrated, but in the end I was pleased with the effect: they stood up straight off the head, very much as they did in real life, and gave the Serpent an alert and listening air. In the half-open mouth lay the white bead I had found on the volcano.

I cupped the bowl in my hands and held it out to the Serpent. "What do you think?" I asked. The Serpent craned its head to the right and left, then circled me to get a view from all sides. It said nothing for a long while. I knew my work was good—the bowl was beautiful—

but as time went by I began to get anxious.

At last the Serpent let out its breath. "It's fantastic," it said, "and I don't say that because you've done me so well—at least, I hope I look like that. Eve, you're an artist, a true artist." It peered again at the bowl and touched it carefully with its tail. "Put it down somewhere safe and let me tell you about God."

In the joy of making my bowl, I had forgotten about God. "What did he say?"

"He wants to see you immediately; he says you're a day late already." The Serpent sighed. "I made you a promise that you would never have to see God again, if you chose not to. I meant that. You have only to tell me."

I turned the bowl in my hands and ran my fingers over the image of the Serpent on its rim. "Thank you, Serpent," I said. "I know that. I've kept it in my heart since you told me in the desert."

"You don't need to be afraid of him. He's understood that he can't force anything on you again. But I'll go with you if you want me to."

I hesitated. "Will Adam be there?" I had decided I could handle God, but was not ready for Adam.

"No," said the Serpent. "I told God it would be better for Adam to stay away a while longer."

"I'll be all right alone," I said. "I'll go this afternoon; I'm ready to see him. I'll set this pot in the sun to dry and have a swim before I leave."

On the ridge behind our hut, where the sun shone for the greater part of the day, there was a small mound of earth. I hollowed out the top and placed the bowl in the depression. I swam, then washed my hair and fanned it dry in the breeze that always freshened in the afternoon.

All the while I thought: *What will I say to God? Will he be angry because I'm late?* Despite the Serpent's reassurance about God reading my mind, I wondered if he would know about the journeys, know the moment he saw me how much my universe had expanded. *If God knows everything,* said a small voice inside me, *won't he know all this? Won't he know what I'm thinking all the time?*

But I was not afraid for long. After all, I had stood against the desert whirlwind and the arctic blizzard (cowered before them, protected by the Serpent, to be absolutely honest, but nevertheless), climbed a high precipice and—again with the Serpent's help—survived a storm at sea.

I can cope with God, I thought, *even without the Serpent.*

Talking to God

AS I ARRIVED at God's clearing, the sun was skimming the trees to the west. The place was still much as it had been when I first saw it, so many moons ago. Some of the plants had grown, and Adam's carved beams were buried in grapevine. God was standing on the edge of the cliff, in much the same position I remembered from that initial visit, gazing over the valley. It was as if no time had passed at all. "Where is that boy?" I expected him to mutter. "What has he gotten up to now?"

But *I* had changed.

"God," I said quietly, stepping from the shadow of the grape arbor into the sunlight. "You wanted to see me. Here I am."

God turned in a flash of white hair and swirling cloud. He drew himself up so that he seemed a head taller than I remembered and took a great breath. In two steps he covered half the distance between us. *Will he want to hug me?* I thought, and shuddered. But he stopped in midstride, his hand raised in that gesture of his, then lowered his arm.

"Eve." His voice was so soft I could barely hear it. "Eve."

It must have been some minutes before either of us spoke. I could not stop staring at God: the great head, the white hair, the heavy, muscled body bound in linen. This being had created all the world I had seen—the sedate, ordered beautiful world within the Garden, the wide, wild world without. Long ago on the mountain, the Serpent had said, "He had to imagine it first." What was it behind his curved forehead that enabled this being, this god, to conjure up, then create: shrimp; leaf; soft jellyfish with dangling tentacles; cold granite afire; flower unfolding bud to bloom; dandelion and polly-wog; frog's tongue leaping for a meal; horse; elk; eagle; bear. Adam. Me.

But not the Serpent.

I could not imagine God conjuring up the Serpent.

God had not moved. It was as if he had never seen

me before, as if I had been a fawn in his forest or a specially bright flower or a sapling that bent to his delight in the wind.

At last he stepped forward and reached out his hand. "Eve," he said again. "I had forgotten. . . . No, something's happened to you. You're more beautiful, even more beautiful, than you were before. You glow. Oh, my dear, come, let me embrace you. . . ." He opened his arms.

I stood still. I saw my shadow spreading away from me across the terrace, sharp edged and uncompromising. God took another step toward me.

"Stop, God," I said.

God stood frozen, arms open, fingers curled, staring at me as if the Serpent had bitten him when he stretched out his hand in greeting.

"Eve!" he said. "Dear child, I want to welcome you, here, to my home. To my heart." He spread his arms wider.

I shook my head. "I don't want to be touched."

"Eve, how can you say that!" God clasped his hands. "How can I not embrace you? You're so beautiful! You're made to embrace! *I* made you to be embraced!"

"You didn't ask *me* about it," I said. "And I don't like it."

"But you can't just say you don't like it! I created

you—you're mine!" God's voice lowered to a growl. His face turned red. "You call out to be held. It's your fault if men—even gods—want to hug you! It's because of you, because of your beauty!"

My beauty. There it was again. What *was* beauty? To *me*? A butterfly, a chestnut, the perfect body of a fly with its delicate transparent wings. To God? To Adam? To the Serpent? I raised my arm into the sunlight: this is my wrist, these are my fingers—are *they* beautiful? Could *this* be beauty?

"Eve," God said again. "Answer me!"

I turned to him. "*You* created me," I cried. "You just told me so. It was you who made me 'beautiful.' Don't blame it on *me*!"

God glowered. "I created you to be a certain kind of creature. *I* decided your role in the world. *I* decided what use to make of you!" He leaned over and shouted in my face, "If you refuse that role, you have no place, no place at all in the world." His hands were balled into fists. I expected him to hit me. I was buffeted once again—by a tornado? A blizzard? I forced myself to stare at him, to look without blinking into his eyes.

After a moment he turned away and began pacing up and down the terrace. Finally he sank onto the bench and took his head in his hands. "How has this happened?" he muttered. "This is not what I wanted." He looked at me. "Eve, I don't want to have these arguments with you. Why have you become like this? Adam, too, doesn't want to do things the way I'd planned." He rubbed his eyes and continued softly, as if he were speaking to himself. "Why do they turn on me? I *made* them. I merely wanted *something*, a distraction to while away the afternoons in the Garden. Some company. It tends to get rather dull at times, lovely but always the same."

God paused.

"What about the Serpent?" I asked. "The Serpent's very good company."

God looked surprised. "Why, of course the Serpent's good company. But we've known each other forever. Besides, I can't tell the Serpent what to do."

"Well, you have the animals. You can tell *them* what to do."

"Yes, but they do it too quickly. They're *too* obedient. And they can't talk." I was about to ask why God couldn't wave his hand and give the animals language, but he snapped out, "Oh, Eve, you haven't changed a bit after all! Stop this foolish chatter!"

God stood up, took a turn around the terrace, and returned to the bench. "I thought I'd create something to amuse me, like the fawns or the butterflies—only I'd be able to talk to them, and they would listen to my stories and laugh." He shifted in his seat as if the wood hurt his thighs. "I didn't want someone to fight with me and turn my words and efforts against me. All that planning of the world and the creatures in it, how they work, especially the humans—how they'd propagate. That was complicated. I spent a lot of time on it. How to get the seed safely to the female. I didn't want seed scattered all around, dozens of offspring—like the frogs or the fish or the dandelions. Just one or two. *I* conceived the instrument that fits so perfectly into the woman that those silly sperm can't help but find the egg. I planned it to be pleasurable, *very* exciting for both, the man *and* the woman." He caught sight of my face. "Well, it *should* be!"

God stayed a long time with his head in his hands. Tired of standing, I sat on a log and watched a long line of tiny brown ants march up and down across the sand. Coming toward me, the ants waved their feelers gaily in the air; going away, each carried a shred of bougainvillea, a minuscule banner. At the edge of the terrace the line disappeared into a hole. I supposed they were lining their nest, preparing a vibrant bridal bed for their queen.

At last God stirred and looked up. When he caught sight of me, he frowned. "Eve! Still here?" He waved his hand. "Go away! I have no use for you."

I remained on my log; the ants had stopped coming for flowers; there was only one line returning home, parading rather wearily beneath their cargo. I waited to see the last ant down its hole.

"Eve!" God said sharply. "Did you *hear* me?"

I stood and brushed the dust from my seat. "Yes, I did, God. I just wanted to make sure the ants get home. They're gone now. I'll go too." I started toward the path. I had been sitting on the bench where Adam and I had spent so many hours while God promenaded before us, teaching his prayers and commandments. On that same terrace God and the Serpent had danced. *Maybe this is the last time I'll come here,* I thought, engulfed suddenly in sadness. As I reached the trees, I turned back. "God," I said. "I don't want to fight with you. I do care a lot for you." I fought back tears. "Can't you find some other use for me?"

God raised his head. His face brightened.

"I can make things," I continued. "Bowls and cups— the Serpent says they're quite lovely. I weave shawls from lambs' wool and make linen towels. I can prepare food. We have delicious meals, and I come up with all sorts of stories."

"Will you sit by my side when you tell them to me? Will you embrace me when you leave?"

I stepped back. To sit by his side, his hand on my hair . . . his beard against my forehead—I shivered. "No, God. I can't. I can't anymore."

"Then go!" God raised his voice to a roar. "Go

before I—" He pounded his fist in his hand.

I wanted to race for the path, run to the Serpent, weep. I was furious and afraid. I wanted to shout back at him, "I hate you! I never want to see you again!" I caught a glimpse of feathers in the sky above God's head—had the Serpent sent the eagle to look out for me? I drew breath and said very quietly, "God, I'm sorry. You know where to find me if you want me."

"I shan't want you!" He pointed to the path. "Get out!"

But I could not take my eyes away. God had caught the last light of the sun. His body glowed red. His hair, crimson, flamed about him. Alpenglow. Godglow.

The sun set. Abruptly the color was gone. God stood, a pillar of white. I turned away.

"All right, God," I said. "Good-bye."

A Storm in the Garden

◖

HE RAIN STARTED before I reached the first turn in the path. Clouds rolled and roiled across the clear sky, and the Garden turned ominous. The branches with their quivering dancing sea green leaves were black and tore my legs as I ran through them. I could barely see the way. Thunder roared, drowning the racket of rain and the din of rushing water in the stream. Lightning flared and screamed in my eyes.

When I arrived at our clearing, the Serpent was skidding down the thatched roof of our hut, where it had added a layer of leaves and anchored them with rocks. "I gather your meeting didn't go well," it said.

"How did you guess?" I replied.

It rained for ten days. The river snarled and spun;

floods of water swept past, carrying branches, wheat stalks, clumps of upturned bushes with roots clawing the air. On the third day the river mounted its banks and devoured the ridge of earth that edged our terrace. Hastily we dragged the leaves and straw from the roof and hauled them up the rise. The bamboo poles were easy to remove: the baked earth we had set them in had turned to mud, and we shlurped them out with a great sucking noise. Our few belongings followed. But when we tried to rebuild the shelter, the poles would not stay in the muck, and gusts of wind tore the straw out of my hands. We finally settled for a lean-to of branches propped against the trunk of an oak, covered with as many leaves as we could bundle together.

"If this continues much longer," said the Serpent as we huddled under the half-built shelter, "we'll have to build an ark." I had no idea what an ark was, and I was too tired to ask.

On the eleventh morning we woke to sunshine, the singing of birds, and the drone of bees rushing to drink nectar from the drenched and opening flowers.

"The tantrum is over," stated the Serpent. "I wonder, what next?"

We set ourselves to clearing the terrace and rebuilding the hut. We placed it a little higher up the hill than before—"Just in case," the Serpent remarked.

When we had finished our lunch—a few sodden bananas we found under a fallen tree—we went to the pond to clean ourselves of mud and leaves. After a short swim the Serpent spiraled onto the bank and shook itself like a dog. Its body, having assumed the colors of the sky, flickered in various shades of blue. "Well, I'd better pay another visit to God," it said. "I must see Adam, too."

I curled the banana peel against my thumb. It wound twice around easily, but I could not stretch it to three. "What for?" I asked.

"I need to talk to him." The Serpent uncoiled its body and lay full length in the sun. "Oh, that feels so good." It opened its feathers, white today, and fanned them out to dry. "Eve," it said, raising its head to look at me, "what Adam did to you was dreadful, and unbelievably horrible for you. But it was also horrible for him."

I raised my eyebrows. "He seemed to enjoy it."

"Yes, for a few moments. But afterward, when he realized what he had done, how much he had hurt you, he must have been in anguish. Embarrassed and confused and lost. Adam's a good boy, basically kind and sweet; it's not in him to hurt anything or anybody."

The Serpent lowered its head and its voice turned hard. "God used him just as much as he used you." The Serpent's tail turned an ugly shade of orange mottled with brown and rapped the ground, sending speckles of muck over us both. "The boy comes in all hot and tired from running with the gazelle—such a beautiful way to spend a morning. God makes him do something unspeakable, something he's never imagined, and hurt you." The Serpent paused and looked at me. "Adam loves you, Eve. You must know that."

I nodded.

"And he enjoyed it; he'll remember that lust, even as he's tormented by the act. You may not be able to see it, Eve, but the experience was in a way nearly as horrifying to Adam as it was to you. No one has spoken to him about it—I doubt very much that God has mentioned it; he probably refused to talk about it. So Adam has no way of understanding what happened."

The Serpent sighed. "I should have gone to see him earlier. But I was so worried about you, so focused on getting you well. And so angry. It warped my judgment."

A breeze came up the valley, splattering me with raindrops from the leaves above, but I was too absorbed to move. How could the Serpent judge itself this way, even consider it had been at fault? *I* was always telling myself that I shouldn't have teased Adam or that it was wrong of me to hold the frog so long in my hands when it wanted to get away. But I thought this self-criticism was a quirk that would pass as I grew older and more perfect. And wiser, like the Serpent. The Serpent could never do wrong.

The Serpent lifted its body and raised its head high above the ground and said, "You know, Eve, I hold myself partially responsible for what happened. I didn't see it coming at all. I let God handle Adam's education without ever considering what he was doing. And I know God well. God is a magnificent and powerful being, a great, no, *the* Great Creator. But he should not raise a young person; he's too impatient, too hot-tempered. And always, the world has to revolve around *him*; he can't conceive of it any other way."

"Would you have brought us both up?" I asked.

"It would have been difficult to persuade God to let me have both of you." The Serpent looked at me as though it had just noticed me. "Eve, I shouldn't be talking to you this way. But you have to learn sometime that not only the young make mistakes; creatures with aeons of experience can do so too. I didn't pay enough attention to Adam. I didn't pay enough attention to what was happening to God, either, how he was getting more and more obsessed with whether his plans would actually work—and how." The Serpent began moving toward the path. "I'll be back for supper, Eve. Have you checked on your bowl?"

I bounded to my feet and pushed my hands through my hair. "Oh!" I cried. I had completely forgotten about the bowl I had placed so carefully on its mound in the sun many days before.

The little hillock was still there, planted firmly on the ridge. Miniature ravines had eroded its sides, so it looked like a tiny mesa. The top was still broad and sloped toward the center like a dish. But there was no sign of the bowl at all. I poked my finger into the earth and found tiny particles of reddish dust, but nothing more.

The Serpent returned late that afternoon. I was perched on the bank, washing beet greens for supper, and it coiled itself by my side. It looked pleased. "Well, God is somewhat placated. We had a long talk. He still has not understood the horror he and Adam inflicted on you; he kept saying it was just in fun. I'm not sure he'll ever understand. But he *is* worried about the future of mankind, and I reinforced that worry." The Serpent grinned. "He *has* decided to forgive you for being so unfriendly—as he sees it—the other day. I told him he was lucky you agreed to see him at all. That did cause him some anxiety!" The Serpent shook its head. "Eve, I'm beginning to take positive delight in upsetting God. It's very bad of me! And I certainly shouldn't tell you about it."

"Well, if God behaves badly, why shouldn't you upset him? Why should he live by different rules and be able to do anything he wants?"

The Serpent looked at me sadly. "Because he's God," it replied.

It was not until we had finished supper and were lying on the terrace waiting for the stars to come out that I asked what I most wanted to know. "Did you see Adam?"

"I did. He's changed—more thoughtful, quieter. God actually complained about it."

"Are you going to see him again?"

"Yes, tomorrow and regularly from now on. I told him I'd take him exploring. In spite of all his running around, there are lots of areas he's never been."

I sat up brusquely. "You're not going to take him outside the Garden, are you?"

The Serpent laughed. "Eve, I didn't take *you* outside the Garden. You took *me*. And what I do with Adam is totally different from what I do with you. The things we talk about, how we communicate. You and Adam are very different people."

I loosened my hair and drew it over my face. "Will they come here?" I asked. I had seen God and he no longer frightened me, but I still dreaded seeing Adam. I remembered him as I had last seen him in the meadow, on his back with his arm flopped across his chest. I shivered; the breeze from the pond felt cold.

The Serpent shook its head. "Sooner or later God will come by, as he did before, but Adam will stay away for now. He's not looking forward to a meeting any more than you are. After he's spent some time with me, and you've settled down from our voyages, it will be easier for both of you." The Serpent waved its ears and smiled. "You can relax, Eve."

I picked up a twig and drew a circle in the sand. "Thank you, Serpent," I said softly. I placed a white stone in the middle of the circle and surrounded it with squiggly lines. "I'm glad."

"You've been busy today too," the Serpent said, raising its head and stretching before taking a tour around the yard. I had spent most of the day picking up branches and debris brought down by the flood and had finished by sweeping the entire terrace. The earth was raked into complex lines: sworls and angles, and an occasional series of spirals that looked like waves breaking on the sea. The Serpent's body made sinuous trails through the design as it passed.

"Eve, my dear, how nicely you've done this. It's lovely. You *are* an artist." Finished with its tour, the

Serpent coiled carefully next to me. "But I haven't asked about your bowl."

"It's gone," I said.

The Serpent looked sad. "I'm sorry, Eve. It was very beautiful."

The Plant

AGAIN THE SERPENT and I fell into a routine. We rose shortly before the sun and ran to the east, watching the sky turn from night to day until the whole world was bright and glowing. After we had eaten, the Serpent left for its explorations with Adam. "We went to the ravine behind the falls," or "We found a new stand of blueberry bushes," it reported at lunch. But it would tell me nothing more about what Adam was saying or thinking. If I asked, the Serpent replied simply, "That belongs to Adam and me." While I would have dearly loved to learn more, it was reassuring to know that the Serpent kept Adam's confidences so well.

I enjoyed my mornings alone. I swept increasingly intricate designs in the gravel of the terrace, then squat-

ted on my heels to admire my work. The order and sym-
metry appealed to me. Sometimes, turning my back to
the yard, I would take shiny stones or nuts, or those hard
red berries that grew in the brambles, and fling them
over my shoulder to see whether this made the design
more pleasing or simply turned order into chaos.

I gathered wool from the sheep and goats and llama,
dyed the strands, and wove them into blankets patterned
after the Serpent's coat. Or I collected soft gray clay
from the stream, patted it into balls, or pounded it flat
into a tray. I attempted to make all kinds of objects: cups
and vases and pitchers to hold water or milk or the juice
I squeezed from the berries, little animals and birds,
even low tables. I did not try to replicate my bowl; I
could hardly bear to think of it and was certain I would
never be able to create anything so perfect again.

Every time I put the clay objects on the knoll, I
glanced at the mound where I had left my bowl. One
morning I caught a hint of green. A minute stem was
bent back on itself with its head still in the ground: a
seedling trying to break free. The following day it had
succeeded. It stood half as tall as a dandelion with two
tiny leaves sticking out from the end of its short stalk.
From then on I spoke to it every time I passed:
"Welcome, little friend. Who are you? And where are
you from?" and touched it tenderly with the soft cup of

my little finger. It felt like the moss on the riverbank. Like water. Like the Serpent's tongue. "How big are you going to be? Will you grow to my knee? To my ears? Will you give me shade someday? Blossoms or nuts? Fruit?" The next day it was twice as tall.

One afternoon as I came up the path carrying my pots, I found God in the clearing. Hands clasped behind his back, he was glaring down at my little plant as if he was outraged to find it there. I'd seen him once or twice since our encounter, but always with the Serpent by my side and, though he seemed to have forgotten his anger, I was reluctant to meet him alone. Before I could turn to escape he spotted me. "Eve! What on Earth is this abomination? I've never seen anything like it before! Where did it come from?"

"It just started growing there," I said. "I found it a few days ago, when I came to set my pots out to dry."

"Oh, yes, I saw your pots. Quite pretty, some of them," he muttered absently. "But *this*! It's frightful!"

"Oh, I think it's nice," I said. "It certainly isn't doing any harm. If it's a flower it will be pretty here in the middle of this empty space, and if it grows into a tree, we'll have some shade. Maybe even some fruit."

"No, no, no!" cried God. "Impossible! Eve, you don't understand, *I* created everything on this Earth. I *know* what I made. I never made anything like this! How did it get here? And what *can* it be?"

I was quite interested in that question myself. Indeed, what *could* it be? And where had it come from? Something niggled in the back of my mind: the plant was growing exactly where I had set my bowl. But it seemed far-fetched. My bowl was made of clay, and clay does not sprout.

"Perhaps it developed by itself, out of something you created, or out of two or three things you made that joined together and became something new?"

God frowned. "Impossible," he said, "Absolutely impossible! Eve, come here." He motioned me to follow him farther up the rise. "Look over there." He pointed across the valley. "Do you see that big cedar on the hill?"

I nodded.

"Well, *I* made that tree. And all the other trees, of course."

"They're beautiful. I love trees."

God looked satisfied. "Do you see the top of that cedar?"

"Yes."

"The very top? I could take that top and lop it off and plop it into the ground anywhere, and it would grow into a tree every bit as big, and bigger, than that one."

I believed him, but I thought the cedar was beautiful just as it was and would look stunted without its crown.

"I can wither any tree. Wither it to the ground. Make it the smallest of the small. See that oak? The one that towers over all the rest?" I knew the oak well. It was the biggest tree in the Garden; I had climbed in its branches and swung on the ends of its boughs.

"I can destroy it whenever I choose. Watch." God raised his arm and pointed his long index finger at the oak. Its top quivered; the leaves curled and turned brown. Some began to fall. The entire tree shriveled before my eyes; it seemed to be sinking into the ground as if some spirit it had inside—that thing that made it not only a tree but this particular one-and-only tree—were seeping away from every crevice in the bark.

"No!" I cried. "God, *no!*"

God laughed. "You see what I can do?"

"But God, you made that tree so well. It's one of the most perfect you've ever created. Why would you ever destroy it!" I turned and looked at him. "Do you have the power to make it whole again?"

"Of course I do, Eve. What do you think?" Once more he raised his hand, palm up, and wiggled his fingers, as if he were calling chickadees to come in to feed. The tree shook itself and straightened and stood as tall and full as before.

"So you've seen what I can do," said God. "I used to do that sort of thing all the time when I was creating the

263

world, but I don't often have the chance anymore."

He turned and walked down the hill to the plant standing in the midst of my little garden of drying pots. "Now that we've settled that, we need to settle *this* upstart." He frowned and shook his head. "I have no idea where it came from. But we'll get rid of it. I'll just yank it out."

He leaned over and grabbed the leaves, but jumped quickly back and put his hand to his mouth.

"Ow!" he cried. "Look what it did to me!" Several short, deep cuts ran straight across his palm. "Evil thing! Well, that settles it!" He raised his great foot in the sandal Adam had made for him and brought it down on the plant, crushing it into the ground. I could see one leaf stretch out from under the sandal and try to reach his heel before it disappeared. God ground his foot into the soil again and again until nothing was left, only black earth pounded hard. "So that is that," said God, and went off sucking his hand.

I hated to see anything, plant or creature, hurt. If I snapped a twig or bruised a flower as I rushed down a path, it saddened me. But when God hugged his bloody hand, my heart swelled with joy. I could think only of the plant he had destroyed.

That evening I reported the story to the Serpent.

Though I usually told it everything that happened to me, I had said nothing about the plant. It was *my* secret, *my* surprise, *my* plant, and I had not wanted to talk about it, even to the Serpent.

The Serpent was captivated by God's reaction to the tiny shoot and asked me to describe every detail of the plant and of God's behavior.

"You say it was growing exactly where you left your pot?"

"In the same place, on a mound that's always been there. I had hollowed out the top to hold the bowl so it wouldn't get knocked down by an animal or blown away by the wind. I wanted a place that would get really hot—you know how the heat builds up in a hollow?—so it would bake well."

The Serpent nodded. "Then it was definitely there." For a few moments it said nothing. The four petals of its velvet tongue swept over its face, reminding me of the leaves on the plant, leaves soft as moss that had turned viciously sharp at God's attack.

"What sort of clay did you use to make the bowl?"

"The clay and sand I brought back from our journeys—you saw me mixing them." I stopped and drew in my breath sharply. "But there were other things in that soil. Remember the white bead I found on the volcano? And a few seeds. Do you think the plant could have grown from something I brought back from one of our journeys?"

"Or from all of them. You told God it could be a new kind of plant that had developed from some of his creations. That's not a bad guess." We sat in silence for some time as the possibilities of such an idea opened before us.

"So even though God says he created everything," I ventured hesitantly, "that there's nothing on Earth that was not made by him, and he knows every detail of each creation—even so . . . he's wrong."

"He's mistaken. He can't conceive that things he created could take on a life of their own. But we've seen that they do. You're certainly not what God had in mind when he set out to make a woman: you've taken on a life of your own. Even Adam, who at first seemed so docile, is not what God expected. Or intended."

I jumped to my feet. "And the tornado, the blizzard, the storm in the sea. All those things got away from God. So why shouldn't it happen with animals, and plants, and trees?"

"Perhaps," said the Serpent.

"Oh, Serpent, who knows what the plant might have become? And now it's gone and we'll never know."

"I wouldn't write it off so easily. Remember how it attacked God!"

"But how could it hurt God?" The idea had just come to me. "You told me God doesn't feel pain."

The Serpent nodded. "It *is* surprising," it said. "I think this plant must have some power of its own." It chuckled. "I shouldn't laugh, but your description of God going off with his hand in his mouth *is* funny. And he deserved it: God should *make* life, not destroy it."

Over the next few days, I ran into God two or three times. Each time he appeared he went directly to the mound and kicked at the earth where the plant had been. After a week or so he stopped coming. I suppose he had decided that the plant was truly dead, so the trip was no longer worth it.

A New Kind of Life

I CONTINUED TAKING my pots to the clearing to bake in the sun. One afternoon, after setting out the day's work, I examined the mound. God had nearly flattened it with his stamping feet. I thought of the plant shoving through the hard earth with such determination. Most trees in the Garden sprouted through soft, crumbly soil that parted easily at the slightest pressure. I picked up a long, flat stone with a sharp edge and began to dig. It was impossible; the ground had been pounded as solid as granite. Across the valley, the oak stood stoutly beautiful in the evening light. I remembered it in all its glory, wilting suddenly, leaves curled and brown, beneath God's raised finger. I looked at the cedar he would have beheaded merely to show off his power to me.

In a sudden fury I sought out a stone I knew to be especially hard and used it to pound the edges of my digging tool until they began to chip away. The sweat ran down my body; my hair was as wet as if I had swum in the sea. I battered the rock with all the will and strength in my body. When it was sharpened on both sides and pointed at the end, I used it to till the earth made virtually impenetrable by God's pride.

Little by little I was able, with this tool, to roughen the surface of the ground. First I dug the depth of a fingernail, then of my thumb. As I went deeper it became easier; the earth was softer and felt damp. I didn't know what I was searching for. It was clear to me that the plant was not there; nothing could survive such a pounding. Finally, I stopped. God was right. The plant was dead.

"If I were you," said a voice over my shoulder, "I'd cover up any signs of digging."

I jumped and fell backward with my seat in the dirt. "Oh, Serpent! Don't come creeping up on me that way. You scared me!" I scrambled to my feet and dusted off my rear.

"What are you looking for?"

"You know perfectly well what I'm looking for," I said crossly. "And you might at least apologize!"

The Serpent nodded its head. "Of course I should,"

it said, "though I think I've hurt your dignity more than your behind. Plus I've given you a lesson you won't forget. It's the easiest thing imaginable for someone to come up unnoticed when you're totally absorbed in something. And I'm not the only one in the Garden."

"God hasn't come for a while," I said. "I think he's lost interest."

"Perhaps. But it's just possible he may decide to check again to be sure."

"I'll tell him I want to plant flowers in the mound. Geraniums. Those deep purple double geraniums."

The Serpent raised its brows. "Eve, I've never known you to lie, and I don't think you'd be good at it."

"I'd lie for the plant."

"To God?"

"Of course. *Only* to God. God almost *makes* you lie to him, he gets so angry. I'd never lie to you." To this, the Serpent said nothing.

"Anyway," I continued, "God's right. There's nothing there. It's gone. He destroyed it."

"Well, that may be. But I'd smooth out that earth you've dug up so nicely and maybe put a jar there and strew some hay around so it looks as if you've decided to use it for a drying mound again."

Fortunately I took the Serpent's advice; two days later God appeared on the ridge. He paused to examine the little figure I had set on the mound: a clay rabbit standing on its hind legs, ears raised, a carrot in its paws.

"That girl is clever," he muttered as he walked off.

Always, throughout the Garden, there was an aura of calm and peace; but as the weeks went by the ridge seemed to take on an even greater depth of beauty and perfection. Every day at dusk I would take my tools and work on the mound. To the digging tool I had added a rake: a very old piece of wood with gnarled, hooked branches like the claw of some immense petrified giant, sharpened until I had an effective implement to turn the earth. I pulled it back and forth across the surface—with care, in case a plant was trying to find its way into the sunlight. If it had not rained, I carried water from a nearby spring. But I turned up only pebbles. There was no sign of any living thing.

Usually in the Garden it rained only at night, a drizzle barely heavier than dew, so soft you could hardly hear it fall. But two or three times a year we had a few days of steady rain that drenched the ground and brought enough water to last the animals and plants for several months. So it was, very early one morning, I heard it begin, the drops pattering on the thatch that covered the roof of the hut. I curled myself into a ball under my quilt and went back to sleep. I loved the long rains and savored the lazy days ahead.

The Serpent and I had rebuilt the hut after the storm even better than before, enclosing it on the fourth side, with wide doors opening onto the terrace, and we were perfectly warm and dry inside. We played games with pebbles, or sketched designs of houses and boats on the dirt floor. I listened to the rain and the silence that lay beneath it and wondered, *Why don't birds sing when it rains?* We made up poems and songs and chants, and told stories, each trying to outdo the other. "Once upon a time . . ." began the Serpent.

"What does that mean, 'once upon a time'?" I inquired. "God used to say it, and I always wanted to ask."

"It means long ago, once and forever: this tale could have happened anywhere, any time." The Serpent settled more comfortably on a quilt, as if the story would last all day. "Once upon a time," it continued, "before there was rain on Earth—"

"There was always rain on Earth!" I cried indignantly.

"Not on *my* Earth. This is *my* story, and I can make it any way I please. Before there was rain on Earth, the birds sang all the time, day and night. But it was dry, and the plants did not grow very fast, and there was not enough for the animals to eat. So all the creatures came together and cried out to the birds: 'Birds, birds, we need you! All the Earth is dry. We must go to God and ask him to give us water. But *we* can only growl and bark and whinny—'

"'If we let the donkeys bray,' interrupted the hyena, 'God will run away with his hands over his ears.'

"The donkeys looked sad, and the elephant whispered to them: 'You have lovely voices, my dears. They're just too loud for most of these creatures. Look at them! Only a few of us have proper auricles'—the elephants waved their great ears and the breeze they created blew the ants into a heap—'and we *certainly* appreciate your song!'

"'Please, birds,' continued the animals, 'go to God with your sweet voices and ask him to give us rain.'

"So the birds went to God and sang and trilled their plea, and God smiled and said, 'Of course I'll give you rain. It was in the original plan; I don't know how it got left out.' And so it rained, not all the time but just enough for the flowers to bloom and the grass to grow and the trees to bring forth their fruit. And all the animals were happy.

"The birds were happy too; they loved the leaves and flowers and all the good things to eat. The only problem was, they could not sing in the rain, for when they opened their beaks, the water flowed down their throats and made them sneeze."

"Sneeze?" I said. "It would make them cough, not sneeze!"

"Sneeze," said the Serpent firmly. "So they went back to God and warbled: 'God, we love the rain and thank you kindly. But when it rains, we cannot sing!'

"God looked at them and said, 'You asked for rain, and I gave it to you. You have done a good deed for the Earth and all the animals. Everyone has profited from your act; only you have lost something—the ability to sing in the rain.'

"The birds nodded sadly.

"'Well, I'm sorry,' said God. 'I liked hearing you sing all the time. But this is a lesson to you. Never expect a reward for a kind deed.'

"So the birds went home chastened, and to this day birds do not sing in the rain."

"What an awful lesson," I said.

"Well, it's not always true; quite often you *are* rewarded for doing something nice. It just means you shouldn't count on it or be upset if it doesn't happen."

"It was a good story until the end," I said.

"Tomorrow it's your turn to tell a story." The Serpent began setting up the stones for a game of checkers. "I look forward to hearing it."

The following day I began: "Once upon a time, the stars grew tired of standing from dusk to dawn in the sky. They saw the planets zooming around, and they thought that looked like much more fun. So the stars ran off to play together, and the night sky was transformed. All the sky was black, except for a crowd of lights dancing at the far end of the heavens, where you could hardly see them. And it got worse."

The Serpent raised its ears. "Worse?" it said.

"Worse," I repeated. "The moon was lonely without the stars. One day, when the sun was shining brightly and no one would notice, the moon ran off and hid behind the volcano."

"A murky situation," the Serpent observed.

"The sun decided it had to do something," I continued. "It went to the moon and said, 'The animals that come alive in the night cannot see to go about their ways. They stay huddled in their holes and do not eat. Dear Moon, please rise and cast your silver light across the Earth again.'

"But the moon said, 'Why should I shine all alone in the sky? Speak to the stars.'

"So the sun went to the stars and said, 'The moon refuses to shine because you are not there. The night is tenebrous—'"

"Wherever did you learn that word?" the Serpent interrupted, tapping its tail in appreciation.

"From God; he used it in a story. It's a lovely word,

isn't it?" I continued with the tale. "But the stars replied: 'We're tired of standing still all through the night, while the moon and the planets are enjoying themselves, stretching their legs.'"

The Serpent raised its brows. "I don't believe stars and planets have legs," it said.

"*My* moon does; *my* planets do. It's my story," I retorted.

The Serpent laughed. "You're right. Go on."

"Well, the sun went off into the desert and thought about the problem, and for a whole day the Earth had neither moon nor stars nor sun. Nothing dared to move, even the wind; there was not a rustle in the trees. The creatures huddled in their holes and dens and nests and wept, believing they would live forever in the dark. But on the second morning, the sun went round to the back of the Earth where the stars spend the day and called them all together, and said, 'The Earth and all its creatures are in despair because the night is dark.'

"'The day, too!' snapped the stars. 'You're not shining either, and you're much more crucial than we are.'

"'Not at all,' replied the sun. 'You are every bit as important as I am. When you do not rise, half of all Time is dark.'

"Though the stars muttered among themselves, they

pressed eagerly around the sun. The first few days of freedom had been fun, but they were beginning to get bored with too much playing. 'What do you suggest?' they asked.

"The sun said, 'Each of you must fetch a shell, the biggest one you can find, from the ocean shore. Today, and once a month hereafter, I will meet you in the far North, and I will shine on that shell so that it will hold its light for many days. And any time you want to go off to play, you will hang the shell in the sky, and no one will know the difference.'

"The stars were delighted with this solution. They hopped up and down and clapped their hands and ran off to the beach to find shells. And from that day on, when you look at the night sky, you never know whether it is truly a star up there, or a shell from the sea reflecting the light of the sun. Though when you see a star twinkle, you can be sure it's a shell."

The Serpent pounded its tail on the floor. "Bravo!" it cried. "That's a great tale. It deserves a permanent place among the myths. You're a storyteller as well as an artist."

As always, I was happy with the Serpent's approval. But even without its praise, I knew my story was good.

For four days the rain fell. Then, as always, came the miraculous morning when everything glowed and all the world seemed new. Birds ruffled the rain from their feathers, plumped themselves, and sang. The air smelled of hay and lilac and climbing roses and the raw, rough scent of a roebuck rubbing its wet hide on a tree.

Though I woke early that day, the Serpent had already left. I bathed, catching my breath in water made cold by days of rain, and ran into the rising sun and back, legs stretched long and supple, back and buttocks taut, arms pumping; I felt invincible. As I neared the glade at the top of the ridge, I stopped. The path, usually bright with sunlight, had a greenish tinge, and the bit of meadow I could see was dappled. Slowly I approached.

In the center of the clearing stood a tree. A bit taller than I, it had many spreading branches covered in bright green leaves. It was a young tree, the bark was smooth and gray, and it was still growing. Before my eyes, the limbs swelled and lengthened, spawned smaller branches, buds formed and expanded into leaves. The main shoot rushed upward; limbs sprouted, leaves unfolded, bark cracked under the pressure of the widening trunk. In moments the tree had grown to nearly three times my height. Then it stopped, quivered, was still, quivered again, and stood motionless in the glade as though it had been there forever.

Sinking to the ground at its feet, I stroked it lightly,

feeling beneath my fingers that wonderful half-smooth, half-rough texture of a young tree, and the velvet of a leaf. I flung my arms around the trunk, my fingertips barely touching on the other side. The tree exuded a sweet-acid smell. Its leaves were soft as moss.

God, I thought, w*hat will he say when he sees this tree? He'll destroy it again!* But the full-grown tree no longer looked easy to destroy.

I tumbled down the hill to find the Serpent returning from its morning with Adam.

"Eve, where have you been?" the Serpent asked, seeing the terrace still covered with the leaves and twigs brought down by the rain.

"Serpent, come with me," I shouted, and caught it around the neck. It looked at me amazed; we rarely touched each other—only on chilly nights when it curled around me to keep me warm. I had certainly never grabbed it before. "Oh, come right away; you *have* to see this! You'll never believe it!" I ran back up the ridge. The Serpent followed without a word, as though it already knew what it would find.

We stopped at the edge of the clearing and looked at the tree. It had not grown any larger, but it seemed even more settled in its place. Broad and spreading rather than tall, it was a hospitable tree, a good tree for climbing. I heard the Serpent draw its breath sharply.

"So," it murmured. "It has come."

"What has come? The tree?"

"The tree, of course. And the time."

I was barely listening. "Isn't it amazing? Have you ever seen anything like it before?"

The Serpent wagged its head back and forth. "Of course I have," it said calmly, "and so have you."

"I have not!" I exclaimed indignantly.

"Eve, look at it. Forget how quickly it grew. It's an apple tree."

"It's *not*!" But when I went close to it again, I could see that it was indeed an apple tree. "Though it *does* have a different look about it. It's not an ordinary apple tree; the leaves are a different green; the bark is amazing. And the leaves: they have such a velvety feel to them."

"You're right," said the Serpent. "It's not a regular apple tree. It's a very special one."

"Did it grow from my bowl?"

"Yes, I think it did."

"All that traveling, all that work. Just to get an ordinary apple tree!"

The Serpent laughed. "You said yourself it's not an ordinary apple tree."

All through lunch the Serpent seemed preoccupied.

"What is it, Serpent? Are you worried about something?"

"Just thinking, Eve." The Serpent waggled its tail on the ground, making odd, irregular crescents in the unraked sand.

"Did you know the tree was going to grow?" I asked.

"I thought it would someday, but I had no idea when."

"When you saw the plant growing, did you know it was that tree, the one you were waiting for?"

"I wasn't *waiting* for it; I thought it might appear someday. And yes, I suspected it might be."

"And when God destroyed it, did you know it would grow back?"

The Serpent shook its head heavily, as if it had taken on weight during the day. "Eve, so many questions. I wasn't certain, but I wasn't surprised."

"Are you *happy* to see it?"

"Happy? No, not really."

"Why?"

"Are *you* happy to see it, Eve?"

I had felt such joy on seeing it that I could not imagine the Serpent feeling otherwise.

"Yes," I said. "When I saw it, I could hardly breathe. But I have no idea why." I plucked some grasses from the side of the terrace and began plaiting them into a rope. I was thinking back over the things the Serpent had said since seeing the tree. "You said it was *time*?

What did you mean?"

"It's time. For change. For a new kind of life. I also meant, we're running out of time. I have to remind myself: it's time to act, there are things that must be done. . . ." The Serpent seemed almost to be talking to itself.

"What things? What change?"

The Serpent sighed. "First we had better decide how to deal with God when he discovers the tree has reappeared, fully grown."

A Plain Old Apple Tree

WE NEVER HAD A chance to discuss that question. As we finished our meal, God strolled up the path, hands behind his back, whistling. For once he seemed relaxed and cheerful. "I'm glad to find you here," he said. "We've been staying in our own corners, haven't we? It's good to have company from time to time."

"God, welcome," said the Serpent, uncoiling itself and waving its ears with its usual courtesy. "Please, sit there on the bench. Eve has added some down cushions. You'll find them quite comfortable."

"Yes, you're a clever girl, Eve. I've seen your little models. The rabbit was amusing." God sat back on the bench and stretched his legs in front of him.

On the excuse of needing water, I scooped up a jug and ran to the stream. God had come too soon. What could I say to keep him away from the ridge? He would surely go home that way. And if he found the tree? Water sloshed over my legs; I was trembling. I wanted desperately to talk to the Serpent, but the Serpent was talking to God. Maybe the Serpent would tell him about the tree. But God would still turn on me; he knew I went to the ridge regularly. And after all, it *was* I who had encouraged the tree to grow.

When I returned to the hut, carrying the jug, God and the Serpent were eating figs.

"Eve, I've asked Adam to join us. I hope you don't mind." God glanced at me, as if my minding or not made little difference. "He's rather at a loss right now."

Before I could answer—I did not trust my voice—the Serpent spoke. "God, you didn't tell me Adam was coming, or ask me if it was all right. You gave me your word that Adam would not come here until I invited him."

God looked discomfited, but he waved his hand as if to brush the remark aside. "That was ages ago, nearly a moon. I thought it was fine for him to come now. You can't humor Eve's whims forever."

"Eve does not have whims, and it's not a question of whims at all. It's a question of your word and mine: a promise made will not be broken." The Serpent nodded curtly toward the path. Its feathered ears were black and lay flattened against its body. "God, you must leave immediately. Find Adam and tell him he is not to come."

Reluctantly God stood up. I expected him to shout at the Serpent, but he did not. *He's afraid of the Serpent!* The thought flashed through my mind and took my breath away.

"Serpent, you're right," God said at last. "I should have checked with you." He glanced at me. "But it's been a long time. Perhaps Eve wants to see him."

In the first weeks after the rape, I could not imagine ever being with Adam again. The idea of coming around a bend and finding him in the middle of the path made me breathless and sick. Then, as time and the Serpent wrought their healing, I came to accept the fact that someday I would see him again. But he was supplanted by the volcano and the desert, rattlesnakes on the rock, boiling torrents miles below my dangling feet, mountains of water, mountains of snow. Our meeting was far in the future and did not loom very large in my life. I had dealt with lava and blizzard and ocean; I had dealt with God. When the time came, I would manage to make *my* peace—I did not care about his—with Adam. In my wanderings about the Garden, if I saw a herd of bison, or spotted an odd cloud in the sky, I almost missed him.

But see him now? *I'm not ready!* I wanted to cry. *Not*

today! Not with God and the Serpent here, hanging on every word—as if the future of the Earth depended on it!

Again, the choice was gone. While God and the Serpent waited for my reply, Adam appeared.

He always had a flair for dramatic entrances—there was a rising or setting sun behind him, or a bit of leftover rainbow crowning his head. Suddenly he was standing in front of me: I had no time to worry about how to behave.

"I'm sorry," he said. "Eve, I'm *so* sorry." His voice broke; he lowered his head and a lock of hair fell over his forehead. I felt my hand reach forward to push the hair out of his eyes, but pulled it back. I could not touch him.

I shrugged. "It's done," I said. "It's over."

Neither God nor the Serpent seemed to be paying the slightest attention to us. God had sat down again, and they were talking about this year's wine, how the Serpent always managed to find the earliest grapes, and whether wine that had been kept in clay jugs was better than that aged in wood.

"Eve," the Serpent called just as I was wondering what next to say to Adam, "bring us some of the wine from the clay pitcher, and some from the oak bowl. And cups for all four of us."

Turning back to God, the Serpent said, "Now we can compare them." God licked his lips and rubbed his hands together.

I brought biscuits and cheese, and olives and figs, ripe and warm from the sun. We sat around the table and ate and drank. God and the Serpent discussed the wine. "The oak is definitely better," God proclaimed.

The Serpent took another sip and nodded gravely. "I think you're right."

God raised the bowl to his nose. "And the bouquet is exquisite. Eve, how did you make the cheese?" he asked. "It's excellent."

"It *is* good," echoed Adam.

"It's goat cheese," I said, "from the goats on the highest hills. It's cooler than anywhere else in the Garden, and there's a kind of clover that grows only in those meadows. It gives the milk a special taste, a little tart but with a touch of sweetness, too."

God wiped his lips on the back of his hand and said, "That was *perfect*, Eve. And your cups and bowls are lovely. Adam, see how clever she is!" Adam turned the cup in his hand; the handle had the form of a squirrel, its tail raised inquisitively, which made him laugh.

"How do you make them?" he inquired.

"I find the red clay on the bank of the river, a bit upstream. Or there's gray clay out by the swamp, you know where the crocodiles live? I shape the cups or whatever I'm making on the flat boulder by the pond, because I can reach the water easily. Then I set them in the sun to dry, but I bring them in every night in case it rains. It takes four or five days for them to bake hard."

"Do you still put them on the ridge?" God asked me, then turned to Adam. "Eve has a ridge where she puts her creations. It's very amusing. A garden of little jars and cups and bowls and occasionally an animal. Last time I was there, she'd made a rabbit eating a carrot! Very well done! We'll go back that way." He glanced at me. "What do you have out there now?"

The Serpent lifted its head.

"I don't use that ridge anymore," I said.

"Whyever not?" asked God. "There's nowhere else nearby that's so exposed to the sun."

"Well, actually," I said, "there's not much sun there now."

God looked surprised. "Oh?"

"There's a tree."

God stared at me, openmouthed. "A tree? Did you plant a tree?"

"No. It grew."

"*Grew?* When?"

"Sometime during the rains," I said.

The blood rose in God's face. "Did it grow where that dreadful plant was?"

I nodded.

God sprang to his feet. I had forgotten how tall he was, how much space he filled with his great body, and his hair and his beard and his muscled arms raised in the air.

"But I *destroyed* it! I destroyed it!" He stamped his foot. "I ground every leaf, every tendril into dust. It *can't* have grown!"

"Perhaps it's not the same plant," I said, though I was fairly sure it was. "It's just growing in the same place."

In two steps God crossed the terrace and shook his fist under my nose. Adam half rose from the bench.

"Why didn't you tell me?" God cried. He turned to the Serpent. "Someone should have told me!"

"Sit down, God," the Serpent said quietly, narrowing its eyes. "We only found the plant this morning."

God lowered his fist and took several deep breaths; then he thumped back onto the bench. Adam looked relieved and sank into his seat.

I stood and looked full at God. "I thought you knew about the tree. You told me you know *everything* that happens in the Garden." Adam stared at me as if I had turned into a different being.

God coughed and glared at his feet. "Well," he said. "Of course I do . . . I must have forgotten about it."

"I thought *you* had put the tree there," I said. "Especially since it grew so fast."

The Serpent lowered its head to the ground.

"*Grew* so fast?" God cried, breathless. "*How* fast?"

"In four days."

"*Four days?* Are you *sure?*"

"Yes, I took my pots inside the evening before the rain started, and there was no tree, just the bare ridge. Then I went back this morning, the first sunny day, and there it was. Quite big, but still growing. Bursting branches out in all directions, popping its leaves open like mad."

God leaned forward. "*Then* what happened?" he said.

"It stopped."

"Stopped?"

"Stopped growing. One minute it was shooting up, and the next it stopped. Like that! It quivered."

"Quivered?"

"Shook itself all over. Then it was quiet, quivered again, and was still. It looks as if it has been there forever. But I'm not telling you anything you don't already know."

God looked uncomfortable. "Well, not the details," he said. "I haven't watched anything grow for ages. I just conceive it." He traced a circle on the ground with the toe of his sandal. "What kind of tree is it?"

"An apple tree," I said. "A plain old apple tree."

I stood and began to rake the terrace, round and round. God and Adam and the Serpent watched me as if the patterns taking shape under my rake would transform the world.

At last God stirred. He stood up, sighing, and began walking home the same way he had come, by the river path, looking dispirited. "I'll see the tree another day," he muttered. Adam started after him but came running back.

"Thank you, Eve. And you too, Serpent. Everything was delicious." He took my hands in his. "Eve, is it all right if I come again?"

I pulled my hands away, but I nodded.

"Of course it's all right!" God shouted impatiently. "You can see her tomorrow. Adam, hurry up!"

Adam blushed. "Are *you* sure it's all right with you?" he whispered. Again I nodded, and he turned and ran after God.

The Serpent raised itself on its tail and peered into my face. "Are you all right, Eve?"

"I think so." Now that God and Adam had gone, I was close to tears.

"It isn't easy, my dear. I know that." The Serpent curled itself at my side. "It's been a rough day today."

Today. Today had gone on forever. The tree, God,

Adam. Suddenly I needed to talk, and the words poured out. "It wasn't nearly as hard to see Adam as I expected," I began. "I was touched when he came up to me straightaway and said he was sorry. I never expected that. And he looked so woebegone, I felt sorry for him." I rubbed at a blot of earth on my thumb. "I dreaded seeing him; I'm glad it's over. I think we can be friends again." I thought of Adam's hands holding mine and shook my head. "But that's all."

"Fine," said the Serpent.

"I'm surprised God wasn't more upset by the tree," I said. I couldn't think of Adam anymore. In my mind I went over God's words and movements and the expressions that had passed across his face. "I was sure he'd have a tantrum, and we'd get another storm. Do you think he knows it's the same plant?"

"I believe he does."

"Did he expect it to grow again?" I asked.

"I think he suspected it might."

"Did he *create* it?"

The Serpent hesitated before it spoke. "He created other plants, and that tree grew from them, as you suggested. He may have known such a tree was possible but hoped it would never grow."

"And now it has," I said softly.

"It took courage to tell God about the tree," said the Serpent.

"I didn't have a choice. He said he was going home that way. There was no way I could lie."

"But you *did* lie to him."

"I *don't* lie!" I cried indignantly.

"Don't you?" The Serpent turned to look at me. "You told God you thought he knew everything that happens on Earth."

I hesitated. "It wasn't really a lie."

"Do you believe that?"

"Not anymore." I sighed.

"Do you believe that God knew about the tree? That he had planned it?"

I pulled at the stalk of a wild onion. "No."

The Serpent lowered its head to the ground. "Well, Eve, that is lying—as much as if you had told God you'd never seen the tree."

"It's different."

"It's a little different, but it's still saying something that isn't true."

"But—" I started.

"You were manipulating God, telling him things you don't believe, things you know are not true—to get him to behave as you wanted."

"But you do that too. So does Adam!"

"Do *what*?" The Serpent raised its brows.

"Manipulate him. You give him wine and get him talking about grapes and figs and other nice things when he gets angry." I could feel my temper rising; blood flowed to my cheeks. "The first day I met God, and he got mad because I interrupted him, you implied that you couldn't whistle the way he did. And then you did, on the volcano, when you whistled up the wind!"

The Serpent looked at me in amazement and laughed. "Such a memory! Of course, you're right. I *do* manipulate God occasionally. And I have less excuse than you or Adam, or any other creature for that matter, because I have no reason to fear him." The Serpent paused and stared at the tree arching over our heads. "Other than my fear of what he can do to you."

For a moment the Serpent closed its eyes. "The things God gets angry about are usually minor. It makes life easier to distract him." The Serpent smiled at me. "If you have a child someday, you'll find ways to turn its attention away from the fire or from your necklace by dangling a toy."

"But God's not a child."

"No. God is God. All-powerful—though apparently not entirely so. And he's getting more difficult."

I started up, surprised. "Has he changed?" I had

always thought God was simply the way he was and always would be.

"Yes. He's always been demanding and impatient. But since he's been dealing with you and Adam, he's become even more short-tempered. The day of the rape was a milestone for God as well as for the two of you. For the first time, his plans did not work as expected. Even more important, for the first time his creatures defied him."

"And you did too."

The Serpent hesitated. "Yes," it said slowly. "but that was not such a surprise. God does not expect me to obey him."

"But he was stunned." I thought of God hovering over my mat in the cave, his face aghast as the Serpent turned on him.

"At how strongly I reacted, how angry I was. Before then, God had never truly realized one vital fact: even he cannot escape the consequences of his actions." The Serpent frowned. "He has, alas, become more dangerous. In fact, God is now very dangerous indeed. An omnipotent being, with all the power of a god, and, all too often, the appetites, and the temper, and the lack of control of a child."

I remembered God in his fury when I denied him a hug.

"It's this God," the Serpent went on, "who holds the future in his hands. The world is at the mercy of his will and of his whim. All creatures have reason to fear such a god, and to do all they can to placate him."

For a long time we were silent. Finally the Serpent turned to me. "So I can hardly scold you for using all your wiles with God. But no matter how disingenuous you are with him, you must be aware of what you're doing. Be honest always with yourself."

The Tree of the Knowledge of Good and Evil

🍎

THE NEXT MORNING when the Serpent and I returned from our run, Adam was pacing the terrace.

"Hello, Adam," the Serpent said. "You're here early."

"Yes. God's at the tree and wants you to come right away. He's in a state."

"We haven't had breakfast!" I exclaimed.

"Oh, dear," said Adam. "He's frantic."

"Come, Eve," said the Serpent. "It's better to see him now."

When we arrived at the ridge, God was planted in front of the tree with his hands clasped behind his back, scowling. The tree had not grown since the day before, but the leaves had filled out and were now a brilliant green, almost as bright as the Serpent's eyes.

"Ah, you're here! About time!" God cried when he saw us.

"Good morning, God," said the Serpent courteously. "I'm sorry you're upset. We came as soon as Adam told us. We didn't even stop to have breakfast."

I was always surprised at the Serpent's effect on God; now he looked discomfited. "Well, sorry to rush you," he muttered. "But this is important." He began marching back and forth with a frown on his face, as if searching for words. My stomach rumbled. At last God stopped and glared at us.

"Adam and Eve!" he shouted, even though we were barely an arm's length away. "I created you and have placed you in this beautiful Garden. I have given you every plant and every tree on the face of the Earth for food. You may freely eat of every one: but of this one tree you may not eat." God lifted his hands and spread his fingers in the air. "Listen well! This is the Tree of the Knowledge of Good and Evil. Its fruit is poisonous, and in the day you eat of it you shall die!"

Adam and I glanced at each other. God lowered his eyebrows and glowered at us. "Does that not put the fear of God into you?"

I searched my memory for anything the Serpent

might have said about "poisonous." Nothing. I shook my head.

"It doesn't scare you? Make you quake as you stand here before this tree?" We bowed our heads, mute. "Before *me*?"

"I don't think they know what 'poisonous' means," said the Serpent.

"Not know what 'poisonous' means? After all the time we've spent educating them! What's the matter with them?" God pounded a fist into his palm.

"Now God," said the Serpent reasonably. "How could they know? There's no such thing as poison in the Garden, nothing that can harm them. They have never"—it glanced at me—"or rarely, felt pain. The very idea that they could be hurt, that something could do them damage—they can not"—again a quick look in my direction—"they can hardly conceive of such a thing." The Serpent curled itself into a tight spiral, raised its head high, and spread its plumes, white today, against the green leaves of the tree. "They do not know evil, or what it means to die."

"Idiots," muttered God.

"But God, there *is* no evil here," the Serpent went on, "or death. How could these children know such things when you have protected them so well?"

God coughed. "Well, why don't you tell them about it?" he said crossly.

We shifted our weight from foot to foot. "Adam and Eve, sit down," said the Serpent, "and I'll try to explain poison and death." The Serpent bent its neck as though it were tired and would like to stretch out with us under the tree. "As you know, all the food that grows in the Garden is good to eat. But someday certain foods may harm you."

"Like what?" I asked.

"A mushroom, the sprouts on a potato, rhubarb leaves."

"But we eat them all the time!" Adam exclaimed.

"But at some time in the future they may contain a poison that will make you ill, or even kill you. In the Garden you're protected."

"By *me*," said God.

"By God, from any pain or illness. Someday God may remove his protection, and then many ills will enter. Disease, poison, death."

"What is death?" asked Adam.

Death, I wanted to cry, *is a baby raccoon floating stiff in a stream.*

"Death, Adam, is the absence of life. The absence of breath, of feeling, of thought. The disappearance of body, mind, and soul." The Serpent swallowed; its tongue flicked across its lips as though it were tormented by thirst. I closed my eyes: the raccoon lay before me, spread-eagled in my hand. The Serpent, I thought, must be seeing it too.

"But why would you withdraw your protection?" Adam looked anxiously at God. "You'd never do that, would you?"

God was annoyed. "Only if you bring it on yourselves. Now," he continued rapidly, "you know what death is, and what 'poisonous' means. The fruit of this tree is *poisonous*."

"Why?" Adam and I asked together.

"I told you!" God stormed. "It will give you the Knowledge of Good and Evil, and that will poison you. You will die."

"Evil?" I interrupted. God had called the eagle evil; the Serpent said evil was the opposite of good, but what did it mean to "know" evil?

God tapped his foot. "Surely the Serpent has taught you about evil!"

"I don't know what evil is either," said Adam. "*You* didn't teach *me* about it."

God frowned, and the Serpent interceded quickly. "It's nearly impossible to explain in the Garden, where evil does not exist."

God pulled at his beard. "Well, try to explain now.

They certainly can't understand how serious this is, the Knowledge of Good and Evil, if they don't even know what evil is."

The Serpent gave God a long look. I thought it might say, "Why don't *you* tell them?" But it did not. "Evil is hurting something, with the *intent* to hurt. Willfully harming another being: flora or fauna. Taking from others because you yourself need what they have. Or want it. . . ."

God raised his arms, fists clenched. "Nonsense!" he cried. "Serpent, you always make things so complicated. 'Willfully harming!'" God stamped his feet angrily, crushing buttercups and violets and clover into the ground. "What do those things have to do with evil? Nothing! Nothing whatsoever!" He leaned toward us, right hand raised. "Listen to me, Adam and Eve. Evil is one thing and one thing only: disobedience to God! And *I* am God!"

I could hardly believe I had heard properly. It was one thing for God to call the eagle evil in a fit of pique; but the idea that evil was purely and simply disobedience to God stunned me.

"But . . . but . . ." I stuttered.

God must have been pleased by the effect his words were having; he turned to me with a smile. "Eve, do you have a question?"

"What about all those things the Serpent said?"

"Not important. Evil," God repeated, "is disobedience to God, *to me.*" He poked his finger into his chest.

"So it doesn't matter about being kind or good? We can treat other creatures any way we want, and we're not evil as long as we obey you?"

"Eve, don't be so literal! Of course it's nice, important even, to treat others well. I'm putting together some rules, you know, guidelines, commandments, about how I want people to behave."

"What are they?" Adam asked.

God hesitated. "Let's see. It starts, I am the Lord thy God. You shall have no other gods before me. You shall not make or worship any graven images—"

("Statues of beings you set up as gods," whispered the Serpent.)

"—or take the name of the Lord thy God in vain . . ."

"Never mind," said the Serpent, "I'll explain later."

"Keep the seventh day holy." God stopped and thought a moment, caressing his chin with one hand. "Let's see, Serpent, have I forgotten any?"

"Honor your father and your mother."

"We don't have any," I said.

"No, but from now on everyone will," the Serpent said.

"Go on, go on," cried God fretfully.

"You shall not kill," the Serpent went on. "You shall not commit adultery; you shall not steal; you shall not covet your neighbor's house, nor his wife, nor his manservant, nor his maidservant, nor his ox, nor his donkey, nor anything that is your neighbor's."

Adam and I looked at each other again. An ox and a donkey we knew, and we had been told about husbands and wives. But a neighbor, a dultery, a manservant? Covet?

The Serpent glanced at our faces and chortled. "It's all right," it said, "I'll tell you later."

"So," said God, "those are my commandments. You must obey them all. For"—God raised his hands, balled into fists—"I the Lord thy God am a *jealous* god, visiting the iniquity of the fathers upon the children onto the third and fourth generation . . . ."

"Yes, yes," said the Serpent, a hint of impatience in its voice. "You are indeed a powerful and jealous god." God scowled at the Serpent.

"But God," I asked. "If evil is bad, why isn't it a good thing for us to know the difference between good and evil? So we can avoid evil?"

God lowered his brows over his eyes and planted himself more firmly in front of the tree. Strands of white hair rose around his head. "Always quibbling, Eve. You're *always* quibbling! What nonsense! The

Knowledge of Good and Evil is for the gods. For *me*. And for the Serpent."

"Is the Serpent a god?" asked Adam.

God turned a deeper shade of red. "I told you," he sputtered. "There is no other god but me!" He paused and drew breath before adding, "But the Serpent's been around for a long time."

The Serpent coughed and swished its tail through the grass. God raised his voice again. "It's not *good* for you to know the difference between good and evil, because it's not good for you to *think*! Not for yourselves, anyway."

The Serpent coughed again.

"Now," continued God. "This is all you have to remember: Evil is disobeying God. *I* am God, and I say to you: *Do not eat the fruit of this tree,* the Tree of the Knowledge of Good and Evil. If you do you will surely die!" God leaned back on his heels, crossed his arms, and glared at us. Behind him the tree shimmered in the sun.

"Well," said Adam. "I guess we better not eat it." He stood up and shook out his legs. "God, we haven't had breakfast. Are you finished?"

"Why—" I began.

"Adam's right," interrupted the Serpent. "We're all hungry. We should go home and have something to eat."

It began to unwind its body. "I think you've made your point," it murmured to God over its shoulder as it started down the hill. "Anything more would be overkill."

"Overkill!" cried God. "Kill! You dare use that fearful word—and join it to another?"

The Serpent laughed. "A new word," it said, "to go with your Lesson for the Day."

The Meaning of Evil

GOD MARCHED OFF with Adam at his heels, but we had barely finished breakfast when the boy reappeared. "I thought I should make sure God had everything he needed; we hadn't eaten either." Adam plonked himself down on the bench and sighed. "I'm really confused."

"I'm sure you both are," the Serpent said. "Let's go to the hill overlooking the volcano. We'll have a picnic and talk." The Serpent, who believed in exercise, especially in times of tension, spiraled rapidly away. I put some food into a basket, and Adam and I followed behind.

"Where are we going?" Adam asked.

"To the hill beyond the river, where the mulberries grow. There's a big meadow there—we go often to see if the volcano's all right."

"Why shouldn't it be?"

"When we were there, it erupted."

"Erupted?" Adam stopped. "When *you* were there?"

"Oh, I forgot! You don't know about the volcano!"

"I know what a volcano is. God told me, about magma and lava. But what do you mean, it erupted?"

"It blew up, and lava rushed down the mountain."

"But you can't have been there; it's outside the Garden and terribly far away. It would take many days to get there."

"A few days," I said. "From the top you can see all the way to the desert and the mountains and the sea."

"Desert, mountains, sea? God's told me about them, but they're at the ends of the Earth."

"They're not. I've been to them all."

"The Serpent would never let you leave the Garden!"

"The Serpent went with me. I couldn't have gone alone."

"I don't believe it," said Adam, setting his lips tightly together.

"Ask the Serpent," I retorted. We spoke no more until we reached the hill.

The moment we arrived Adam burst out: "Serpent, Eve's telling me stories about leaving the Garden and going to the volcano and a lot of other places. It's not true, is it?"

The Serpent answered mildly, "I don't blame you for having trouble believing it, Adam. But it *is* true."

Adam looked stunned. "Why didn't you tell me about it?"

"It's Eve's story to tell, Adam," the Serpent replied firmly.

Adam looked at his hands. "Yes. Of course," he mumbled. "I'm sorry."

"*You* tell him," I said to the Serpent. "He'll believe *you*." So the Serpent told Adam about our journeys, and Adam sat with his hands covering his ears to shut out the murmur of the wind and the *chuck-chuck* of the quail and all the other sounds around. I thought he would say, as he had when God told us the tale of Anansi the Spider, "That's impossible!" but he did not. Mouth agape, he listened speechless to the very end.

When the Serpent had finished, Adam gasped and shook his head. "Oh!" he said. "I'd love to see those places! Serpent, will you take me? Take us together?"

Shaking its head, the Serpent replied, "My days as a guide are over. But we didn't come here to talk about our adventures outside the Garden. You had questions for me, Adam."

"Yes," Adam said, suddenly quiet. "Death. The tree.

The Knowledge of Good and Evil." He sighed. "I *do* know what evil is. What I did to Eve was evil."

For a few moments the Serpent said nothing. I felt heavy in the silence. All at once I remembered the great weight on my stomach the day I first woke to life.

"I guess"—Adam's voice broke—"*I* must be evil."

"Adam," the Serpent asked quietly. "Do you *feel* evil?"

I glanced at Adam. His eyes were scrunched shut, his hands clenched over his ears. "Let me think," he muttered. Then he opened his eyes and sat up. "I feel bad," he said, "but not evil. Is that possible?" He pushed a lock of hair from his face.

The Serpent turned his gaze on the boy. "Of course. Adam, what you did was evil, but you are not. You were urged to act by God, your mentor—the same God who defines evil as *disobedience to God*! Even Eve encouraged you. She said the act must be beautiful, because *I* had told her it was! Then you were swept away by passion. You had no idea that what you were doing was bad, or that you were hurting Eve. And when you did, God ordered you to continue. So Adam, no, you are not evil."

Adam breathed a great sigh, as if the world had been taken off his shoulders.

"And God," I said softly. "Was God evil, that day?"

Briefly the Serpent shut its eyes. "Eve, will you unpack our lunch? It's late; we're all hungry."

I emptied the basket and set the food on the grass: bread wrapped in grape leaves, cheese, tomatoes mixed with basil and olive oil and sprinkled with salt. Adam grinned when he saw the bowl that held them: on the rim sat a chipmunk with a fluffy tail.

As Adam and I ate, the Serpent spoke. "God," it said, "was far more at fault than Adam. He knew what he had planned was not right, not at that time. He knew I would not approve and made sure I wouldn't be there. But he couldn't see anything wrong in encouraging Adam to make love to Eve. For him it was not an act of violence, but the natural outcome of two young creatures spending time together—all those lovely afternoons in nature—the act of procreation that guaranteed the future of humankind."

The Serpent bent its neck and took another olive. "God too was swept away by passion—a different kind from Adam's—his passion to find out whether his invention would work. God was selfish, egotistical, insensitive. But evil?" The Serpent shook its head.

"If an elephant rushes down a path to reach her calf and knocks you over, is the elephant evil?" I remembered being brushed aside by a mother bear following her cub. "God is like that elephant, only he's not following a calf; he's completing an experiment. Nothing else matters." The Serpent stopped; its feathered ears drooped along the side of its body. "I'm afraid, however"—its voice fell to a whisper—"that in his single-minded passion, God is capable of inflicting a great deal of harm."

"Is passion an excuse for evil?" I asked.

"No," said the Serpent. "Nothing excuses evil."

"God *must* have known how it was for me!" I cried. "He created everything, everything, all this glory"—I waved my arms at the valley and hills, and the volcano in the distance—"down to the tiniest swirl on a butterfly's wing. He made our bodies and gave us our minds. How can he not know what we feel?"

The Serpent answered slowly. "That's a big question, Eve, and I'm not sure I know the answer. It's troubled me more and more as I've come to understand God's view of the universe." The Serpent swept its eyes across the landscape and shifted uneasily in its coils. "God started with an incredible vision of the world he wanted to create. He's a fine craftsman, and he did a beautiful job. His creations are certainly wonderful. But once they were done, his imagination could go no further."

The Serpent helped itself to a tomato from the bowl and patted the chipmunk's head with its tongue. "Take this bowl, Eve. You saw it in your mind, you worked and shaped the clay and made it as it is now. You don't expect the bowl to change shape—to be rectangular instead of round, or the chipmunk to sit up and complain that its tail is too long."

I giggled. "What a fantastic idea! I'd love it if the chipmunk told me what kind of tail it wanted!"

"That's silly, Eve," said Adam, but the Serpent flapped its ears in appreciation.

"God doesn't see it the way you do, Eve," it continued. "In his view he created a perfect world. There's no reason for it to change."

"He always wants things to stay the same," agreed Adam.

The Serpent nodded. "God had a plan for every plant and every creature he made, and he gave each what it needed to fulfill its role in his world. To trees he gave roots and leaves to draw nourishment from the soil and the sun. Cows and sheep and deer have several stomachs so they can digest the rough plants they eat.

"God gave you and Adam everything you need to accomplish what he wants you to do. He gave you those useful hands with thumbs, and he had you walk on two feet instead of four, so you can pick fruit and climb trees and tend the Garden. He made your bodies in all their miraculous details. What he did is extraordinary." The

Serpent paused and glanced at us. "But for all his creative power, God cannot imagine the pain of a skinned knee."

"He felt it when the tree stung him," I said.

"Yes." The Serpent turned to me. "But God has forgotten that; I'm sure it went out of his mind immediately. It was not in his plan, and therefore it *did not* happen. So he still has no conception of pain."

"That's why he didn't believe me when I said it hurt!"

"Exactly." The Serpent took another olive. "Beyond those marvelous bodies, God gave you speech and intelligence, so you could enjoy his stories and discuss things with him. He gave you emotions: love and joy, so you'll be drawn to each other and have children, and those children will prosper and populate the world."

"So we'll love him too," said Adam.

"And adore and worship him," I added.

"Adore and worship him," the Serpent agreed, "and feel joy in the Lord and in your mate and in your children and in the beauty around you, and your greatest desire will be to care for them all."

I thought of the joy I felt when I saw the sunrise, or rubbed my fingers across the moss on a tree, or heard water fall on rocks. And the love I felt for the Serpent, a love so deep that I could never fully express it. Did God know that? The Serpent smiled at me as if once again it could read my thoughts. "Is it God who made our feelings so strong?" I asked.

"I don't believe so. God gave you enough emotion to accomplish *his* ends. I don't think he conceived of passion, just as when he made the wind, he didn't envision the tornado. He never thought intelligence would extend to such depths of reflection or that the mind would become so analytic or poetic or imaginative."

"What about the soul? Did God make that?" I asked.

The Serpent was still, head tilted, eyes fixed far away. "God did not wager with the soul, I think," it answered at last, "or expect it to assume a life of its own."

"So that's something else that got away from him. . . ." I said.

"Like the tornado and the blizzard," whispered Adam, as if the very words would bring the wind into the meadow.

No one spoke for a long time. Adam wandered away to pick some flowers, returned, and began counting them languidly. After a while he dozed off in a nest of hay, mouth open, one arm flung to the side. In his hand he clutched a bouquet of scarlet poppies; as he relaxed in sleep, the flowers fell one by one from his fingers and slipped to the ground. The Serpent stretched itself under a tree and closed its eyes, but if it slept it was a troubled sleep; from time to time it moaned as if, behind the hooded lids, pictures passed before its eyes—pictures it did not want to see. I watched them, two of the three beings who filled my life. At last I shook them awake.

"It's late," I said.

Adam sat up and rubbed his eyes. "We haven't talked about death," he said.

"We'll deal with death another day," replied the Serpent. "And the soul."

Suddenly, across the valley, the volcano began to glow.

Apples

FOR THE NEXT FEW days we forgot about death: we were absorbed by the tree. It filled out rapidly; the leaves were thick, and on every branch buds formed and swelled. God had warned us about the fruit, but he had said nothing about staying away from the tree itself. We could not have obeyed him if he had, for we were drawn to it irresistibly, like hummingbirds to the nectar of a honeysuckle flower.

At sunrise Adam came striding down the path, and he and the Serpent went off on their explorations. I was happy to have the morning to myself. After tidying the hut and raking the terrace, I turned to my own explorations. In the mulberry bushes I had discovered a kind of worm that spun an unusual thread: it had an inner shine to it and shimmered in the sun. I was trying to collect enough thread to weave into cloth.

When the Serpent and Adam returned, I put my work away and the three of us swam and had lunch. Then Adam and I ran off to the tree.

"Serpent, will you come with us?" I asked. But usually the Serpent had other things to do. "I'll stop by later," it said. "Enjoy yourselves."

So each day we settled under the branches of the tree. At first I stayed well away from Adam. Even as I watched a pipit explore the meadow, tail pumping up and down, I felt Adam's presence: he was flexing his toes, brushing long brown fingers through the grass, pursing his lips, with his brows drawn low over his eyes. Gradually I grew accustomed to having him nearby.

We talked of things we had never discussed: the time before we had known each other, when we had built our huts and discovered the Garden and all its creatures. I told Adam about falling down the cliff, and he told me about being caught in the midst of a herd of elephants. Adam plied me with questions about our voyages, and I recounted every detail of each trip, sometimes jumping up to act out a scene. And then I described my beautiful bowl with the Serpent around the rim, how it grew into a little plant, how God had trampled it into the ground—and how the leaves cut his hand. When I told him about God shriveling the great oak and making it grow again, I felt cold and shuddered.

Adam squeezed his eyes shut. "What's the first thing you remember?" he finally asked. "About coming to life?"

I told him about awakening with the Serpent sitting on my stomach, about our morning runs, the hut, the Serpent's lessons.

"What about you?" I asked.

"The first thing I remember is standing in a meadow surrounded by flowers, wide awake, with God staring at me."

"Then what happened?"

"God shook me and said, 'Well, boy, can you talk?'"

"What did you say?" I asked.

Adam giggled. "Nothing. I started to sneeze. The field was full of goldenrod."

I had forgotten. "Oh, I sneezed too!" I cried, and we rolled on our backs in fits of laughter.

The tree exuded some quality we had never known before, though we could not say what it was. When we were near it, we felt at the same time excited and immersed in calm. Our thoughts were clearer, our conversations more profound. We laughed a great deal, and wept, for under the tree everything moved us more deeply than anywhere else. The eagle, I knew, could spot a berry from the sky; when I sat under the tree, I felt I could see into the heart of every flower.

God came too, nearly every day, but the tree seemed to affect him in the opposite way. As he neared it he walked more slowly, more heavily, as if he were slogging through mud and each step added muck to his sandals. When he saw us he muttered, "Evil tree! Remember what I said!" but he did not proscribe our visits.

"He's so glum," I said as God stomped out of the glade.

"He's always glum these days," said Adam. "He used to be more relaxed and sometimes even fun—you remember our lessons. But from the first he's wanted me to do things his way, and he's always been so critical of me."

"The Serpent never criticizes me," I said. "Or not so it makes me feel small, only so I see how to do things better. The Serpent's happy to have me try things out. I think it likes guessing what I'll do next."

Adam groaned. "You're so lucky! God gets furious if I have *any* ideas of my own. I have to agree with him on everything and obey him instantly."

"He does that with all of us, not only you. Me, and all the animals. Do you remember the parade? He wanted the creatures to follow his every signal. He got angry at the eagle when it didn't obey him."

Adam nodded. "How do *you* feel about God?" he

asked, as if the question had just occurred to him.

Adam had never asked about my feelings before, and I was surprised he would be interested. I was not sure anymore how I felt about God. Once I had loved him—not the way I loved the Serpent, but I had enjoyed being with him, enjoyed his stories, his voice, the joy he took in our music and dance. Whenever I saw him, be it on a cliff top or napping on his bench, I felt a trembling in my breast. Even when God got angry and shouted—behaved badly, as the Serpent said—he filled me with awe. He was the Great Creator.

But now?

There was a rustle behind us. The Serpent had come up the path and settled itself between Adam and me. "We're talking about God," I explained. "Before . . ." I could not bring myself to say "the rape." "Before that day, I really enjoyed being with God. There were things we didn't like—all those praises—but looking back on it, we had a lot of fun. The music and dancing—and his stories were wonderful. I didn't care much for his hugs, but at least I knew he liked me, and that was nice. I liked *him* too. Sometimes I thought I even loved him—not like the Serpent, but a little, especially when he was in a good mood. He stood tall; he was impressive and wonderful. I held him in awe, but he didn't really frighten me." I stopped and brushed my fingers through the clover. The Serpent, coiled at my side, listened carefully as it always did. Adam had his hands over his ears. His eyes were nearly shut, but I could tell he was watching me.

"Since . . . since that day, I'm still not scared of him, not really. I know he won't do anything bad to me again." I turned to the Serpent. "You made sure of that. But now when I see God, something inside of me begins to shake." I shuddered.

Adam tugged at a dandelion.

"It was such a betrayal!" I went on, suddenly nearly in tears. "I trusted him fully, and he trapped me! No one should behave the way he did to me, even the Great Creator. It's wrong." My voice was shaking. "I can never respect him," I said. "I can never love him again." The tears overflowed and ran down my cheeks. Adam stared at his toes.

"Dear Eve," said the Serpent, patting my hand. "Of course you feel that way." It pulled up some grass and wiped my face. I leaned against its warm coils, as I had in my early days in the Garden, and closed my eyes.

"I didn't mean to interrupt your conversation, you two," the Serpent said after a time.

I raised my head. "Serpent, you know I have no secrets from you. I'm glad you came. And I'm really glad *you* brought me up, not God."

"I wish you'd brought *me* up!" Adam exclaimed. "How can you and God be so different?"

"We have different views of the world, that's all," the Serpent replied. "Come, there's a baby kangaroo in the meadow, that's what I came to tell you. Let's go see it. You've been sitting around too long."

That night the buds burst open and the tree bloomed.

It was God who alerted us. His bellow brought the Serpent at full speed from the river and Adam and me at a run from the copse by the pond, where we had been picking berries for lunch. When we arrived at the glade, panting, God was standing in front of the tree, arms raised, trembling. There was a red tinge about him. *He's turned red with rage,* I thought, before I realized his white skin and hair and robe were reflecting the color of the tree.

"It's blooming!" he roared, and the tender leaves of the aspens encircling the clearing quivered with his cry. "Serpent!" he shouted as he saw us. "Look at it! The damned thing is *blooming*!"

"Of course it's blooming, God," the Serpent replied calmly. "What did you expect? It was covered in buds." God's face turned crimson. "It's an apple tree, and it's spring," the Serpent continued and, as God drew breath, the Serpent added nearly in a whisper, so Adam and I could barely hear, "Come, God, calm yourself. All the shouting in the world won't blow those blossoms away." In a louder voice it added, "Look at that tree. What a thing of beauty it is."

The Serpent's voice had its usual effect: God stopped shouting and let the air trickle through his lips, though I could tell he was still angry. We stood in front of the tree and stared.

The blossoms were a color I had never seen before on any other tree: the deep, clear red of a ruby, sparked with white. A few buds, still tightly wrapped, waited to burst. Others were half-open, petals still half-curled protectively around the stamen. But most were open full, eight or ten flowers on a stem, amidst a whorl of leaves. The petals curved gently outward; clear crimson, white, white flecks. From the center of every bloom filaments rose, deep purple; at the tip of each filament flared an anther, airy as a cobweb and green as the darkest emerald sea.

"An outrageous and wondrous tree," muttered the Serpent.

"And so beautiful," I breathed.

For two weeks the tree bloomed. Each day we went—Adam and the Serpent and I—to admire it. We sat under its boughs or climbed as high as we could into its branches and looked out on the world through the ruby petals. Always we felt overcome with happiness and calm—light, buoyant, like the very petals themselves. But after that first visit, God did not appear.

One evening the wind rose, and in the morning we woke to find the earth covered in red. The petals had flown on the wind; they seemed to blanket the whole Garden. We scuffed through them. Soft and light, they rose around our ankles in crimson clouds and settled back to the ground without a rustle. The tree was green again. Not a blossom remained, but tiny swellings promised fruit.

The fruit grew fast. Each time we visited the clearing the apples looked more round, more plump. In a few days most were tinged with color. Like everything about the tree, the tiny fruits were different from any other— perfectly round, and joined to the branches by velvety emerald stems. Not red, or green, or yellow, the fruit was golden: the gold of a buttercup, or corn plucked from its stalk at the height of summer.

"At this rate," the Serpent stated, "tomorrow they'll be ripe."

The Meaning of Death

THE NEXT MORNING, when the Serpent and I visited the tree, the apples were gone. The grass was trampled flat; a few broken branches were strewn about, and there were signs that something had clambered up—scratches on the bark, leaves torn.

"God!" I cried.

"God," echoed the Serpent. "He's removed temptation."

Adam arrived at a run, breathless. When he saw the tree, he clapped his hand to his forehead. "Oh, God *was* here!" he cried. "I was hoping. . . ."

"What happened? Adam, what happened?" I shook his shoulder; he was dripping with sweat.

"When I woke up this morning, God wasn't there.

He does sometimes go out early, so I didn't think anything of it. I went to the big rock above the falls to watch the salmon—they're coming upriver to spawn—and I heard something on the path. I thought it might be God—animals never make that much noise—so I rolled under the bushes and hid."

"Why did you do that?" I asked. I often wanted to hide from God, but I was always afraid he would find me out. I could envisage him lifting his nose like a hound, sniffing and saying, "Eve, I sense you there. What are you doing? Come out immediately!" And I would have to crawl from my hiding place, brushing away the dirt and pulling twigs out of my hair.

Adam looked embarrassed. "I hide from him because I don't like him knowing what I do all the time." He rubbed his arm across his nose, adding a streak of red earth to the dust that coated his face. "I didn't want to explain what I was doing there, or why I love watching the salmon jump. God's always poking into my business, into my mind. I can't stand it!"

"Then what happened? You hid and—"

"God stopped at the top of the falls. He had a big load on his back, wrapped in one of your blankets, Eve. He put it down on the edge of the rock. I couldn't see what was in it, but it was lumpy. Then he lifted one side and shook the cloth, and all the apples came tumbling out." Adam shoved both hands through his hair. "They fell, all of them, into the river and were carried over the waterfall."

I could see the apples tumbling over the falls, golden globes mingled with prisms of spray. "Are you *sure* there weren't any left? Maybe caught in the bushes?"

Adam shook his head. "As soon as he left, I went over the whole area. I even climbed down the cliff to search the riverbanks below. There was nothing—not a bashed bit or a fleck of skin." He glanced at the tree. "Are they all gone?"

"Yes. I looked," I said shortly. I was ready to cry.

"Why did he have to climb the tree anyway?" Adam asked, running his fingers over the scratches on the bark. "Why didn't he just wave his hands and make the apples fall, the way he did with the oak tree?"

"God doesn't have that kind of power over this tree," the Serpent replied. "If he had, he would have killed it long ago."

"Then how did he get the apples?" I asked. "The tree always stings him."

The Serpent examined the trunk. "I don't think God did the climbing. He must have had the monkeys help him. See, there are bits of fur caught on the twigs."

"What do we do now?" I asked.

"We go back to the hut and have breakfast," said the

Serpent. "We'll be able to think more clearly when we've had some food."

Once we were settled at the table with a bowl of fruit in front of us, the Serpent peered into our faces. "After all, is anything different? You weren't planning to eat the apples anyway."

"Well . . ." Adam and I said together, and looked at each other, startled.

"Have you changed your minds?" asked the Serpent.

"We haven't talked about it," I said, "but I've been thinking. How do we know if God's telling us the truth? Will we really die if we eat the apple?"

The Serpent answered slowly. "Die right away? I doubt it. I think God means that if you eat the apple, you will lose the protection you have in the Garden. Maybe he wants to remind you that whatever he gives can just as easily be taken away."

"I still don't understand death," Adam said, popping a last section of orange in his mouth. On the table, the peel shone orange in the sun. "You told us it's the absence of life. But how does life disappear?"

The Serpent looked north as if trying to see the glacier or the mountain peak red with alpenglow. "When death comes," it said slowly, "everything that makes a being alive suddenly vanishes. You can no longer move, or feel or see or hear, walk, laugh, breathe. Or think. Everything goes."

"Including the soul," I said.

"You were going to tell me about the soul," said Adam.

"The soul is the essence of what we are—" the Serpent began.

"What goes on in your head, and in your heart," I interrupted, closing my eyes. The Serpent's words came back to me, with the heat of the desert and the cool, sharp spine of the cactus. "The part of you that thinks and feels, that has wants and needs and desires, and knows the difference between right and wrong. It is the soul that reflects, and sees the beauty of the world, and loves. The soul is the core of your being. It is who you are."

The Serpent stared at me in astonishment. "Eve, how did you remember that?"

"I'll never forget it," I said.

"So what's left of us?" asked Adam.

"A body that no longer has any meaning, an empty shell," replied the Serpent, brushing the orange peel with a feathered ear.

"What happens to the body?" Adam asked.

"Well, the skin and flesh and organs dry up inside, and you're left with bones: a skeleton."

"Ugh," said Adam.

"The body turns to dust, which returns to the Earth,

and from it grows trees and flowers and grain and many other plants."

"From me? A flower will grow from me?" Adam looked down at his sturdy body. "You're making it up, Serpent! Anyway, how would you know? No one has ever died."

"Not in the Garden."

"In the river we found a baby raccoon that was dead," I said.

"Dead?" Adam exclaimed, staring at me. "Are you sure?"

"It couldn't move," I rubbed my eyes. "It was stiff."

Adam shivered. "How awful!" He picked up a twig and started tapping it on the ground. "I could never eat the apple if it means I have to die."

Could I? I wondered.

"More than anything else," the Serpent said, "death is sad. Eve felt that sadness when she saw the raccoon, even though it was a little creature she had never known. When someone you love disappears from your life— which is what happens when death comes—it's a very deep sorrow."

"But how do you know?"

"I know how it will be." The Serpent stared at the circles I had raked that morning in the sand. "But there *is* a positive side to death. It's not all bad. Where there is no death, life also must be limited. There can be no renewal, no regeneration, only a static world. Even in the Garden leaves wither and die, and those that fall are replaced with new ones, and buds and flowers. And fruit.

"If there were no death," the Serpent went on, "most beings would be very old. The ancient would rule, for they would have the power. And they would believe they know best."

"Like God?" asked Adam.

"Yes, a bit like God," the Serpent agreed. "The Earth would be quickly overrun. You could not have a succession of beings progressing through life, each generation learning and growing and giving in its own way, rediscovering beauty, taking joy in the world around them. Death makes way for the young."

Suddenly the Serpent laughed as it had laughed when it rescued me from the bottom of the sea—a peal of pure, infectious delight that rang like a clarion through the air. Shocked, Adam and I stared as though it had gone mad. "You've never seen children," the Serpent exclaimed. "You've never *been* children. Children are wonderful! The essence of joy." It looked at us and laughed again. "Wait and see."

Dreams

THAT NIGHT all we had talked about in the last weeks—evil and apples and death—whirled in my head. Stretched flat on my mat, I lay rigid, hands folded on my breast, and tried to shut out the cuckoo, the moon glow behind my eyelids, the rustle of reeds by the stream. I sought to stop my breath and feel the worms gnawing on my heart.

I dreamed.

Adam is my husband, and we're living some-where, outside the Garden. We have two baby boys. Sweet they are, we named them Cain and Abel, and I tend them as I tended the plant that grew into the golden apple tree. Cain was first born; I cradled him in my arms, and his little mouth fastened to my breast, his wee hands patted me gently, gently. Then came Abel—not a year had passed—and he drank greedily and, when he could, pushed his brother away.

They played together, and sometimes fought as brothers will, but they meant no harm. I knew they loved each other. From the first Abel was strong and bold, climbed higher, threw the javelin farther, even though he was the younger. Adam always asked Abel, never Cain, to go hunting. Cain loved the garden, and all the plants; he touched them tenderly as he passed by, and talked to them too. He had a temper, my Cain, quick to come and quick to go, perhaps because he had trouble saying what he wanted, stumbling and stuttering over his words, so that his father always took him for the guilty one when he and Abel got up to mischief.

Now they've grown to men. Cain is the gardener, and Abel the shepherd. Cain works so hard, planting seeds and pulling weeds and carrying water from the well, while Abel sits on a rock and watches the lambs gambol around him, blowing into those pipes of his—he does make nice tunes. He mocks his brother sometimes *about all that drudgery, only teasing, of course, the way brothers do, but I can see it's hard for Cain to keep his temper.*

There's a holiday of some sort—God's always having holidays—and my boys are preparing gifts for him. Cain picks his fruits and vegetables and arranges them in a basket lined with grape leaves. I've never known such succulent fruit, or vegetables so delectable. My mouth waters just looking at them. Cain offers them to God with his face aglow.

Abel cuts wood and builds a fire. He slays one of his lambs, and cleans it, and lays it on the flames to cook. The odor wafts across my dreamland, and suddenly the meadow is ringed with animals: wolves and lions, tigers and foxes, their mouths open, tongues hanging out. When the meat is cooked, Abel bears it to God on a great wooden platter, with the gleam of pride in his eye.

God leans over the platter and inhales deeply. "Aaaah," he sighs, and smiles. But he turns from Cain's offering with barely a glance.

I creep up beside him and whisper in his ear, "Oh, God, he worked so hard to please you. Could you not say something to Cain, some word?"

"Bah!" says God in a loud voice. "Those pesky fruits! And vegetables! Women's food!" He pushes the basket aside, and grapes and eggplants and fat tomatoes scatter on the ground. "Raising them is women's work!" He makes ready to eat the lamb, dripping juice on his yellow robe. "Eve, at least one good thing has come out of your disobedience, you and Adam!" he says to me, pointing at the lamb. He stuffs a wedge of meat into his mouth and begins to chew. "I don't understand how I could have eaten only fruits and vegetables all those years in the Garden!"

Cain rushes off, his face drawn up in rage. I hurry after him, but he is gone. Later in the evening, in the fields, I see them together, my sons. Cain is bent over, pulling weeds from among the onion plants.

Abel throws his head back and laughs. "You heard God," he said. "It's women's work."

Cain stops still. Then a great cry bursts from his throat. He seizes a rock, sweeps it into the air, and brings it down on Abel's head. Abel falls to the ground. His hands scrabble in the earth. Then he lies motionless, his face buried among the onions.

Alas! Alas! I've lost them both, my boys. God

has banished Cain, sent him forever into the wilderness with a mark on his forehead. And Abel, oh, Abel is dead.

I woke. My head throbbed. I was hot and kicked off the covers. After a while I slept and dreamed again.

I am another woman, not Eve. I am standing knee deep in a pool of water with my daughter at my side. It's raining, it has been raining for days. Water is everywhere. It fills the valleys, blanketing the vineyards on the upper slopes; it puddles at the foot of trees and rises until it drowns them. All around me people struggle in the mud with panic in their eyes; men and women and children cling to the topmost branches of the tallest trees.

I take my child and climb with her into the hills, to a high mountain peak. Still the water rises, covers our feet, creeps up our legs. When the child is waist-deep I lift her into my arms and the water sweeps us away. She cries; I calm her as best I can while I swim.

Suddenly through the rain a boat appears, a great ark. A rope hangs down its side. I take hold of the rope and lift my daughter so she can shimmy up—she's strong and climbs like a monkey. A man calls: "There's someone trying to climb up!"

and he leans over the side with a broom and begins to strike her.

"Let her be!" I yell. "It's only a little girl!"

"She can't come up," bellows a voice from above. "We have a full contingent, all our two's. We're not allowed to save anyone else!"

"Who says so?" I shout.

"God," comes the answer. "It's God's command." The broom handle strikes my daughter full in the face. She falls back into the water and I cannot reach her. Soon I too am engulfed by the waves and float with all the others in the immense and endless sea, eyes open, tendrils of seaweed clutched in the puckered fingers of my hands.

I woke drenched with sweat. I pulled up the covers and lay shivering, looking at the stars. Though the bed smelled sweet, of mint and marjoram, my mouth was bitter with the taste of bile and stagnant water, as though I was still living the dream. I longed to stay awake, to dream no more, but I could not. Again I fell asleep, again I dreamed.

I'm hauling a ram up a hill. The ram keeps digging its feet into the ground; its hooves carve deep grooves in the mud. At the rear the Serpent butts the creature in the rump and tickles its flanks with its feathered ears.

I'm an old woman—not Eve, not the mother in the flood. My husband and I are both old, but our son is young. After many childless years, I gave birth at a great age—truly a miracle, truly a joy! But today I am filled with dread: this morning my husband went off with the boy, and manservants, and donkeys carrying fagots of wood; he told me that God had ordered him to take our son into the wilderness. Since the child's birth, my husband has been more and more possessed by God; he's always on his knees in the dust with his hands raised, blabbering away with a wild look in his eyes. I know something dreadful is about to happen.

"Move," I shriek. "You stupid creature, move! Will we be in time?"

"It's only a little farther," cries the Serpent. "Pull harder! Such imbeciles, both of them," it grumbles through its teeth. "He's the only male with any brains in ages, that boy. And God has to test his father by asking him to sacrifice his son!" The Serpent gives the ram a shove, and the

creature hops a few feet forward. "Why God needs more proof that everyone's scared to death of him, I do not know!" It gives another bump to the ram's rear. "As if sacrificing your child were proof of anything"—thump—"but idiocy!" The ram stumbles over a stump and falls to its knees.

"Come on," I scream, yanking the rope.

"We're here," the Serpent calls, and there is my husband with a great knife in his hand, his arm raised over the heart of our son, and God looking around saying, "Where is that ram? It was supposed to be here!"

The Serpent grasps the animal in its coils and flings it on top of the wood piled at God's feet, then whooshes fire from its nostrils. The pyre bursts into flame. God looks relieved, and tells my husband to let the boy go. The old man sinks to his knees and buries his head in his hands, weeping. "Thank you, God, thank you, All-Merciful God," he babbles. The knife clatters to the rocky ground and shatters; the shards gleam silver in the sun.

Before God speaks I have the boy in my arms—he is white and bloodless as if the blade had already descended. I rock my son as though

he were a babe again and croon comforting words
in his ear. But in my breast, my soul screams.

The Earth trembled. I woke. The Serpent was shaking me. "Eve," it said. "You're here. Safe, in the Garden. You were dreaming."

"No," I said. "It's real."

The Serpent Is Troubled

○

*I*N THE MORNING I had only the vaguest memory of my dreams. The Serpent appeared troubled. It answered questions in monosyllables; from time to time it shook its head and sighed deeply. Its brows were furrowed; its eyes half-shut, fixed on a point far away.

"Some bread, Serpent?" I asked, waving a fresh sunbaked loaf under its nose. "The very best blackberries. They're so ripe my hands are purple from picking them."

The Serpent did not answer. I doubt it even heard me.

I put my arms around its neck, feeling the thick power of its muscles under the dappled skin. "Are you all right, Serpent? Can I help?" Still it was silent. Finally it shook its head as if coming out of a deep sleep and squeezed its eyes shut.

"We're running out of time, Eve, running out of time. I must *act*." It looked full at me. "Dear Eve," it said.

After breakfast the Serpent announced that it would be gone all day. "Adam won't be around either; God wants him to build another pergola and bring in some fresh hay. Why don't you cut some hay too, and make yourself a new bed? The field is full of clover and geranium, ripe to be cut."

So I spent the morning in the meadow, swinging my scythe back and forth, back and forth through the long, sweet grass that fell in neat rows along the swath I had made. I let the grass dry in the sun for a few hours at midday, then carried it back in my arms. The straw tickled my nose, stuck to my skin, and caught in my hair. But it smelled fresh, of clover and geranium as the Serpent had said, but also of basil and honeysuckle, marjoram, rosemary, lemon mint, dill weed, and thyme.

Usually the Serpent slept on the covered porch outside the hut; it preferred the fresh air and hard-packed earth to a mat. Today, however, I wanted to do something special for it. It was so clearly worried—I suspected on my account, mine and Adam's. So I put a bundle of hay on the porch, and my favorite blanket. Whether the Serpent slept there or not, it would know I had thought of its comfort.

The rest of the hay I piled in the corner of the hut where I made my bed.

Evening: The Potion

○

THE SERPENT AND I ate our evening meal by the pond, watching the trout jump and the frogs flip their long tongues to flick seeds from the air. When we had finished, the Serpent went to the stream and, after a few moments, returned with a steaming cup in its mouth. The brew was green, with a dusting of yellow powder around the edge.

"What is it?" I asked.

The Serpent raised its head to watch a swallow swoop above the trees. "It's a special tea, made from the herbs I picked today. It will bring you only good dreams tonight."

I poked the tea with a twig. "I don't remember seeing this yellow stuff before." I wrinkled my nose.

"It's an herb, that's all. It tastes like orange. Eve," said the Serpent, "drink it and have a dip, and get to bed early."

I stood. "Drink your tea," said the Serpent.

"I'll take it with me," I lifted the cup and started toward the stream.

"I'd rather have you drink it here, now," the Serpent said, an edge to its voice. "Those are rare herbs; it's not easy to find them."

I turned and stared at the Serpent, but I could not catch its eye; it was still following the swallow in its flight.

"I won't spill it," I said. "I'll drink it after I bathe."

But I did not bathe immediately. I sat on a rock, my feet in the water, holding the cup in my hands. When I lifted it to my face, the vapor warmed my cheeks. The tea smelled like chocolate, with a touch of orange; perhaps that was what the yellow stuff was, orange zest. Everything about it was delicious, inviting. My mouth watered, my lips puckered and reached of their own volition toward the rim. Quickly I set the cup down beside me on the grass.

Never before had the Serpent failed to look me straight in the eyes. Never before had I heard such an edge in its voice. *What's so special about this potion?* I thought. *Why is it so important that I drink it? And why is the Serpent being so mysterious?*

Again I raised the cup and held it level with my eyes. The tea was as appealing as before. *I will not!* I thought. *I will not be manipulated! By anyone!* I waded into the stream until the water reached my knees. *Not Adam! Not God!* My hands shook. *Not even the Serpent!* I held the cup high, tilted it, and poured the brew into the water.

I plunged in and swam fast. Arms churning, I cut through the current, muttering angrily in my head: *I will not! I will not!* And then: *Horrible Serpent!* Tears of rage dissipated in the cold water. It had never occurred to me that the Serpent—*my* Serpent—would mislead me in any way. If it could—what *else* was possible? What was *not* possible? And, in all this, where was I?

Little by little I slowed my pace. *The Serpent,* I thought, *would never lie to me.*

But that tea, so strange? And it practically ordered me to drink it, and wouldn't look at me.

Even so, even so. There must be a reason. The Serpent would not lie. Unless . . . unless . . . it involved something so important for me, that the Serpent felt it had to mislead me for a while.

I stopped swimming and floated downstream. *What could it be?*

Slowly I paddled back to the pond. The sun had set and the sky was black, sparked with stars. Later there would be a moon, but now there was a mere ghost of a glow over the eastern hills. As I waded to shore, my eye caught white flashes and bits of yellow froth on the water's surface. I reached out to touch: petals, I thought, floating from upstream. But they were fish, dozens of small fish, belly up on the face of the stream. I picked one up. It flicked its tail and opened an eye; it was asleep. *Indeed,* I thought. *The Serpent wants to make sure I sleep soundly tonight. Why is it so important? What will come in the night?*

"Well," said the Serpent as I appeared, wringing out my hair. "You certainly had a long swim."

"Yes. It's such an unbelievable evening, and the water's perfect. I haven't swum at night for ages."

"How was your drink?" it asked, too casually.

"Good," I answered. "Delicious, in fact. What did you put in it?"

"Several things. Did you drink it before your swim?"

I thought of the fish. "No, just now," I replied. "Thank you." I yawned. "I'm very sleepy. I'm going to bed."

"Sleep well," said the Serpent. "And thank you for making me such a nice sleeping mat."

Love

THE HAY I HAD PILED in the corner for my bed smelled sweet and fresh. I tucked a sheet of linen over it so the grasses would not tickle me, added a blanket, and settled in the nest. *I won't sleep,* I thought. *I'll just close my eyes until something happens.* But I had mowed the meadow and carried home the hay and had a long swim. I fell asleep almost immediately and slept as soundly as the fish. The dreams I had—if they should pass as dreams—were extraordinarily beautiful.

There was the touch of a feather, or an eyelash, on a nipple. I stirred and brushed my hand across my breast. Gone. And then on the other nipple, the slightest barest brush. A voice, soft, calm, loving; a voice I knew but did not know: *Eve. Let go, let go, I am with you.* A movement at my shoulder, down my arm, my waist, my hip; a slight warm feel, as of water eddying in a shallow stream, against my side.

For a while I lay straight and still on my bed of hay, as sweet caresses touched every part of my body—fleeting, delicate, light. The gentlest massage—I could not resist, every muscle in me softened, melted. Whatever it was, I could not say—but it began to play with me, plucked a tress, a foot, a finger, blew softly in my ear. I stirred and shifted on the bed, twisted my waist, raised my body to the caress. A softness on my lips, in my mouth, on my tongue. A movement over my belly. I moaned, and stirred, twined my arms around another's body, whispered *come, come,* though I knew not what I meant. And finally, *finally* when I thought I could stand it no more, I felt it enter gently, delicately, with great tenderness.

Whatever god visited me that night made love to me till dawn. At first our contact was sweet and slow; a loving, a drift of sleep, held tightly, safe; wakened again by soft touches and tender moves. I stirred, moaned, reached out to draw my lover in. Little crying sounds came from me. I grasped the body next to mine and held it close. I heard a laugh. *So!* it cried. I let my passion go, let it take me where it would. All night we made love—sometimes with great tenderness, sometimes so wild!

The skin against mine was soft, smooth. It was legs I felt twined in mine, arms that embraced me, fingers that worked their magic across my body. It was a head I held between my hands and kissed; ears I tickled with my tongue, hair I caught in my fingers. A mouth I kissed, that kissed me: a man's lips, a man's tongue, a man's teeth. This was a woman's lover.

Through the hours moonlight sparkled on the edge of the bed, I saw hay escaping from the rumpled linen, my feet twisted in the sheet. But all the while my lover stayed, shrouded, a mist in the dark.

At dawn, clean swept, I murmured, "I love you."

"And I love you, Eve," came the reply.

Morning

I WOKE TO A DAY more glorious than any other I had known in Eden. On every tree, in every hue of green, each leaf stood out against a sapphire sky. Butterflies trembled yellow black-dotted wings above the goldenrod; a warbler shouted its joy atop the aspen tree. The fish leaped higher than ever before, as if their sleep had rested them particularly well.

The Serpent was nowhere to be seen. I sat on the bank of the pond, waggling my toes in the water and tossing bits of bread to the fish. They rose eagerly to catch them in their round pink mouths. I felt too lazy to run, but I waded into the water, floated idly on my back, and watched the clouds. *The way I did on my first day,* I thought. So long ago.

When I returned, the Serpent was lying in the boughs of the willow. It looked relaxed and half-asleep; one looped coil brushed the surface of the water, swinging slightly to and fro in the breeze. As I climbed the bank under the tree, the Serpent grinned down at me.

"Turning into a great swimmer, aren't you?" it said. I splashed water in its direction; it pulled up its coil quickly and swooshed me with its tail.

"If you were less lazy, you'd have a swim too," I said.

"Swimming is too easy," replied the Serpent. "I've been climbing trees."

I barely heard what it said; I was picking bananas and blueberries and daisies along the path. "Come for breakfast," I called. "I'll only be a moment."

But when I stepped into the hut to dry myself, I saw the rumpled sheet and bits of hay strewn about. I remembered, and went still.

"Eve," I heard the Serpent call. "Are you coming?"

For a moment I could not speak.

"Eve," it called again.

"I'm coming. Just drying off." My voice sounded gruff, muffled. I clutched a cloth and came onto the terrace rubbing my head, with strands of hair over my face. Not looking at the Serpent, I put fruit and bread on the table, fetched a jug of milk from the cool shallows of the stream, and poured cups for myself and for the Serpent.

We ate. I watched the shadows of the oak and the maple blend and part on the table in front of me.

"Eve, are you all right?" asked the Serpent.

I stuffed half a banana in my mouth. "Yes, I'm fine," I mumbled.

"Look at me," the Serpent said. My face burned.

"Ah," said the Serpent. "I wondered why the fish were sleeping belly up this morning."

"I don't know what you mean," I replied.

"Don't be ridiculous. Of course you do."

"Why did you lie to me?" I snapped.

The Serpent tapped its tail on the ground and looked away. When it spoke again, its voice was calm, low, but with an undertone of tension I had never heard before.

"I lied to you about the potion, which I prepared so you would sleep soundly, and remember only dreams. I have never lied to you before."

I traced a spiral on the ground. "I know," I said.

"I'm not a good liar," said the Serpent, "especially to you."

"I knew there was something strange," I said. "But why did you want me to sleep?"

Again the Serpent hesitated, as though it were not sure it should go on. Finally, it spoke. "I thought it would be easier for you that way. I didn't really want you to remember—more than a dream." It pushed a blueberry across its plate—it had eaten nothing. "When Adam raped you, you were left with such a horror of him, of anything to do with love and sex. Remember our talk in the desert?"

I saw again the sand, the sun, the cactus with its thirst-quenching arm.

"You said you'd be willing to see him again. But you couldn't bear the thought of anything more. You shuddered—you were white as the lily of the valley there. I took your hand; it was ice cold. In the desert, at the height of day! Do you remember?"

I nodded.

"When you stopped shivering and spoke, you said that anything to do with sex was disgusting and you never wanted to talk about it again." The Serpent looked at me. "You know, Eve, you *are* the mother of humankind. If you refuse sex, it *does* present a problem."

My cheeks flamed. "Is that why—you mean, it had nothing to do with me, all that nonsense last night? You rigged it so humankind could get started?"

The Serpent laughed and shook its head. "Eve, Eve. That was only part of it—a small part. If you decide you want nothing to do with Adam again, I will defend that choice. You know that, don't you?"

I did know it. "Yes," I said.

"But love—physical love—is a great joy, and I want *you*—Eve, *my* Eve, not the mother of humankind—to know that joy, and not banish it from your life on the basis of one painful, humiliating experience. My dear, to me your happiness, your fulfillment, are every bit as important as all the rest. If you do not know passion, you will never fully understand the human heart." The Serpent peered at me. "Do you believe me?"

I knew instantly that it was true. In all the Serpent had ever said and in its every act, its belief in the individual rang out, clear, overpowering.

I was also certain of its love for me.

"Yes," I said.

The Serpent squinted its emerald eyes. "Last night you were touched by miracles! Can you truly believe it was rigged, a bit of manipulation by God, by me?" With its tail, the Serpent raised my chin and looked me in the eyes. "Eve, can you honestly say it was *nonsense*?"

I turned away and gazed over the valley. Memories of the night flooded through me.

"No," I answered at last.

The daisies lay on the table, where I had tossed them on my way from the pond. I began plaiting them into a crown, twining the green stems in and out, smoothing the white petals with my fingertips. My eyes on the flowers, I said at last. "Serpent, was it you last night?"

For a time the Serpent did not answer. I was not sure it would. At length it drew breath and spoke slowly.

"You know, Eve, I am many creatures, many things, with many forms. It's almost impossible to say what is I, what is another." It looked at me and sighed. "But yes—last night it was me. In one form or another."

"I thought so." I completed the crown, carefully tucking in the ends.

"Serpent?"

"Eve?"

"Will we do it again? Will you make love again, to me?"

The Serpent was silent. I watched an eagle circle in the sky.

"No," it said at last.

"Oh . . ." I cried.

"But you and Adam will make love. And you'll see. He'll give you great pleasure, and you will give him pleasure too. It *will* be beautiful, for both of you."

"But—" I started.

"Eve. Listen to me. Try to understand." The Serpent pressed its tail flat against the ground. "You are Woman. You are Eve. Eves are not made for Serpents. Serpents are not meant for Eves."

It was my turn to be quiet. After a few moments I said, "Serpent, last night. It was so . . . beautiful . . . for me. Was it for you?"

The Serpent smiled. "Oh, Eve, my dear. It was, it was."

The Choice

ADAM APPEARED LATE in the morning with blisters on his hands. "I'm not used to working so hard anymore," he said. "It took all day to put up the pergola, and then I had to cut the hay this morning." He sank onto the bench. I gave him bread, and soft blue cheese to spread on it, and peaches, and sat opposite him while he ate. His face was smudged with earth, his fingernails dirty and torn; a glob of cheese was stuck in the corner of his mouth and peach juice dripped down his chin. *Is this the man,* I thought, *who will be my lover? Is there something in him I do not see?* But try as I would, I could find no lover there—only Adam eating a peach.

When he had finished, the Serpent, Adam, and I

walked to the glade. It was a hot day, but even though the sun sizzled overhead and leaves hung limp on oak trees and aspen, our tree was as vibrant as before.

"How amazing it is!" Adam exclaimed. "Three days ago it was covered with apples and now they're gone. You'd think it would be drooping, but this tree still looks happy. Let's climb up; maybe it will make *us* feel better."

Adam and I scrambled into the branches. The bark was mauled and scratched in many places, as though rough creatures with sharp claws had clambered about, oblivious to the tree's beauty.

"Surely they were monkeys," said Adam. "Nothing else could get around so well."

I shook my head sadly. "I never thought monkeys were so destructive," I said.

"They must have found it very exciting," the Serpent said thoughtfully. "The fun of it all, picking those beautiful apples, tossing them to God."

"I've found some fur," cried Adam, three quarters of the way up the tree. "It's definitely monkeys." The branch he stood on groaned.

"You're too heavy, Adam," I cried. "Let me go up."

I climbed past him. *I wish I could leave him in the dust for once* flashed unexpectedly through my mind. I stopped abruptly halfway to the next branch, startled. *That's not the way I am; that's not me.* I shook my head; but it *was* a satisfying thought. Climbing on, I sent a powdering of bark onto Adam's head.

All along the trunk, fragments of leaves clung to the bark. Unlike the leaves we knew and rubbed like velvet moss on our lips, these were slate hard with jagged edges, as if the tree had defended itself against the invader.

"Eve, be careful, you're getting very high; you'll break a branch," the Serpent called. As it spoke, the limb I was standing on gave an alarming crack. Nevertheless I hauled myself a little higher, using both arms to distribute my weight. From there I could see into the highest boughs, a filigree of brown and green spread against the sky. And a glimpse of gold.

I held my breath. It was gone, I had dreamed it, there was only green. No, it was real. Gone. In the slight breeze, the delicate top branches moved to and fro and hid and revealed: a butterfly; a bee; a yellow-breasted warbler—perhaps I had seen one of those. But no! Something else, another yellow, deeper: gold. A golden orb. An apple.

I shouted and clapped my hands. My body began to slide, the bark scraped my skin. I grabbed wildly at a branch and clung, heart pounding, against the trunk.

"Oh, Serpent," I cried. "Adam. There's an *apple*."

"An *apple*!" shouted Adam. "Are you sure?"

"An apple," repeated the Serpent, and it did not sound surprised.

"You're sure it's an apple?" Adam repeated.

"Yes. There's no mistaking that color. Serpent, can you come up? I can't reach it."

The Serpent wound its way gracefully up the trunk to the bough next to mine.

"Can you get it?" Adam was standing on tiptoe a few branches below me, dancing with impatience.

"I think so," said the Serpent. Looping its tail around the branch I was standing on, it began to elongate its body as it had on the cliff, with the vine curling around its face. Its neck, thinner and thinner, extended and stretched, while its head, ears, and feathers raised, rose slowly into the upper branches of the tree.

"It is indeed an apple," it said. "Round and perfect. I'll bring it down." And its neck retracted until its head was again level with mine. Cupped in its fluted velvet tongue lay a golden apple.

I reached out and curled my fingers around the fruit. It was unlike any apple I had seen: not much larger than a plum, and golden, with a long stem that seemed too fine to hold even a buttercup, and two tiny velvet leaves. I pressed it to my nose, inhaled: a scent of sandalwood, cinnamon, basil, coriander. Like the tree, the tiny fruit exuded a sense of peace and joy. It made all the world seem bright.

"It's wonderful," I whispered.

"Yes," said the Serpent. "But you'd better climb down before you drop it. And Adam, you'd better get down too before you break the branch."

Adam scrambled quickly out of the tree, and pulled the apple from my hand before my feet had touched the ground. He went through the same motions I had, eyes squinted, feeling, smelling. "It's an apple all right," he said. "But it certainly is different! I've never known anything so nice." He cradled the golden fruit against his chest as though it were a newborn fawn.

"What do we do now?" Adam asked. "Suppose God comes?" He looked at the apple in his hand. "Where can we hide it?"

"What are you going to do with it?" asked the Serpent.

Adam and I looked at each other.

"I don't know," I said.

"Put it in your basket, Eve," said Adam, glancing at the two paths into the clearing. "We can't stay here. God may be on his way now. Serpent, what should we do?"

"We need to talk," the Serpent said. "Someplace where God won't disturb us. There's a thicket to the east, a rabbit warren; it will be perfect. Come."

We walked through all the glory of the Garden, beneath the chattering fronds of palm trees, along brooks that somersaulted over rocks in a confusion of waters, bearing with them dappled trout, acorns, chaff. We passed otters swimming and cavorting in streams. Horses stood head to rump in the shade and swished their silken tails at flies. Insects flitted on the surface of the lake, insouciant—for in the Garden no creature feared any other. Adam and I stepped carefully, avoiding twigs that might snap under our feet. A sense of fore-boding oppressed us, as though we were being hunted and eyes watched us from behind rocks or high in the trees.

At length we came to a thick mess of brambles. There were rabbits everywhere, and small birds.

"Follow me carefully," said the Serpent. On hands and knees we crawled down well-worn rabbit tracks until we reached a small meadow, where an ancient wil-low dipped its branches in a stream. Adam and I sat under the tree and I drew the apple from the basket and placed it on the grass. The Serpent coiled in front of us. As we watched, it changed its morning coat of diamonds in crimson and emerald and azure to gold: gold as the apple, gold as sunflowers in late summer, gold as the sun. When it moved, its body was caught in the light; sparks of gold shot out and flickered across the trunk of the willow, the grass, the leaves, and across our bodies and faces and hair. The Serpent held its ears high; its crimson feathers quivered with each word it spoke. Its tongue—its marvelous, magical tongue—passed across its lips and, from time to time, reached out and touched the apple.

"What *is* this apple?" asked Adam when we were settled. "I've eaten lots of apples, but just looking at this one makes me feel different. Not so much happy, but light and free. Serpent, do you know for sure what will happen if we eat it?"

"If you eat the apple? Nobody can be sure."

"Not even you, Serpent?" I asked.

"Not even, as you put it, I. I know God would be very angry—angrier than you've ever seen him."

"But will we die?"

"I believe God will no longer protect you from death," said the Serpent. "You'll grow old and weak and, yes, eventually die—from old age or disease, or an accident." The Serpent stretched its neck as if it were stiff. "In the Garden you're immortal, until God decides otherwise or you leave the Garden."

"But why should we leave the Garden?" Adam stared at the Serpent, his mouth half-open. "There's no reason to leave. We have everything we need."

"I think," said the Serpent, "God might decide he doesn't want you in the Garden anymore. If you disobey him, he may well throw you out."

"Throw us out!" cried Adam. "Why would he do that? How would he get along without us? I do so many things for him, so much that makes his life comfortable, all the gathering of food, and the hut, and furniture. He doesn't do anything for himself!"

The Serpent knit its brows. "Don't underestimate God. It's dangerous. God enjoys having you around, you're an amusement for him much of the time. . . ."

"Amusement!" cried Adam.

"A distraction," added the Serpent, "and you *do* make his life comfortable without his having to put out any effort. But he's quite capable of getting along without you. Not that he wants to."

"So he doesn't need us, but he doesn't want to throw us out?"

"That's right. God made you, and all the other animals, with the idea that you'd be here forever."

"What about populating the world?"

"As God sees it, when there are more people, some will live outside the Garden, but you and Eve will always live here."

"As an amusement and distraction," muttered Adam.

"And a convenience." The Serpent laughed. "Don't be upset, Adam. That's just the way God is."

"You mean God would throw us out of the Garden for *eating an apple*?" I asked.

"For disobeying him."

"But still, it's because of an apple."

"A very special apple. The apple of the Tree of the Knowledge of Good and Evil."

I shook my head. "How much more can we learn from an apple? And why doesn't God want us to know?"

The Serpent shifted its weight, sending golden sparks in all directions, "If you eat the apple, in certain respects you'll resemble God. You will no longer be innocent: you'll know good and you'll know evil, and be able to choose between them. You'll be responsible for your actions. And you'll be free to choose the course of your lives." It lowered its head and looked at each of us in turn. "You, and all people, for all time."

"What's wrong with that?" asked Adam.

"*I* don't think there's anything wrong with it; on the contrary. But God doesn't see things that way, and your freedom comes at a price. You'll have to work for your survival, and bear the results of your actions, good or bad. You'll have to deal not only with evil committed by others, but with your own—the evil you do—and the evil that may be within yourselves. With guilt and conscience. With the suffering of all people, including those you love."

The Serpent sighed. I had seen it give one of its great sighs only a few times, and I was always enthralled. First it inhaled. Its body swelled from head to toe, and whatever pattern it had assumed that day expanded: diamonds grew immense; dots became wide circles; simple, wavy lines became sweeping, sinuous curves. It remained, swollen and still, for several moments, then gradually deflated, growing thinner and thinner as the air trickled through its nostrils and the patterns shrank to their normal size. When the Serpent sighed, I felt it was lamenting all the ills of the world—those ills we did not know in the Garden.

"No matter what I tell you now," the Serpent continued, "you'll never understand how difficult life will be outside the Garden. Here, you chafe at God's demands. Outside, you'll have other masters. You may be slaves; you may be soldiers forced to fight for causes that are not your own. You'll work endless days and not reap the fruits of your labor. You'll suffer pain and anguish and hardship. And at the end of such a life only death awaits."

"You make it sound *terrible*," said Adam.

"Much of it *is* terrible," the Serpent responded. "And you *must* be aware of that before you make your decision. But much will be beautiful also. In the outside world, the abilities and talents God gave you will be free to flourish and, like the wind, take on lives of their own. You'll feel your emotions more deeply, you'll experience love beyond what is possible here. Because you suffer, your happiness will be more intense; sorrow will give deeper meaning to joy. The mountain that rises from the shadows of a chasm is always the most magnificent." The Serpent looked at me. "Remember, Eve, the alpenglow, after the storm?"

I nodded. The granite glowed again, scarlet, before my eyes.

"God's world will still be there for you to enjoy," continued the Serpent, "and you'll make gardens of your own, and know yourselves the excitement of discovery and the joys of creation."

"And you'll be there to help us," I said.

The Serpent shook its head. "No, Eve, I won't. I can't go with you. At least not so you'll know it."

"Oh, Serpent!" I jumped to my feet. "How could you not come with us? We'd never be able to get along without you!"

"Of course you would, Eve. You'd thrive, you and Adam. You've already managed very well outside the Garden, as we both know."

"But you were there! I couldn't have done anything without you."

"That was the first time. Everything was new. You'll learn how to live on your own; you'll find more hospitable lands than those we saw."

I sank to my knees and buried my head in my arms.

"But Serpent, how can I live without you," I sobbed. My body shuddered; my fingers twisted in the grass. The Serpent sat, immobile, impassive, immense.

"How can you let her cry that way?" Adam shouted, glaring angrily at the Serpent. He came over and put his arms around my shoulders. "Say something to comfort her!"

Silence. The Serpent did not move from its place; beyond my sobs I heard the rhythmic tap of its tail on the dry fallen leaves. Adam's arms lay heavy on my shoulders; after a short time, he drew them away and sat next to me. I felt the warmth of his thigh against mine, but it did not comfort me. For a long time I wept; my hair grew heavy with tears.

Above me an owl shifted its talons on a branch; a leaf fluttered to the ground. At long last, my weeping done, I lay gasping short, ragged breaths, one cheek buried in the leaves. Finally the Serpent spoke, its voice rough as though it too had wept.

"Eve, I've taught you everything I can. Now it's time. Time for you to make your own life."

The Serpent uncurled itself. I thought it would come to me and hold me in its coils, as it always had when something upset me. But it moved a few measures closer to the apple and settled again in its golden heap.

"Stop now," it said quietly. "The Garden is not a place to grieve."

"How can I *not* grieve!" I cried. "I am *filled* with grief!"

"I know, Eve," said the Serpent. "So am I." It stared straight ahead, eyes fixed, watching in the thicket something I could not see. Beyond the cover of the tree, the shadow of an eagle passed across the dappled grass. The Serpent plucked a bunch of clover. "Here," it said, extending it to me. "Wipe your face now."

I blew my nose and mopped at my eyes with the clover. Adam ran to the stream and brought water for me in his cupped hands, then pushed the tangled hair from my face. He held my chin and looked at me carefully, tilting his head.

"You have some dirt here," he said, and swabbed my forehead. "That's better, it's gone." His fingers brushed my cheek lightly. "Eve, you know, we don't *have* to eat the apple. We can stay here, and the Serpent will always be with us. With you."

I nodded, but I knew it was not true. We had come too far. In a way we had already left the Garden.

"Now," said the Serpent when we were settled once more against the tree, "it is time to decide."

We looked at the fruit that lay, golden, on its bed of leaves. The Serpent scrutinized each of us in turn.

"Think carefully, Eve. Adam, reflect on this: In the Garden you are safe. If you leave, you will never be safe again."

"Suppose we just forget about the apple? Bury it, throw it away. Would we be all right?" asked Adam. "Would God know we had found it?"

The Serpent answered slowly. "If you did that, God might never know."

"Adam, do you really think you *could* forget about it now?" I cried. "Go back to your life as it was before and never think of it again?"

Adam knelt next to me and took my hand. "Eve. What do you want to do?"

For a moment I could not answer. What *did* I want?

When I thought of leaving the Garden, my heart sang. I recalled glimpses of the outside world: the glow of rock, pigs rooting on the riverbank, the wildness and the beauty of the sea. To return to that great, undisciplined, outer world: build my house, plant my garden—radishes, yellow beans, grapes, pomegranates, willows and pear trees; explore to the ends of the Earth! Run free across the desert, leaving footprints in the sand.

When I thought of leaving the Garden, my stomach twisted and tore. Our house, cozy and comfortable, the morning runs, the animals I knew and that knew me, that reached out for a scratch on the neck as I passed. And somewhere in the Garden, the dog—I kept hoping he'd reappear. And the Serpent—*how could I leave the Serpent?* Impossible to waken every day without its great presence by my side, impossible not to tell it of a frog I saw, a butterfly of a different color (and the Serpent would change its skin to match the butterfly, saying, "Like this?" "More green?"). Who would answer my questions?

Who would ask questions of me?

Then there was the tree. The tree that had struggled and fought to break ground, to grow, to defend itself from God's attacks. The tree that exuded beauty and tranquility and joy; that called to us and drew us in. Was this, as God said, a wicked, dangerous tree, its beauty there to beguile us unto death? Or was that beauty the embodiment of happiness?

God created the world, but when he was done he remained in the Garden, and in that outer world things took on lives of their own. Lava, tornadoes, blizzards, the storm at sea. Terrible and glorious. For all the shrieking, for all the danger, they were what they were meant to be: themselves.

"If we stay in the Garden," I said, pausing between words to find my way. "We'll be like the animals, obeying God, turning to the right and the left as he moves his hands. Like the monkeys, stealing golden apples from the enchanted tree. Comfortable, but not *free*. Always we'll be under God's control." Through the willow's cascading branches I caught a glimpse of the sky. "I'd rather be like the eagle. He refused to join the parade. He's not afraid to go beyond the Garden: he brought us food on the mountaintop and saved my life in the sea." I drew in my breath sharply. "He defied God, to do what was right—to tell the Serpent what God and Adam were doing to me." I twisted a willow wand around my hand. "I want to be one of the things that gets away from God and takes on its own spirit. A force. Like the eagle." I reached my hand toward the Serpent. "Dear friend," I said. "I can't imagine life without you." I was afraid I would cry again. "But I can't stay in the Garden anymore."

"I know that, Eve," the Serpent replied.

Adam spoke hesitantly, with a quaver in his voice. "I'll come with you."

"You don't have to leave just because I do. You can stay here if you want. I can go alone."

"I couldn't possibly stay here without you." The quaver disappeared. "*You* can't imagine life without the Serpent. Eve, *I* can't imagine life without *you*." He pulled the willow wand from my fingers. "I can't say it the way you do, but I feel the same. No matter how terrible things are outside, I want to be free, like the tornado, to choose myself what I will be and what I will do." He stood. "Besides, I want to see what it's like outside the Garden. We *should* eat the apple." He reached to pick it up.

"Wait," said the Serpent. "We have things to do first. I have to teach you how to make fire, so you can stay warm and cook."

"What does fire have to do with hunger?" asked Adam.

"Outside the Garden, many plants need to be cooked—heated over a fire—before you can eat them. And then"—the Serpent hesitated—"you'll be eating animals, and it's much better to cook them."

"Eating *animals!*" Adam and I looked at the Serpent in horror. "Never!"

"You will before long. And animals will try to eat you, too."

"Oh, no!"

Sighing, the Serpent said, "Do you remember, Eve, I told you God gave each animal the body it needed to survive: beaks to birds, multiple stomachs to ruminants, and so on."

I nodded.

"At the time of Creation, God decided that some animals would eat plants and some would eat meat—that is, other animals, fish, birds. In the Garden we are all vegetarians—we eat only seeds and vegetables and fruits—but when creatures leave the Garden, the carnivores—meat eaters—will start to eat the flesh of other animals."

"Why did he *do* that?" Adam cried. "It's awful!"

"I think God may have felt it was an efficient way to organize the world. But it's far too complicated to go into right now. Find some dry twigs and bring them into the sun."

All afternoon we twirled sticks among dry leaves, blew when we got a spark, added small twigs. After a long while, a tiny fire blossomed among the leaves.

"Good," said the Serpent. "Do it again." And we did it, again and again until our hands were raw. Finally the Serpent was satisfied. "At least you won't die of cold or hunger."

The Serpent shook itself from head to toe as if it were stiff. "Now we need to discuss how *you* will deal with the world outside. You'll have to make weapons to protect yourselves. Eve, weapons are a bit like the tools you made to tend the tree, a sharp stone or a branch. When you push or throw it into an animal, you have a good chance of killing it, so it won't kill you. Then you can use it for food."

I felt sick. Adam shook his head. "Never, never!"

"Adam, like it or not, humans are carnivores, and sooner or later you'll probably eat meat, though you can certainly survive without it. You'll learn to grow vegetables and fruit, so you don't have to hunt for them in the wild. You take seeds from the corn and the wheat and oats and barley, dig the earth to make it soft, put in the seeds, cover them, make sure they have enough water."

"Just as I did the tree," I said.

"Exactly. Animals: some you may keep around as friends—the dog, the cat. . . ."

"Of course, the dog . . . "

"And others you may keep near you—cows, goats, sheep, pigs, llama, camels. And birds: chickens and ducks and geese. Tend them, feed them, give them shelter. In exchange they'll give you their milk and eggs, feathers and wool, and you may take their meat."

Adam again shook his head in disbelief.

"Some of the bigger animals can carry things, pull things, even carry you." The sun was beginning to drop toward the horizon. The Serpent stretched its neck and brushed the golden orb with its tongue. "Adam, Eve, look at this apple. Will you eat it? Are you certain that is what you want?"

"Oh!" Adam buried his head in his arms. "Death! Eating animals! I don't know which is worse!" He sat hunched over in the grass; tiny red ants climbed back and forth across his toes, carrying specks of grain, but he did not notice them.

Death, eating animals, death, eating animals, rattled around my head. The raccoon was dead: would *I* have been able to kill it? Could I have eaten it? My senses whirled.

Finally Adam sat up, shook his hair out of his eyes, and straightened his shoulders. "*I* won't die," he said firmly. "Or if I do, not for a long time. And I'll come back, too, if I want to; I'll find a way. And *I'll* never eat animals—you can, Eve, if you want to!"

I stared at him. I had trouble imagining myself dead, but I knew that what the Serpent said was true. If we left the Garden—if we ate the apple—we *would* die. But, as Adam said, not for a while. And I too was perfectly content with fruits and vegetables.

"Before you eat the apple," the Serpent said slowly, "you must reflect again. Everything I have told you about life in the outside world is true." It looked at each of us in turn.

"I'll eat it." My voice shook, but I put out my hand.

"Adam?" the Serpent asked.

"I'll eat it too," said Adam firmly. The Serpent handed me the apple, and I bit into it. Tart with a slight touch of lemon, it tingled on my tongue and in my throat.

"It's delicious," I said, and gave it to Adam, who bit into it as well.

"It's the best thing I've ever tasted!" he exclaimed. "You must have some, Serpent."

The Serpent shook its head sadly. "I know good and evil well enough already."

So Adam and I took turns finishing the apple, bite by bite, until only the seeds were left. These I put in the basket I still carried around my neck, thinking, *I might grow another tree, outside.*

When we were done, the Serpent grinned at us. "How do you feel?"

We looked at each other. "No different. *Are* we different?"

"*Should* we be different?"

"Of course you're different," said the Serpent. "You don't notice it yet, but you will soon. You've made a choice: you're free."

Adam stood and stretched, and looked at the sun. "It's getting late. We should be going back," he said.

"God will be looking for me." Without waiting for the Serpent or me, he started off, brushing the brambles aside. The Serpent laughed and motioned me to follow.

"Is that the apple's doing?" I murmured, but the Serpent only waggled its ears.

So we walked home, and everything seemed the same. As always, the clouds turned crimson and orange, and our shadows stalked behind us as we marched into the sinking sun.

"Go home, Adam, and come back in the morning," the Serpent said casually as we turned onto the path that led to our house.

Suddenly Adam's confidence was gone. "What do I say to God?" he stammered.

"Say hello. Ask him if he had a nice day. He won't notice anything, and nothing will change until he does."

Climbing the arbor to get grapes for dinner and fetching the bread, I felt dazed, as though I were moving in a dream. I placed olives and cheese on the table, and a good wine. Without a word the Serpent and I ate, and I cleared the things away. Afterward I sat cross-legged on the terrace, idly drawing designs in the sand: a square, a circle, two triangles.

"Serpent." I traced a line around my signs, a squiggly line that did not quite join at the ends.

"Eve?" The Serpent came over and coiled beside me.

"Why didn't you comfort me when I was crying?"

The Serpent answered slowly. "Eve, my dear, before all else, I'm your teacher. Friend, companion, mentor, guide . . ."

"Lover."

After a pause the Serpent said, "If you like. But teacher first. Today you needed to learn two things that will be crucial for you in the future. One, I won't be with you anymore."

I drew my breath in a sob.

"And two, how to deal with life on your own, without any help from me."

"Always, then, will I be alone? When things are hard? Only myself to rely on?"

"You have Adam. And in the ages to come, there'll be others. But finally, yes, you're alone."

"You'll *never* be there again?"

The Serpent was silent for some time. When it answered, its voice was so low that I had to strain to hear. "Not so you'll recognize me, but I'll be there somewhere. You can reach me, if you learn how."

"Tell me," I begged.

"That you must find out for yourself." The Serpent turned away. "Sleep now. Tomorrow will be a long day."

"Serpent?"

"Eve?"

"Please, won't you make love to me tonight, once more?"

The Serpent moved toward the door. "You know the answer to that, Eve, and in your heart of hearts you know it's right." It looked at me with a mischievous glint in its eyes. "Don't tempt me, Eve," it said, and went off laughing outrageously; I could not fathom why.

The Last Day

THAT NIGHT IN THE small hours, cold began to seep into the Garden. From the low valleys, the beds of slow streams, the thickets of the deepest woods, the cold spread across meadow and prairie to the farthest, highest hills. Among the hazel shrubs, deer drew close for warmth. In the trees, tanagers and finches plumped their feathers and buried their heads under wings. I woke shivering, dragged two blankets to my mat, and fell back to sleep.

The Serpent woke me before dawn. "Let's run; we probably won't be able to later."

I drew the blankets over my head. "It's too cold."

"It *is* cold," said the Serpent. "And that's very interesting. Wrap one of your blankets around you. You'll warm up quickly once you start running."

We ran. Frost twinkled on blades of grass. The entire countryside was shrouded in mist. The precious landmarks passed by as though they were moving, not I. *Will I truly not see that elm again? That boulder, how strange it looks in the cloud; will I never climb on it again?* I glanced at the Serpent, gliding smoothly beside me as though it had no care in the world. Tears sprang to my eyes.

"Don't cry, Eve," it said, flicking its tail. "I'll race you to the river."

I lost, of course. I always did. The Serpent was the fastest being in the Garden, and it never slowed to let me win.

As we sat down for breakfast, Adam arrived, blue with cold. The Serpent quickly heated a bowl of milk for him, and I fetched a blanket.

"What's happened?" he asked, teeth chattering.

"I think eating the apple started something," the Serpent said. "Maybe the Garden's defenses have been weakened. What did God say?"

"He didn't seem to realize it was cold."

The Serpent nodded. "Like me, he doesn't feel it. But you'd think he'd notice the mist."

"Oh, it wasn't misty up there, only near the river. He asked me what I did yesterday."

"What did you say?" I asked.

"Nothing. I mean that's what I said— 'Nothing.'"

"Was he satisfied with that?" asked the Serpent.

"Yes. That's what I always say." Adam hugged the cup in both hands and held it to his chest. "This feels so good. And *tastes* so good." The blanket slipped off his shoulder. He twitched it back. "How do you keep this thing on?" he said.

I jumped up, forgetting to hold my blanket, and it fell to the ground. "I'll put a hole in the middle, the way I did with the clothes I made to go North. Then it fits over your head." This was quickly done with my stone knife, and soon Adam and I were outfitted in many-colored woven rugs.

"You're beginning to look like me," the Serpent exclaimed.

"We don't look too funny?" asked Adam.

The Serpent tilted its head from right to left and took a turn around us. "Not at all," it said. "You look elegant. And warm."

Is this real? I kept thinking, as we drank our milk. *Is this really me, getting ready to leave the Garden? Will I never come back? Will I really not see the Serpent again?* I shook my head. My dreams came back to me. *Maybe this is a dream,* I thought, *which will pass. I'll wake up and all will be as it was before.*

I looked at the Serpent. It was discussing patterns of rugs with Adam. "How can we get a diamond shape? And that crimson there?"

"You could try raspberry juice, or currants, or maybe both mixed together," the Serpent suggested, bending its neck to peer at the red circles on its back.

"You're silly, both of you!" I cried. "Our last day!"

"How do you know?" asked Adam. "Maybe God won't notice and we'll stay here."

"Last day in Paradise," sang the Serpent. "Where would you like to go?"

"To the tree," we called out together.

"Wait," I said. I tied a vine around my waist and gave another to Adam, to hold our robes together.

"*Very* smart," the Serpent declared, and off we went.

"Why are you so happy all of a sudden?" I asked the Serpent. With a pang, the thought came: *Maybe it's glad to be rid of me.*

"Certainly not, Eve," said the Serpent, as though I had spoken aloud. "You know that as well as I do. A final lesson, my dear, for life's difficult moments. When everything is decided, and it's out of your hands, once you've had your cry, it's easier on everyone to laugh."

We had just reached the tree when we heard God: "Adam, Eve! Where *are* you?" he roared.

The Serpent raised its ears. Adam and I stood frozen.

"Come here, I want to speak to you! I haven't seen you in days."

"He saw me this *morning*," Adam muttered.

"Eve! Adam!" The words thundered through the trees.

"Come," I said, taking Adam's hand. We went forward to meet God, the Serpent following behind.

God stood just above the hut, apparently forgetting his irritation for the moment.

"Such a lovely spot," he mumbled. "Eve does a nice job with the gravel and flowers." He leaned forward and frowned. "But why is it misty? I've never seen the pond that way before."

"Hello, God," I said. He turned. A series of expressions flashed across his face: amazement, confusion, anger. Rage. Pure rage.

"What's that you've got on?" he growled.

"Blankets."

"Why do you have blankets on?"

"Because we were cold."

"*Why* were you cold? You've never been cold before!"

"It got cold in the night. We didn't have anything to keep us warm—we were naked," I added, remembering the word with pride.

God gulped a great breath and bellowed: "Who *told*

you you were naked? You must have eaten the apple! But I got rid of them, all of them!" He grabbed Adam with both his great hands and shook him. "Tell me! *Who* gave you the apple?"

Adam turned his head away.

God pulled him forward until their faces nearly touched and shouted, "Who?"

"Eve did," Adam stammered, "but . . ."

God jumped toward me, hands raised. Suddenly the Serpent was at my side, erect, still.

"God." A voice I barely recognized sent shivers up my spine.

God dropped his hands and stood shaking with rage. In a choked voice he said, "Eve, who gave you the apple?" I shook my head. God shouted, "WHO GAVE YOU THE APPLE?"

"Answer him, Eve," the Serpent said softly.

"The Serpent—" I said.

"Ah!" shouted God.

"But we both decided, Adam and I—"

"*You!*" cried God, turning on the Serpent. "*Traitor!* You *traitor*!"

"It's not that way, God!" I ran forward. "God, *listen* to me." I clutched his arm. "Adam and I decided to eat it. There was only one left, at the top of the tree—"

"Oh, *treachery!*" God cried, shaking me off and

striking his forehead with the palm of his hand. The Serpent coughed.

"We asked the Serpent to bring it down for us because we couldn't reach it. But it was *our* decision. Adam's and mine!"

"But *you* handed the apple to Adam."

"I did."

"But—" said Adam.

"And *you*," God turned to the Serpent, "*you* gave it to Eve."

The Serpent sighed. "I did."

"And you, Adam, *you* ate it?"

"I did."

"So did I," I said, "but the Serpent didn't."

"The Serpent has no need to eat the apple," God said. He frowned and for a long time was quiet. I was surprised. I had never known him to keep silent when he was angry, and he was surely very angry indeed. He appeared to be fuming; his white hair stood up around his head like tendrils thrashing in the breeze. His fists, and every muscle in his body, were clenched hard as stone. At last he spoke again, and this time it was our fates he told.

Pointing to the Serpent, he cried, "Because you have given the apple to Eve, you are cursed!"

The Serpent raised its great body and, looking God

straight in the eye, cried, "Yahweh! Of my own free will, I accept your curse and all its consequences."

God looked stunned. "You do?" he said.

"I do. Go ahead."

"Er," said God, "where was I?"

"Because you have done this, you are cursed more than all cattle?" the Serpent suggested.

God glared. "Yes, and more than every beast of the field. Every one!" he shouted. He picked up confidence as he went along. "Because you have done this, on your belly you shall go, and you shall eat dust all the days of your life, and I will put enmity"—"Hatred," muttered the Serpent to me, out of the side of its mouth—"between you and the woman, and between your seed and her seed"—"Children," the Serpent explained—"he shall bruise your head, and you will bruise his heel"—"You'll kill me and I'll bite you."

I looked at the Serpent, appalled.

God turned to me, eyes red with rage, and waved his fist in my face. "I will greatly multiply your sorrow. In pain you shall bring forth children, and your husband shall rule over you."

"That's going to be hard to escape," said the Serpent sadly.

"As for you," God cried to Adam, "because you hearkened to the voice of your wife—"

"It wasn't that way!" cried Adam. "And she's not my wife!"

"—and have eaten of the tree, which I commanded you not to eat: I curse the ground you till. You will toil all the days of your life, and bring forth thorns and thistles, and in the end return to the ground." God pointed his long finger at Adam. "For dust thou art, and unto dust shalt thou return." Then, to my great relief, he turned and stomped away.

"It's worse than I expected," muttered the Serpent.

"Oh, Serpent!" I was stunned. "What will he do to you?" But something was happening to the Serpent; its body seemed smaller, the diamonds and circles on the skin less brilliant, the face less round.

"Serpent, Serpent!" I cried.

"Eve, don't fuss," the Serpent said, but its voice was muted and coarse. Its head, the lovely oval with the wide mouth and emerald eyes, thinned; the nose grew long and flat. The patterns faded and dissolved, and all the colors merged to gray. The feathered ears were the last to go; valiantly, they waved above an ugly flattened head, and then, crinkled and dry, fell to the earth.

I threw my arms around its neck. "Oh, Serpent," I sobbed. "Your beautiful body, your beautiful skin." I ran my hands down its thin sides. "Your ears, those plumes! How can God do this to you?" I threw back my head and screamed, and my scream echoed from the canyon walls at the far end of the valley. "Oh, God, I hate you!"

"Eve, stop now," said the Serpent firmly. "That's not important. Come sit on this rock for a moment. We don't have long. Adam, you too." Since God's curse, Adam had not moved; he stood like a stone beside me.

"I didn't think God had any power over you," I moaned.

"He doesn't really." The Serpent smiled. "But even *my* choices are limited. I could have stayed in the Garden. . . ."

"In all your beauty?"

The Serpent chuckled, the old chuckle I knew. "As you say, in all my beauty. I could even have left the Garden and remained as I was."

Adam found his voice, but the words came out as a croak. "So why didn't you do that?" he asked.

"Adam," the Serpent replied, "if I had made either of those choices, I would have lost the right to help you, and Eve, and all the others to come. Intervene for the good of humankind, put up a small defense against evil and chaos." The Serpent shook its ugly head as if the feathers still danced at its top. "It seems to me that such power is worth the loss of beauty."

God did not reappear until late in the morning. He was calm—perhaps he was spent by his rage—and looked sad when he saw us, as if the Garden would be less cheerful without us. Clutched in his arms were what appeared to be shreds of weed. "Adam and Eve, here, you'll need something to keep you warm outside the Garden. Put away those rags." (We were still clutching our blankets around us; it had grown colder as the day went on.) "I brought you these." He threw his armload at our feet.

Cautiously, we approached. "What are they?"

"Skins."

"No!"

"Skins of animals, to keep you warm."

"Skins," stuttered Adam. "What happened to the animals?"

"Why, I killed them of course. What do you think?"

"Killed them? How?"

"I hit them with a bolt of lightning. How else? Put them on, put them on." Reluctantly, we drew the skins over our heads. They were, as God said, warm, and surprisingly soft and comfortable, but we kept the blankets around our shoulders.

"Now you must go," said God. He turned to the Serpent, which was coiled in its diminished state beside us. "Serpent, because you and I have known each other such a very long time, I am ready to overlook your . . . transgressions and allow you to remain in the Garden."

"But Adam and Eve are banished?"

"Certainly."

"God," said the Serpent, raising itself as high as it could and speaking in a raw, rasping voice. "I understand that Adam and Eve must leave the Garden. They have disobeyed you and eaten of the Tree of the Knowledge of Good and Evil. They knew the consequences would be severe. But banishment from the Garden is punishment enough. Why must you add to their pain by cursing their existence forever?"

"I must and I will!" God cried, his voice rising. "It is just! They disobeyed me!"

"They did," the Serpent replied. "There is no denying it. But God, there is not only justice, there is mercy. You taught these children to pray to a just and merciful god. Be merciful now!"

God's face turned from red to crimson. "Adam and Eve do not deserve mercy. They have defied me!" he shouted, and stamped his feet. "They are *evil*, *evil*! They will work, and suffer, and die, and return to dust. It is my will!" He swept his arm across the landscape as if he would wipe us from his world. Then he turned to the Serpent and his voice softened. "But to *you* I will be merciful. It will be lonely here without those two. So *you* may remain."

The Serpent glared at God through narrow eyes. "I

have no wish to stay with the god you have become. I will go into the wilderness with them."

God drew in a great breath as if he would explode. "Then go!" he shouted, and pointed to the South. "Get out, get out! Go!" With every cry his rage grew. In two steps he leaped to the top of a high rock. Putting his fingers to his mouth, he whistled, and the call echoed back and around the hills and valleys of the Garden, and the animals came running and flying, crowding together in their haste.

"Out! Out! Out!" he cried. With each word he seemed to gain in stature until he stood a giant on the cliff. From the ground, he tore a young aspen up by the roots and twirled it over his head, shouting: *"Out with you! Out with you all! Go on! Get out!"*

The animals, all the animals in the Garden, rushed down the valley toward the southern border, running, scurrying, flying, crawling, leaping. "Move!" cried the Serpent. "Quick!" I scrambled toward the bushes.

"Adam!" I called, but Adam was lost in the dust. The ground shuddered. Mouths wide, eyes red with fear, ears flattened, nostrils flared, hooves beating, pounding, rushing, tails whipped the air. Wolves bit one another in their panic; a bull swung its head and thrust its horns through a panther's throat. Was that the dog I glimpsed racing between two red foxes, fear in its eyes? Kangaroos leaped through the air, crushing woodchucks and rabbits as they landed. Elephants trumpeted, trunks outstretched. A giant cobra and a Percheron, dappled gray, raced side by side, desperate. The horse reared, its hoof came down; the snake's gleaming body curled and uncurled, thrashing the hard-packed earth in agony.

I clutched my breast as if it was *I* that had been cut in two. I forgot the racing, dangerous horde and rushed toward the snake. Suddenly I was caught round the waist and thrown to the ground, just out of reach of the stampede. The Serpent clutched me in its coils.

"Let me go, let me *go!*" I cried. I could not believe the strength in the diminished body. "Don't you see the cobra's hurt?"

The Serpent held me fast. "Eve! If you touch it, if you go near, it will bite you, and you will *surely* die." As I watched, the snake snapped out in its paroxysm and caught a zebra's leg in its fangs. The zebra stumbled and fell, and lay still.

"You see," said the Serpent in its strange new voice. "You must learn. There is danger everywhere."

It came to me then, as if a voice had spoken: Eve! This is *your* doing. I fell to my knees in the dirt, all the animals pounding around me, and pulled my hair, and beat my breast, and screamed, *"What have I done!"*

Then for the first and only time, the Serpent hit me:

with its tail, a sharp tap on the thigh. "Eve! Never say that! Never think it!" It glared at me from the narrow yellow eyes I did not know, but whose spirit I knew well. "You and Adam chose freely, both of you, and it was brave. Never doubt that it was the right choice: in the Garden you would have been God's chattels forever. This"—it nodded at the chaos around us—"is not your doing. It is God's."

The Serpent brushed its tail lightly across my cheek and spoke more quietly. "My dear, remember what I say. No matter what lies ahead, keep it in your heart. It is not suffering, or injustice, or evil that you have brought into the world—though they have come. It is freedom."

"Yes." I put my arms around the Serpent's shrunken neck. I had never loved it so well. "Serpent," I gasped. "You said I could still reach you, even after I leave the Garden. You *must* tell me how."

"Eve," the Serpent replied. "You will find me, ever, within yourself: in the deepest regions of your soul."

I groaned. "That's not enough."

"Somewhere, sometime, I will visit you, my dear." The Serpent smiled. "And I will always watch over you."

"Serpent, oh, Serpent." I sat in the sand and wept while the animals raced by on every side.

"Eve, look at me!" the Serpent called as it had when I was climbing the cliff. "Don't cry. Stand proud!

Because of your choice, all humans are free, now and forevermore. Though"—the Serpent stared at the turmoil around us and laughed—"it may not seem like such a good decision right now."

It pulled me to the edge of the path. "Good-bye, Eve," it said, and glided off through the ferns in its strange new skin as if we would meet again that evening, for supper by the pond.

Adam came running through the dust. "Where were you? I was afraid you'd been trampled." He hauled me to my feet. "Which way should we go?"

I looked around. A thicket of thornbushes barred our way. "I think I remember—there's a path behind those shrubs." Though the spiny shoots ripped our skin, we managed to creep through them on our hands and knees. Finally we reached an open glade and collapsed on the grass. Lying on my back, I stared into the leaves above. An eagle passed overhead, circled, and passed by again. I closed my eyes.

After a time I was aware of Adam beside me, breathing hard. I turned my head and squinted at him. He lay with his knees bent and his arms stretched above his head, eyebrows drawn together in a frown. The sun glinted on his body. He looked larger than I remembered, as if, in leaving the Garden, he had gained some of God's strength. I shivered. I felt I hardly knew him.

What am I doing here, I thought, *alone with this man?*

For some time we stayed quiet under the trees. Gradually the clamor of pounding hoofs and the screams of animals abated. We sat up and stared at each other.

"You have blood all over you," Adam said.

"So do you," I replied.

"Scratches from the thorns," said Adam. "I didn't even notice."

"Let's see if we can find some water."

We wandered rather aimlessly through the trees. Everything around me seemed unreal, as though I had returned to a dreamland: insubstantial trees that would skitter away if I blew on them, stones underfoot ready to spin into the air. No sound other than our footsteps, not a bird, not a creature, anywhere. Only this man I did not know beside me. Perhaps he too would disappear.

At last we came upon a trickle of water, and washed our scratches, and drank. I sank into a pile of leaves.

"I can't go any farther," I said.

"Neither can I. Let's stay here for the night." Adam lay down next to me, which surprised me, but I did not move away: his body was warm. We huddled together under our skins and slept as only the young can, for we were still very young, barely more than children. Just before dawn I felt an animal creep up and lie beside me. A tail wagged against my legs; a warm, rough tongue licked my ear. It was the dog, returned at last.

In the morning we came to a river and walked along its banks, through a silent forest, through vacant meadows and plains, with the dog at our heels as if it had never been away. God truly had emptied the Garden: no animal, no bird, no fish remained. "What will he do all alone here?" Adam mused. "He'll get bored."

"He'll come and bother us," I said morosely.

In a while we arrived at the narrow passage between the great redwoods, where many moons ago the barricade had blocked our journey to the South. The earth had been trampled bare, and the bodies of several animals, barely recognizable, lay crushed on the ground.

"Poor things," said Adam, but we did not go near them. Ahead we could see the plain, yellow and endless as I remembered it. I glimpsed what looked like a herd of goats far out on the prairie, but I said nothing: it might have been a mirage.

"Not very inviting." Adam sighed.

"Perhaps we'll find a valley," I replied without much hope. "At least there'll be water. This river must go somewhere." But as we walked hand in hand through the redwoods, we felt very low.

Suddenly the forest was behind us and we were on

the plain. High above, a pair of eagles floated together and away, riding the currents of the wind. Behind us, to the north, lay the Garden. In front, an expanse of waving, dappled grass stretched south as far as we could see. To the east, where the river tumbled through a sun-filled valley, was a grove of apple trees, in full bloom.

The blossoms were a color I had seen only once before, on any tree: the deep, clear red of a ruby, sparked with white. A few buds, still tightly wrapped, waited to burst. Others were half-open, petals still half-curled protectively around the stamens. But most were open full, eight or ten flowers on a stem, amidst a whorl of leaves. The petals curved gently outward; clear crimson, with white flecks. From the center of every blossom filaments rose, deep purple; at the tip of each filament flared an anther, airy as a cobweb and green as the darkest emerald sea.

"Glorious trees," I murmured. "So beautiful."

"God's apples, those he threw over the falls," said Adam.

God's apples? I thought. *No.*

I turned to Adam. "*Our* apples," I said. "Our trees."

AUTHOR'S NOTE

The idea for *The Garden* came to me several years ago, in church. The lesson was the third chapter of Genesis; when God accuses Adam of eating the apple, Adam replies: ". . . but the woman gave it to me." (Eve then turns around and blames the Serpent, which is equally reprehensible.) That day the familiar response—such a cop-out!—launched me into *The Garden*.

After that day in church, I could not get Eve out of my mind. It has always seemed wrong that, in religion as in mythology, woman is so often blamed for the introduction of sin into the world. As I thought about Eve in Eden, the characters stirred and grew in unexpected ways, and the story took on a life of its own. I was excited by the ideas and questions that came up: Was the Garden of Eden Paradise? Is that what Paradise is: a beautiful place where all one's physical needs are met? Can we evade moral responsibility through blind obedience to a "higher being"? Why have we been given minds?

My depiction of God in *The Garden* was influenced by a stay in Santa Fe, where I became interested in the development of the atom bomb in Los Alamos. The brilliant scientists who created the bomb were passionate about their work—totally absorbed, exhilarated, drunk on intellectual excitement. But, geniuses though they were, they never considered the moral implications of the bomb, or the suffering it would bring. I began to think God could in some ways be compared to the Los Alamos scientists: a creator focused on his creations, impatient to prove his theories right (or at least make them work as he had planned), with no understanding of the human cost. I have certainly taken liberties with God, but I do not think his behavior is out of character. The God of the Old Testament is a choleric and impetuous being.

As I delved further into the Garden of Eden, it became clear to me that the Serpent is the hero of the story, the Prometheus of the Gardenites, so to speak. Prometheus brought humans fire; the Serpent gave them the capacity to reason. Had it not been for the Serpent, Adam and Eve and their progeny might have sat around in the Garden forever and never made use of those minds of theirs. Perhaps the Serpent is Wisdom, who, according to some ancient texts, was with God at the Creation.

I did not write *The Garden* to upset anyone. I have great respect for much religion and for personal faith. But I part ways with organized religion in crucial areas. I cannot believe in an exclusive god, one who, like the old tribal gods, protects only one group of people. I cannot reconcile an omnipotent god with the suffering that exists in the world. Nor can I believe that people are inherently evil. Like the Manicheans, I view the world as a struggle between the forces of good and the forces of evil, and humans as capable both of great evil and great good. And like Eve, I do not understand why a great god should need so much adulation.

Though in my *Garden* Eve is quicker and more adventurous than Adam, I do not consider this a feminist book. *The Garden* is a different perspective on Eden; Eve is the protagonist and has central place. This may be the Eve we would have seen if the Bible had been composed by a less patriarchal society.

No matter how we look at the Bible—as the word of God, the history of a people, or the attempt of those people to make sense of the world around them—it has for centuries been a vibrant, crucial text. It has inspired countless narratives and reflections. My *Garden* is a novel, not a work of theology—a novel that departs from one of the oldest and best-known tales on earth, in which I have tried to explore questions of personal responsibility, justice, and freedom.

It took me seven years to write *The Garden*. The story and the characters—and I—changed over that period. When I began I had no clear idea of where I would finish; I knew only that, at the end, Adam and Eve would find themselves outside the Garden.